PRAISE FOR CONSTANCE O'DAY-FLANNERY

"She proves that love is timeless." —Nora Roberts

"She is a remarkable talent." —*Rendezvous*

"Not just uplifting but downright smart."
—*Publishers Weekly* on *Best Laid Plans*

"O'Day-Flannery slowly and carefully builds the suspense, and a relationship, maintaining a deliberate pace that finally yields a happy ending." —*Booklist* on *Colliding Forces*

"*Shifting Love* is unique, thrilling, and chock-full of emotion, proving O'Day-Flannery is still at the top of her game!" —*Romantic Times BOOK*reviews
(4 ½ stars) on *Shifting Love*

"*Shifting Love* read like Deb Smith's *Alice at Heart* crossed with *Touched by a (Sexy) Angel*. The dual heroes in the book—Julian and Marcus—will leave you guessing until the very end." —*Science Fiction Romance*

TOR ROMANCE BOOKS BY
CONSTANCE O'DAY-FLANNERY

Shifting Love
Colliding Forces
Best Laid Plans
Twice in a Lifetime
Old Friends

Old Friends

CONSTANCE
O'DAY-FLANNERY

tor paranormal romance

A TOM DOHERTY ASSOCIATES BOOK
NEW YORK

OLD FRIENDS

Copyright © 2007 by Constance O'Day-Flannery

A Tor Book
Published by Tom Doherty Associates, LLC
175 Fifth Avenue
New York, NY 10010

www.tor.com

Tor® is a registered trademark of Tom Doherty Associates, LLC.

ISBN-13: 978-0-7653-5405-1
ISBN-10: 0-7653-5405-5

First Edition: December 2007

Printed in the United States of America

0 9 8 7 6 5 4 3 2 1

Dedication

This book is dedicated to women—all women, past, present and future—and in particular those women who have graced my life as mother, daughter, sister, sister-in-law and friend.

Old Friends

Chapter

I

SOMETIMES THERE WAS NO GOOD REASON TO EXPLAIN the emotions that played with one's heart and mind. You could wake up feeling great and, unexplainably, you might be suddenly overtaken with an odd heaviness that seemed to have attached itself to your shoulders. It was as if something decided to hitch a ride without your permission and you were the ass carrying the burden. Was it a feeling of foreboding, or just the blahs? Ever since the Gang had arrived, she'd felt it.

Claire looked around the dining room table and was filled with a mixture of gratitude and sadness. Sadness wasn't exactly right. She didn't feel the need to cry or be wrapped in someone's arms for consolation. Maybe the heaviness was emptiness or perhaps loss . . . for somehow all of her precious friends were happy, partnered, content, on purpose, living "La Vida Loca," and she was . . . well, alone and probably just plain loco, hung up on a stupid dream. She couldn't get that childhood dream out of her head, nor the feeling of elation she'd had upon waking. She'd felt young again. Filled with hope and excitement, ready to throw open the back door and find adventure—

"So that takes care of the business portion of the meeting, ladies. Anyone have anything to add?"

"Claire?"

"Hey, are you with us?" Cristine asked with a grin.

She blinked, drawing herself back to reality, back to the circle of friends surrounding her. "Oh, sorry," she murmured with an embarrassed smile. "I think using women in prison on work release to operate the food bank is a great idea, Tina. They've got enough street smarts to weed out anyone trying to work the system. And I'm amazed, Kelly, that you got so many of the chain supermarkets to donate food."

"Actually, it wasn't as hard as I thought it might be," Kelly answered. "Once one donated, the others actually wanted to get in on it. You were right. Great publicity."

"It's your meeting, Claire. Are we finished?"

She nodded quickly, smiling at the five women around her. "That's it," she stated, pushing back her chair from the dining room table. "Good productive meeting, ladies. Now who wants that chocolate cake?"

"I do!" Isabel said, rising with Claire and walking into the kitchen. "I swear, ever since Hope was born I'm craving sweets."

Claire grinned as Tina yelled out, "I never turn down anything chocolate and sweet."

"And that includes the good Dr. Ramsey," Kelly answered with a giggle.

Claire could hear Tina's laugh from the kitchen.

When the cake and the women returned to the table, Tina cleared her throat. "Actually," she began with a shy smile, "I do have some personal news."

Claire, who was about to cut the cake, stopped and stared at her dear friend. "What? Good news, I hope."

"Don't keep us in suspense," Isabel added.

"Well," Tina began in a teasing voice, "I just might be needing all your help in this."

"What is it?" Cristine demanded, moving in closer to the table and staring at Tina.

"I think I may be getting married," Tina whispered in disbelief, then burst into nervous giggles as shock was replaced by happiness.

Claire sank to her chair and simply held the knife in her hand. Tina. Married. Her favorite partner in crime. The one she could always count on to catch a movie or try out a new restaurant or hop in the car and head to New Hope just because the sun was shining. Gone. Snatched up. *Married.*

The heaviness was identified. She had known *something* was coming. Maybe she was psychic. Nah . . .

"Married!" Kelly exclaimed. "When?"

"Oh, Tina, I'm so happy for you!" Isabel whispered as tears came into her eyes.

"How could you wait this long to tell us?" Paula asked with a big grin while shaking her head with happiness.

"I wanted to wait until we finished foundation business," Tina answered, blinking rapidly to stop the tears from sliding down her cheeks.

"Married . . ." Claire whispered in shock, though why she should be shocked was a mystery. Tina had been dating Louis Ramsey since he'd delivered Cristine's baby almost two years ago. "When? What are your plans?"

"Well, that's just it. I haven't said yes yet."

Cristine's jaw dropped. "Why the hell not?"

"He's wonderful, Tina. You two are perfect for each other," Isabel said.

"He's gorgeous, intelligent—"

"And a doctor!" Paula interrupted.

"And a doctor," Kelly repeated.

"And he loves you," Cristine whispered with a tender smile.

Tina glanced up at Claire.

She swallowed the tightness in her throat and nodded. "They're right, Tina. He's perfect for you. Why are you hesitating?"

No longer able to stop her tears, Tina sniffled and sighed. "Because I wanted your approval. All your approval. When a man marries a woman, he marries her family and you guys are part of my family, my soul family."

"So say yes, woman," Claire commanded. "Say yes before he finds out how nuts the Yellow Brick Road Gang really is and runs for the hills!"

Everyone laughed and then Paula said, "We're not truly nuts. Are we, Isabel?"

Isabel, the oldest and wisest, grinned, then shrugged. "Well, we *are* outside the box of perceived normalcy. Some would judge that as nuts."

"I am not nuts!" Kelly insisted, motioning to Claire to start slicing the cake.

Tina laughed. "That's what nutty people always say."

"We're *unusual*," Paula replied. "There's a difference."

The group began discussing the difference while Claire cut the cake and smiled at the others surrounding her dining room table. Five women, wonderful women, who had come together nine years ago as a book club and had transformed themselves and then their small slice of the planet by forming a foundation that supported women in need. There was Kelly, red haired, lovely mother of a teenage daughter. For the last eight months she'd been dating a good guy, John Lawson, the host of *AM Philly*—who had been interviewing Isabel when her water broke and they'd all rushed the stage to accompany her to the hospital. Isabel, the oldest, was sitting back smiling and listening to the group, content with her life now that Joshua had given her the daughter she'd never thought she could have. Motherhood agreed with her. She looked younger, happier, vibrant. Paula had finally cut her long hair to shoulder length. Mother of five, finishing her thesis to get her master's in anthropology, Paula at last looked happy, rested, as if she had found her path. As Cristine had . . . meeting Daniel, winning the lottery, giving birth to an extraordinary daughter who was delivered by Tina's maybe-new-fiancé, and also coming up with the idea for the foundation. Cristine too was on purpose.

And then there was her . . .

What was her purpose?

Was she always going to be delegated to the supporting role, cheering the others on?

She hated to admit a part of her felt left out. Everyone else had found happiness and she was truly thrilled for them, but still . . .

Was it ever going to be her turn?

And the most important question . . . did she even want a turn? Too many years without a man in her life had left her fiercely independent. Was she willing to share her life with a male again?

"Okay, enough of this!" Isabel finally said, bringing Claire back into the present. "We're all forgetting Miss Tina here just announced she is getting married. You *are* going to say yes, aren't you?"

"You'd be certifiable if you said no," Kelly added. "I mean, what more could you want in a man?"

Tina sighed heavily, running her hands through her curly black hair and pulling it back from her face. Her large, expressive dark eyes seemed even more lovely surrounded by perfect creamy mocha skin. Tina was an exotically beautiful woman who now appeared frightened. "It's such a big decision," she said, letting her curls fall back around her face. "I . . . I mean I've waited so long."

"And he finally appeared!" Claire said with a laugh, placing a big slice of cake in front of her. "Why don't you just get it out, whatever it is, and then we can settle it and begin making wedding plans?" Sitting back down in her chair, she smiled tenderly at her friend, her buddy in more crazy schemes than any of the others. "What is it? What's bothering you?"

Tina looked down to the plate in front of her. "His profession," she whispered.

"What? He's a doctor!" Kelly exclaimed.

"He's a gynecologist," Tina stated. "He looks up into women's bodies all week long."

Claire burst out laughing. "It's his *job*! Or are you scared you won't measure up?" She giggled, then sobered quickly when she saw she'd struck a nerve. Shaking her head, she added, "It's bad enough women dress for each other, starve themselves to fit into a size zero, spend a fortune on creams so they'll never have to show their age, and now you're feeling insecure about your vagina? God, is there *any* part of our bodies that we can feel good about?"

"How would you know, Claire?" Tina countered, her face rigid from holding back tears. "Look at you. You're tiny, petite. You've got naturally blond hair, and you don't even have to wear makeup and you'd still look like a miniature Charlize Theron. You have no idea what it's like to be thirty pounds overweight. You can eat like a truck driver and you never gain a pound."

Claire shut up, trying not to feel attacked, because Tina really was scared.

"So she's got a great metabolism," Cristine said to fill the silence. "And enviable genes, but I agree with Claire. When are we going to be allowed to feel good about ourselves? How long are we going to put up with the media telling us we aren't good enough because it sells ad space and promotes women spending billions of dollars trying to live up to an impossible image?"

"I like my eyes," Kelly murmured, as the rest of the group contemplated Cristine's words and fell into silence.

"The eyes are the windows to the soul," Isabel whispered. "And you all have lovely eyes."

"You know this is the only culture that does this to women," Paula stated. "The Western world can be so cruel to women. We like to think we're so liberated, but I actually overheard these young women at college saying another student had an old-school crotch. Well, they didn't use the term *crotch* exactly. But an old-school crotch? I wondered, what the hell is that? I finally figured out an *old-school* crotch is one that isn't waxed into a landing strip."

"Ouch," Isabel muttered and the others grinned in sympathy.

"See what I mean?" Tina complained. "I'm not the only one giving this some thought. The times are a changin', ladies."

"Good God," Cristine said. "We've taken something so private and made it into a fashion statement."

"And men expect it now," Kelly added. "I get a bikini wax every few months and it's painful as hell, but I have to keep up."

"Why?" Isabel asked. "Why put yourself through that torture?"

Kelly shrugged. "It's . . . just the way things are now."

"Do you really think a man cares that much whether it's a triangle or a landing strip?" Cristine demanded. "From my experience a man's just happy when you don't say no."

Since Claire hadn't had a man in her life in . . . God, was it four years now? Well, she hadn't had to make that painful choice in some time. "I think we should start a new fashion statement and expect men to wax their genitalia. Let them experience it and see if they still think women should do it."

"All you'd have to do is start an ad campaign saying it made them look bigger and they'd be lining up," Paula stated.

Everyone laughed and Claire turned to her good friend. "Tina, the man loves you. *You!* You are so much more than your vagina and if you weren't in such a state, you'd know it. Think of it this way. He looks at vaginas all day long and he chose you and yours."

"Right," Kelly agreed. "Must be special."

Tina groaned with embarrassment.

"And the weight thing?" Claire continued. "You're almost six feet. You're a statuesque beautiful goddess of a woman. Louis already loves you. He asked all of you, including those thirty pounds, to be his wife. And if you look at those damn charts about height and weight, we'd all be dieting for the rest of our lives. Will you just forget about comparing yourself to anyone else? Your gorgeous doctor didn't ask anyone else to spend the rest of her life with him. He asked you, right?"

Tina shrugged.

"Right?" Kelly asked.

"Right?" the rest of the group demanded in unison.

"Right," Tina murmured. "But it's so hard. Why couldn't he have been a podiatrist?"

Isabel laughed. "Then you'd be worried about your feet. Let it go, will you?"

"I bet he's a great lover," Kelly murmured with a sly grin. "No road maps for him. Must be well informed on *the* erogenous zone."

"Lucky girl." Claire said with a giggle. "Why can't you just accept you hit a grand slam and be happy?"

"Because it doesn't last, that's why!" Tina muttered, wrapping her fingers tightly around her fork. "This whole marriage thing. What are the chances? Really? Less than forty percent now?"

"Do you *want* to talk yourself out of this proposal?" Isabel asked gently. "You're right about your statistics, but what if you and Louis are part of that forty percent that makes it?"

"And how will you feel if you don't give it your all?" Cristine asked. "Tina, I know you. You'd regret it the rest of your life, especially if it's fear that's keeping you from grabbing your well-deserved reward."

"When have you failed at anything you really wanted?" Isabel asked. "You went to the University of Penn, then Wharton School of Business. You run a highly successful real estate company. You're an accomplished woman, Tina, and you're letting low self-esteem hold you back from what you know in your heart is your gift from the universe. You waited for the right man to show up and he did."

Cristine sighed. "You know the night I won the lottery I had some moments of thinking I didn't deserve it and later that night my purse was torn off my shoulder with the ticket inside. Daniel got it back, but he taught me that if you believe you are unworthy, your reward will go to someone who's will is stronger and thinks it should it be theirs. Do you want another woman to claim Louis?"

Tina looked up from the rosewood table. "God, no . . ."

"Then you'd better believe in every cell of your luscious body that you deserve him," Cristine said. "And you do, my friend. You so deserve him."

"She's right," Paula whispered, sitting next to Tina and stroking her back.

"So what I want to know is when you're telling Dr. Ramsey yes and when we can begin planning this wedding," Claire said with a smile for her dear, insecure, complicated friend.

Tina smiled back. "I knew you women would make me see the truth."

"Even if it ain't pretty," Kelly said, then quickly added, "I mean you are. Pretty. Just your thinking stinks."

Isabel laughed. "I think she got that, Kelly. It's okay for our thinking to stink, as long as we can smell it out, or have people who love us just the way we are point it out."

"The Yellow Brick Road Gang," Paula murmured with gratitude. "Where would any of us be without it?"

The women looked around the table at each other and their bond became even stronger with recognition. They really were a soul family, Claire thought, brought together to help figure out this bizarre adventure called life.

"So what about this wedding, woman?" Claire asked, finally digging into her chocolate cake now that the crisis had passed. "And who's going to be the maid of honor? Considering the state of my love life and that Kelly will probably be engaged to Mr. TV Personality in a few months, that leaves me. The aging maid."

"*Maid?*" Kelly asked in friendly disbelief. "A little long in the tooth for a maid, aren't you? Besides, doesn't a maid signify a virgin?"

Claire didn't even bother to swallow. "Now that would leave everybody out at this table. And, since I haven't had sex in over four years, good sex in more than a decade, I'm practically a virgin."

Cristine laughed. "A born-again virgin. Claire. Of all people!" she said with a teasing grin. "I think we'd all agree on matron of honor, whoever Tina picks."

"I don't want any bad feelings about this," Tina stated. "That's why we're going to put all your names in a hat and pick one. That's the fairest way." She paused and her eyes became teary again. "Because I couldn't choose. I love you all."

"So there *is* going to be a wedding, right?"

"Of course there is. She just needed to get her insecurities out."

"Don't you think Louis might want to know?"

More laughter.

"He'll know soon enough. Claire, get some paper, a pen and a hat. Might as well make this real."

"The boys are at baseball practice and with Hank away again, I have to pick them up, so I'll have to leave soon."

"Me too, Paula," Cristine said. "Daniel and I are thinking about putting a pool in the backyard, and if I leave it up to him, he'll already have the dirt moved."

"A pool?" Kelly asked. "He wouldn't start that without you."

Cristine glanced at Isabel and laughed. "Oh, yes he would, just to surprise me."

"Aren't you afraid, with the baby?" Tina asked. "Or does she already know how to swim? I swear that daughter of yours is a prodigy, Cristine. She's already walking and talking. She actually asked me if I loved spiders."

"I know," Cristine said with awe. "For some odd reason Angelique's fascinated with insects right now. I found her squatting down in the backyard staring at a spiderweb. She stayed there for almost fifteen minutes. And as for the pool . . . I brought her over here last week and took her into Claire's. She pushed out of my arms and started swimming like a fish. She loved it and didn't want to get out. Figured I could use the exercise so we've been talking about it."

"Good for you," Kelly said, then added, "Claire? Hurry up, will you? I have to run too. I have a date tonight."

"And I'm going to start leaking breast milk," Isabel said, "if I don't get back to Hope soon."

"And I've got to tell a man he's about to be a husband."

"Okay . . . Tina wins. She's got the best reason for hurrying this thing up," Cristine said with a laugh. "Claire! You've got some impatient women here!"

Claire heard it all as she picked up a sheet of paper from her printer, grabbed a pen and made her way to the foyer closet to get a baseball cap. Everyone had plans.

Except her.

Saturday night and what . . . she was going to rent a movie to watch by herself?

Bringing everything back to the table, she reminded herself that was her choice.

She was alone by choice.

Was it just Tina's announcement that made her wonder if she'd made the right one?

"Okay, everyone write down their names," she said, tearing the paper into five pieces. She wrote her name, then passed the pen on to Isabel. Folding the paper into a square over and over again, she almost crushed it making it so tiny. She didn't think she really wanted to be Tina's matron of honor. She didn't want to help plan a wedding right now. She would assist any way she could, but the thought of all the details, all the hearts and flowers and love sentiments might just nauseate her . . . and then her big mouth would surely get her in trouble and spoil this special time for Tina. It was best someone else took this assignment.

When they all had thrown their names into the pale blue Phillies baseball cap, Kelly held it out to Tina. She took a deep breath, closed her eyes and stuck her hand into the cap.

Claire watched as Tina brought out a folded piece of paper. She exhaled in relief, seeing that the paper wasn't folded as many times as hers. *Got out of that one,* she thought.

Everyone watched as Tina opened the paper.

"Who is it?" Isabel asked.

They all waited until Tina refolded the paper, threw it back into the hat and grinned.

"Claire," she announced, smiling so brightly across the table at her that Claire didn't have the guts to protest and tell her she'd cheated someone else.

Everyone turned to Claire and grinned.

"Perfect!" Cristine said, standing. "She's so organized."

"Meant to be," Paula said.

"You two always were good with plans," Isabel added. "Just tell us how to help."

Kelly rose and pushed her chair back to the table. "Right. Anything you guys need, just yell." She grinned at Claire. "But you ain't no maid. Face it. You're forty-three years old. Like the rest of us, you're officially a matron."

Stunned, Claire forced a smile. "That's me. The aging matron."

She waited until she'd escorted everyone else out the door, then pulled on Tina's arm to keep her from walking out. "I need to speak with you."

Tina seemed surprised. "Sure, Claire. What's up?" she said, waving to the others as they got in their cars.

"That's what I want to know. That wasn't my name on that piece of paper. Mine was folded much smaller."

Tina looked guilty and grinned sheepishly. "God, Claire, only you would question me. It was Paula, okay? How can I ask Paula with her tribe of kids and going back to college to help me plan a wedding? She doesn't have the time, or the energy."

"But it was her name," Claire answered. "You cheated her of the chance."

"I thought it was kinder not to put her in that position. You know how busy she is. This would have been one more task to add to her already overcrowded life."

Claire didn't want to agree. Not yet anyway. "But you lied."

"Okay, so I'm not as enlightened as Cristine or Isabel. I'm not above using a little sleight of hand to save a friend. Or . . . don't you want to be my maid of honor?"

Now it was Claire's turn and she tried not to appear guilty at being found out. "It's matron, remember? As was pointed out, my maid days are long gone." She grinned, to hide her own feelings. "And of course I want to be your helpless slave as you drag me to bridal shops and order me around and make me wear some hideous organza nightmare. I'm honored."

Tina narrowed her gaze. "You sure? I mean, if this is a—"

"Yes, I'm sure," Claire interrupted and stood on her toes to kiss Tina's cheek. "Now go find your gorgeous doctor and tell him yes, will you?"

Tina laughed and wrapped her arm around Claire's shoulders. Hugging her, she murmured, "God, I hope I'm doing the right thing."

Claire squeezed her back. "Stop worrying, will you? You and Louis are going to be so happy it'll make me sick with envy."

Tina pulled away and looked down at her. "Honey, your time will come. Your man is out there, waiting for you."

"Who said I want one?"

Tina grinned knowingly. "You want one. You just want the right one."

Claire simply nodded as she let go. "Now get out of here and go put poor Louis out of his misery."

Nodding, Tina took a deep breath. "You're right. It's time to get on with my life."

"Congratulations, Tina. Really. I know you're going to be happy."

Tina kissed her cheek and walked out the door.

"Good God," she muttered after closing the front door. She was going to be a maid of honor. No, *matron* of honor. She probably wouldn't even have a date, just to make her singleness even more obvious. Hopefully, Tina wouldn't get married for a few months.

That ought to give her time to rustle up a man.

A wedding.

She was getting used to bizarre childbirths, but now . . . *a wedding.*

Chapter

2

CLAIRE WAS WALKING PAST THE CURRENT RELEASES with couples, families and all the other singles who found themselves alone on a Saturday night. That heaviness she'd felt earlier increased as she passed a young man and woman holding hands and giggling while one of them tried to read the back cover of a DVD. Dressed in jeans, a white T-shirt and a Phillies cap with her ponytail hanging out the back, she steeled herself against the couple's cuteness as she viewed the movie titles on the wall. She wasn't in the mood for an Asian woman's memoirs or the story of an aging male virgin. Nothing current appealed to her, so she left the crowded perimeter of the store and headed for the older titles. Maybe she should drive over to the mega bookstore, but even that could prove depressing as more singles wandered the aisles looking for something of interest, be it found on the pages of a book or someone of the opposite sex.

There ought to be a place, besides a video or bookstore, for forty-somethings who were content with their lives and just wanted some entertainment for the night. Sometimes she wished she lived in the city. Philly had a thriving cultural life, but she always balanced that out with less traffic in the suburbs and the close proximity of the Gang. A part of her knew she was looking for a diversion tonight so she wouldn't have to deal with being the odd one out in the Gang and now the designated matron of honor for Tina's upcoming nuptials.

Tina. Married.

It still had the power to make her stomach muscles clench. Too bad she'd already seen *The Wedding Date*. It would have been perfect tonight for the way she was feeling. Maybe that's what she should do—hire someone, someone great looking, sexy and funny. Who cared what he did for a living? She just didn't want to show up alone as a true matron.

What a word, Claire thought, heading for the comedy section of the store. Matron. It reminded her of some old woman with warts on her chin who whipped female inmates into submission. She wasn't a matron.

Sighing, she admitted she also wasn't a maid.

What was the term for someone no longer virginal and not yet using Depends?

Middle-aged. Forty-three makes you middle-aged.

How could *she* be middle-aged? When had that slipped up on her? She swore that in her head she was only in her late twenties, still young and full of life and . . . looking for a DVD to rent on a Saturday night? Sounded middle-aged to her. Depressingly middle-aged.

Don't think about being middle-aged, she scolded herself and shook her head slightly to clear her mind as she perused the shelves. But why was Tina's announcement hitting her like this? She was happy, truly happy for her friend, but it meant change . . . and not only for Tina. The Gang was changing. She could feel the shift into coupleness and motherhood circling around her. Even Kelly was finally in a serious romance with a good guy.

Cripes . . . romance. It had done in more intelligent women than leg warmers and shoulder pads in the eighties. The things you do for love . . . or what most people thought was love. It was simply a chemical reaction and she was no longer addicted to the chemical. Romance. It was scientifically proven those chemicals in the brain wore off after two or three years. It's the carrot that's dangled in front of you to lure you into a relationship where you end up making crazy decisions and losing your identity. No thanks. She'd tried it all, and it was someone else's dogma. Besides, she'd realized that no man could ever put up with her independence or her views. And marriage? Keep it far away from her. She'd done that too. Got the T-shirt and the mug on that one.

A picture of Brian's face raced across her mind and her muscles tensed automatically. Damn, she hadn't thought of him in years. Well if she did think of him it was fleeting . . . her husband, ex-husband. Born and bred into Philadelphia's Main Line society. Handsome, funny, intelligent—and a manipulator and a liar. Quite a combination, and someone else's problem by now. Years ago she'd divorced his cheating Main Line spoiled ass and closed the door firmly behind her. Since then she'd been off men, as if they were bad seafood that caused food poisoning and she wasn't about to chance another serving. It wasn't that she had been devastated by the divorce. She'd known about his cheating, even if she'd been in denial. Somewhere, with her head buried in the sand, had been the nagging feeling he'd been fooling around for years. And she had been right, very right . . . with his receptionist, several of his clients and a prostitute he'd been supporting for three years.

The Gang had gotten her through the divorce, and she had to admit that her overwhelming resulting emotion had been gratitude. She was free.

Finally free of pleasing anyone other than herself.

Women are biologically programmed to find a suitable mate, make a nest and procreate. Men are biologically programmed to spread their seed for survival of the species.

She was done thinking men could be monogamous creatures. Only the ones with self-control and respect didn't cheat, and they were rare, she thought, picking up a movie and looking at the cover. She put the movie back and kept strolling down the aisle.

Maybe there was hope . . . for Cristine and Daniel, Isabel and Joshua. Maybe for Paula and Hank—and now even for Tina. God, she really hoped Tina was one of the lucky forty percent. Forty percent . . . ? How many of those stayed together because of convenience or fear of surviving alone? She didn't have the courage or trust to try it ever again. What for? She'd already made her own nest and not everyone on the planet had to procreate. Considering the state of the planet and the size of the population, it seemed like a wise decision.

She had a good life. A good job. A great home. Wonderful friends. A terrific little vibrator. What more could a reasonable woman want?

So she would play the Auntie Mame character for the rest of her life. So what? Take everyone's kids out on adventures, get them into some harmless trouble and then return them to their parents without all the fuss of—

"Excuse me. Have you seen this movie?"

Brought out of her wandering reflections by a deep male voice, Claire blinked and looked over her shoulder. "I'm sorry?"

He stood next to her, dressed in jeans and a crisp light blue shirt with the sleeves rolled up. He was about five ten with curly brown hair, blue eyes and a friendly smile. "Do you know if this is a good movie to watch?"

She looked down to his hand. *Ghostbusters.*

"You've never seen it?" she asked, wondering if he'd just arrived from Mars.

He smiled and shook his head. And for some crazy reason, Claire felt there was something familiar about him.

"Yeah . . . it's good the first time. Funny." She stared at him, trying to see if she knew him from her years in the financial field. "Do I know you?"

He grinned. A nice grin. "Do you think you do?"

She couldn't help grinning back. "I don't know. You look familiar, but . . ." She shook her head. "Enjoy your movie," she murmured and headed down the aisle. Time to find a movie and get out. Maybe she would call the Italian restaurant and pick up something really delicious to eat. As she reached into the pocket of her jeans for her cell phone, her gaze rested on the perfect movie.

Saving Grace.

So what if she'd already seen it a couple of years ago? She could count on a few good laughs. She grabbed the DVD with one hand and flipped open her phone with the other. In her contact list, she found the number for Guiseppe's restaurant and highlighted it, then pressed the call button while walking up to the long line of customers waiting to pay for their viewing choices.

"Hi. I'd like to order takeout, spaghetti and meatballs with the blush marinara sauce. No salad, rolls or soup, thanks." She listened as her order was repeated then was given her order number. "Thanks. About twenty minutes?" When the time was confirmed, she thanked the person on the phone again and shut her cell.

"Sounds good."

Now in line, she turned and was about to grin when she saw it was the *Ghostbusters* guy standing behind her. Shrugging, she said, "Carbs and laughter. A perfect Saturday night."

"What movie did you choose?"

She looked back at him, again thinking there was something vaguely familiar about him. Holding up the DVD, she said, "It's pretty funny."

"Saving Grace," the man repeated. "Wonderful title. Is it . . . religious?"

She couldn't help laughing. "Hardly. It's about a middle-aged widow growing pot to save her home from creditors."

"Pot?"

She lowered her voice. "Pot. Weed."

He simply stared at her with a confused expression.

"Grass?"

"Grass?" he asked, appearing even more perplexed.

She looked at those people ahead of her in line and those behind the man, then leaned her head toward him and whispered, "Marijuana." Why was she even explaining this to a stranger?

He looked up to the ceiling for a moment and then nodded his head. "Ah, yes, an herbal plant that produces a feeling of well-being."

Claire sort of shrunk away from him as the line moved about three feet. He sounded like a scientist and, come to think of it, he sort of looked like a science teacher. He wasn't exactly good looking. Definitely not great looking. Decent looking. A little nerdy. Maybe a lot nerdy if he'd never heard of pot. Putting him out of her mind, she stared at the woman's head in front of her, wishing she had that kind of curly hair. Why was it that she always seemed to want what she didn't have? Tina had told her horror stories of straightening her hair with chemicals and flat irons, until she'd given up and had accepted curls Claire had wanted since she was a child.

"You don't use marijuana any longer, do you?"

Her breath left her body in a rush and her jaw dropped as she spun around to him. "No!" she stated emphatically and looked around to see who else had heard him. People seemed to be in their own little worlds as they waited to get their movies. "Look, I don't know you, okay? Enjoy your movie." She turned back to the line ahead of her. Really! Some people just thought they could invade one's life and—

"But you seemed to think you knew me."

Again she blew her breath out in frustration. She was

used to being hit on by strange men who thought she should be thrilled by their attention, but this guy was too pushy.

Ignore him, she told herself. He would get the hint . . . if this damn line ever moved! She looked down at the DVD. How much did she want it? She could always put it down and walk out of the store. But why should she let a geeky weirdo deprive her of a movie she wanted to watch? Besides, she had fifteen minutes to kill before picking up her dinner. And she wasn't about to be harassed into fleeing by some horny male who thought because she had spoken to him it gave him the right to—

"I do know you, Claire. I know when you were in college you enjoyed this herb greatly. It is nothing to regret or hide, is it?"

This time she spun around and slapped his too-near chest with her DVD. "Back off, okay? I don't regret anything, except maybe speaking to you." She turned around to the line and moved a few feet ahead, hating that she was making a scene. Maybe she should walk out and go to another video store or . . . hold it. How did he know her name? She hadn't told him.

Her heart began slamming into the wall of her chest. How did he know her *name*?

"You have nothing to fear, Claire," he whispered behind her.

His voice was close. Too close to her ear. Every instinct was telling her to run, to get as far away from him as possible. He might be a stalker, or a rapist or—

"I would never harm you. Calm down, Claire."

She couldn't move. She was frozen with fear. He seemed to know her thoughts! Her hands, tightly holding the DVD, began to shake. She should yell out, run, call the police . . .

Suddenly she felt a hand upon her shoulder and his voice was so close to her ear that she could feel his breath as he spoke.

"Let us pay for your movie and we can speak outside the store. I promise I mean you no harm. Please believe me."

A weird, though pleasantly warm sensation seemed to radiate from his hand into her body. She felt . . . calm. Calmer. Her stomach muscles unclenched and her diaphragm relaxed. Her mind seemed flooded with . . . well-being, as if . . . somebody had just passed her a joint! Everything seemed all right with the world. The people around her were no longer slow and impeding her exit from the store. They were . . . fellow travelers in life and she felt a kinship with every single one of them.

It was her turn to step up to the counter and she barely recognized that the geek still had his hand on her shoulder, as if they were together as a couple, renting a funny movie for the weekend. Who cared if he was a geek? Smiling at the clerk, she handed over her movie and took her membership card and her money out of her pocket. She offered her card.

"Did you find everything you wanted?" the woman behind the counter asked, processing Claire's card through the computer.

"Yes, thank you," Claire murmured, slipping a five-dollar bill onto the counter while thinking the woman looked tired but had a nice smile. Claire wondered how she felt working on a Saturday night. Was there a husband and children waiting for her? Claire hoped she was happy and her family appreciated her when she got home.

Irrationally, she had to fight the urge to give the tired woman a hug. Instead, she kept smiling. A part of her knew she was thinking irrationally, like some stoned-out hippie wanting to give everyone the peace sign. What was she going to think next? That she should start singing "All You Need Is Love"?

Whatever bizarre thing was happening to her, she wasn't ready to stop it. It just felt so good. No worries. No past, no future. Just truly enjoying the present moment and everyone around her. She took her change, thanked the woman and walked with the geek still beside her to pick up her movie on the other side of the counter. He pushed open the door for her and when she was standing outside she allowed him to walk her to her car in the parking lot.

"Please listen to me, Claire. It is time we meet. I have something very important to tell you."

Still mellow, Claire looked up at him in the darkened parking lot and swore she saw tiny white lights surrounding his head. She stopping walking and gasped in awe. "Who . . . *are* you?"

"You may call me Michael," he said, smiling down at her.

"Michael . . ." she repeated, thinking the name fit him. "Are you like a science teacher or something?"

"A science teacher?" He seemed to think about it for a moment, then said, "I'm more . . . something, Claire," he answered, staring into her eyes with the most friendly expression.

"You know out here in the dark . . . in the parking lot you look . . . different." She couldn't stop staring at the beautiful lights around his head. *How did he do that?*

"How so?"

She grinned. "Not so . . . nerdy, ya know?" Then, realizing she had spoken out loud and probably insulted him, she quickly added, "Not that you're nerdy or anything. You're kinda cute in a . . . I don't know, studious way."

"And that is a compliment?" he asked with amusement.

She tilted her head. "I'd take it as one." Why was she speaking to the man like this? Like she was flirting with him? But those lights, those beautiful lights . . . swirling faintly around him and—

"Claire," he interrupted her thoughts, bringing her back to the conversation. "If I take my hand away from your shoulder, will you allow me to speak to you without getting upset?"

She simply nodded, yet when his hand lifted she slowly began to feel . . . less mellow, wondering why she had permitted a stranger to touch her, lead her about, take control of her. Her body stiffened and she reached into the pocket of her jeans for her car keys.

"Claire, the time has come for you to step into your life in a more meaningful way. There are . . . issues . . . you can heal now and I have come to assist you in any way I can."

She blinked, feeling more like herself, more normal. What the *hell* had she been doing even giving this man the time of day? Embarrassed, angry, mostly embarrassed, she straightened her shoulders. "Is that it? Can I go now?" Her other hand was ready to flip open her cell and dial 911.

"That is it for now. I can see you are frightened again. We will continue our discussion at a time when you are more calm."

"Fine."

She opened the door of her BMW. Getting inside, she put her key into the ignition, closed the door and locked the car. Before she backed out of her parking space, she lowered the window a fraction and called out, "If you ever come near me again, I'm calling the police. Stay away from me!"

And then she threw the car into reverse and backed up so fast she didn't even check her rearview mirror to see if she hit him. Slamming the car into drive, she left tire marks and squealed out of the parking lot and onto the highway.

What the hell had happened back there? Her heart was pounding. She could feel her pulse in her temples and even in her fingertips as she clutched the steering wheel. Her mouth was so dry that she had to gulp several times to bring moisture back into it.

Who was that nutcase?

What did he say? There were issues she could heal now? What kind of person spoke like that? It was perhaps the worst pickup line she'd ever heard. Shaking her head, she suddenly realized that she hadn't turned on her head-lights.

"Shit!"

Scared, she flipped them on and released her breath. God, he'd rattled her so much she was now a road hazard.

She drove to Guiseppe's like a student driver, in the slow lane, looking in the rearview mirror every few seconds, hands clutching the steering wheel, her rigid back not resting against the seat cushion. She realized she didn't have her seat belt on, but was too scared to attempt buckling it while driving.

A few minutes later she pulled into the crowded parking lot of the restaurant. Finally finding a parking space in the back, she turned off the car and just sat, staring out the window into the night. Now it was safe to think . . .

What had he done to her? What was with that hand on her shoulder, making her feel so . . . so mellow and peaceful? It really was like some kind of drug had entered her bloodstream and had rushed over her mind and body. And even if she wasn't ready to admit it yet, she knew it had felt wonderful. It was as if she'd had no will to resist it. Hell, it hadn't even occurred to her to resist it, because it had been years, lots of years, since she'd felt that . . . free . . . of worry, self-doubt, isolation. For a few moments there in that video store and in the parking lot she'd felt lifted, out of the mundane everyday struggle of life and into—*what*?

She didn't know, but it had been lovely to drop her usual protectiveness with strangers, to feel connected to everyone around her, to see others with compassion and . . . peace.

Peace?

She sighed and got out of her car.

Whom was she kidding? Peace was great, but it was the hardest thing to achieve in everyday life. Too many things annoyed her, like ignorant or rude people, or off-the-wall geeks who accost you in video stores.

But what was with those lights, those beautiful dancing lights around him?

Scared, because she might have just had a delusional episode, Claire muttered, "Who cares?" *Get dinner and get home,* she told herself. Where it's safe. Where the only craziness comes from the Gang whenever *their* lives go off the charts.

Her life was supposed to be an even keel.

Isn't that what she had worked so hard to achieve? No craziness. No sudden violent episodes that make you curl up into a ball of helplessness—

Damn that geek! His stupid talk about healing issues had brought up shit from her past that she'd dealt with and buried a long time ago.

Who the hell was he to have invaded her head like that?

Pushing open the door to the small Italian restaurant, Claire was determined to clear her mind as she walked up to the hostess. "Hey, Carmen," she said with a big smile. "Hard to find parking out there, so business must be good. How's that gorgeous man treating you?"

The older woman grinned. "Takeout again, Claire?"

Claire shrugged. "Number eleven, and what can I say? I'm addicted to Tony's sauce."

Carmen, dressed in a stylish black dress, gave her a knowing nod. "I'll go back and see if it's ready."

"Okay," Claire answered, taking out her bank card as Carmen walked toward the kitchen.

Claire looked at the crowded tables in the dining room. Families. Couples. Everyone looked happy. Again, she felt like an outsider, an observer. She saw an older man reach behind his wife's chair and stroke her back as he listened to the conversation of the couple across the table from him. It kind of tugged at her heart to witness his tenderness. Now see, she wouldn't mind that . . . some attention, some tenderness. Trouble was it wasn't until the testosterone dropped in an aging male that he realized what women have always known, that relationships are more important than empires.

"So when am I ever going to seat you at a table with a man?" Carmen asked, placing the box with her dinner on her hostess table. "You're too young and pretty to be eating takeout alone."

Claire grinned as she handed over her bank card. "Ah, Mamma Carmen," she answered in a teasing voice, "all I need to be happy is Tony's blush marinara sauce."

Carmen took the card and raised her eyebrows. "If all you want is the sauce, you miss out on the real meal. Stop fighting yourself, Claire," she said, running the card through the register. "One cannot survive on appetizers alone. It's time to decide on the main course, no?"

Shrugging, Claire took her card and stuffed it into her pocket. "Some people go their whole lives without deciding."

Carmen grinned as she waited and then placed the credit receipt in front of Claire to be signed.

Claire picked up the pen and scribbled her signature.

"But not you, Claire. You are a woman meant to be cherished."

Sliding the receipt back, Claire picked up her box. "Are you cherished, Carmen?"

Carmen tilted her head. "I haven't stayed married to that man for twenty-three years for his sauce."

Claire grinned. "Good for you," she said, and meant it. "See you soon, Carmen."

As she turned away, she heard Carmen say, "Not for takeout, I hope. Bring a man."

Claire simply waved as she walked out the door.

A man . . .

Why was everything in her life right now shoving her man-less state in her face? She'd known Carmen for years, so she didn't take offense. Carmen was always treating her like a daughter, thinking the only path to happiness was through a husband and family. She was old school, and she was cherished. If you think you've found the solution to anything, you wanted to share it with others.

Cherished.

That word brought a lump into her throat.

Had she ever felt cherished? *Ever?*

Sadly, Claire couldn't remember and figured the answer was no.

Chapter
3

CLAIRE WAS STARTING TO BELIEVE IT MIGHT NEVER have happened, at least not the way she remembered it. There simply couldn't have been some weird guy who seemed to have magic in his hands, who told her she had issues to heal, who had beautiful tiny lights dancing around his head in the dark. This stuff just didn't happen in her life, in anyone's life. Really . . . when she thought about it, the whole thing was absurd.

So don't think about it anymore, she told herself, slipping into the cool water of her pool.

She had finished her movie, half of her dinner and had tried to sleep, but that bizarre encounter at the video store seemed to haunt her. Finally, she'd decided that a vigorous swim would tire her and it was a perfect night for it. Summer was not her favorite time of year. It was better than winter, which could be brutal, so when she'd bought the one-story contemporary, the first major expenditure was having a pool installed. In her mind, it was a necessary luxury.

Summers in the northeast could be stifling with humidity, where the air seemed so heavy you literally had to suck it in to breathe, so she went from an air-conditioned home to an air-conditioned car to an air-conditioned office. Still, being enclosed all the time when she spent a small fortune on landscaping seemed too restrictive—so the pool. It provided exercise and she could enjoy her backyard in comfort.

It wasn't that she was spoiled, she thought as she took pleasure in the cool water that lowered her temperature and her anxiety. She really did suffer with the humidity ever since she was a child.

Slowly swimming out to the deep end, Claire stopped. Treading water, she looked at her home in the darkness and smiled with satisfaction. It was her own little slice of paradise with a wide stone patio for entertaining. Two steps down she used a smaller patio for sunbathing, though no one really sat in the sun anymore without 40 SPF. Even though the summer sun was no longer a friend to her skin, she did love summer nights.

Summer nights . . . like the first time she was kissed in eighth grade by Mike Murphy. A shy furtive kiss at a friend's pool party. Both she and Mike tried to make it seem like in the movies, but she just remembered fearing Mike was going to suck her lips into his mouth. Too bad he'd never learned how to kiss . . .

Mike's whole family had died in a car accident before that summer was over. Claire sighed at the loss. She'd been stunned, beyond shocked, that Mike and his younger sister had been killed along with their parents on vacation in Wyoming. At thirteen you think you are invincible. Sure you somehow know that everyone is going to die someday, but you can't even picture yourself graduating high school, let alone becoming an old lady who's lived a full life.

Blowing her breath out slowly, she looked up at the stars, twinkling against the dark sky.

Kind of like those lights around the weird guy in the parking lot . . .

Stop thinking about him, she scolded herself and resumed her swim. When she reached the tiled cement wall, she pushed off and started her laps. Back and forth across the pool she glided, loving the feel of weightlessness and her own power to command her body. She especially loved the feeling right after pushing off the wall, the silent surge through the water until her lungs demanded she surface. There was no time to think of anything other than being in a supportive element, moving her arms and legs and breathing on every third or fourth stroke. Time disappeared. Gravity altered. There were no outside forces demanding her attention. She even lost count of her laps.

When she felt the burning in her arms and legs, Claire stopped at the deep end and hung on to the wall for a few moments to catch her breath, then pushed herself backward and just floated, looking at the stars. It was the reward she earned for her laps, cradled in the water like a baby in the womb. If she stayed in the moment everything seemed right in the world.

Closing her eyes, she let the feeling sink in deeper, relaxing her to the point where she wished it were possible to sleep just like this . . . but it wasn't. She would have to surrender soon and get out, strip off her panties and the sports bra, towel off and fall into a dry bed. Opening her eyes, she listened to a frog in the distance and grinned as she heard an answering call of another frog. Even the cicadas had begun their nightly chorus. Nature . . . God, it was beautiful on nights like this.

And then her gaze narrowed as she tried to make out a cluster of stars that she hadn't seen before. And the more she looked at them, the closer they seemed to get. Startled, Claire stopped floating and swam backward, all the while watching as the stars became clearer and closer, seeming to leave the sky and head right in her direction!

When her arms touched the cement steps, she sat on the second stair and watched in awe as the stars seemed to float in the air as they descended . . . closer and closer.

Meteor shower?

Aliens?

Claire had no more time to think as the stars seemed to come right out of the sky and hover above her pool! Stunned, frozen, she didn't move, except for her jaw dropping in astonishment as they swirled above the water not ten feet away.

They were beautiful orbs of dancing light, sparkling in all the colors of the rainbow, like a shattered floating prism. The water seemed to light up with their brilliance. Amazing! Stunningly beautiful!

And coming closer to her!

Internally, she fought her fascination and her fear. What the hell was going on?

She tried to back up to the next step, to get out of the water, to save herself, when suddenly the lights surged toward her and she found herself surrounded in breathtaking color.

She gasped in awe as she was filled with a sensation of pleasure. Threads of joy raced through her body, shooting out her fingertips and toes, filling up her torso until she moaned and felt herself go weak with desire. And then . . . unbelievably, her entire body arched toward them, welcoming them as surge after surge of exquisite pleasure exploded within her. Her mind, if she still had one, vaguely put together the image of a mind-blowing orgasm, leaving her weak with joy and fulfillment. From somewhere outside herself, she realized she seemed to be floating into the lights, carried out of the water, placed on a chaise lounge and covered in a towel. She tried to open her eyes in disappointment when the pleasure abruptly ended, but all she could do was gulp air into her lungs as she lay on the chair like a puppet whose strings had been cut.

She couldn't move.

"Claire?"

She heard her name whispered, yet was too afraid to turn her head.

"Claire, don't be afraid. I've tried to show you that you have no need of fear. It will, in truth, make everything so much more difficult."

Her head moved like a robot's, jerking in tiny movements until she saw who was sitting in the other chair.

It was him!

The nerd!

She gasped in shock. *"You!"* she muttered in an accusatory tone. "Those lights! You!" And then she blinked a few times. "Why aren't you wet?" she gasped, closing the towel around her as tightly as she could manage with weak arms.

He smiled, seemingly very relaxed in the midst of madness. "Would you like me to appear wet? I can, if you wish it. I will do whatever it takes to communicate with you."

She shook her head, still staring at him as though one of them had just crossed the line into insanity. "That . . . *that* was you? Those lights?"

He nodded. "That is a more accurate appearance of who I am."

"Who *are* you? *What* are you? Are you . . . like an alien?"

He grinned. "Not by what your conventional perceptions of that label would describe. I am a being from another dimension. A sentient being like you, Claire, full of energy and information. You, your energy, vibrates at eight hertz and mine vibrates much more quickly, thus I am able to do things you might think of as alien."

She swallowed, trying to make sense of it all. He can't be what he says. It isn't possible and—

"I am exactly who I say I am, Claire," he said, as though he could read her mind. "I am not here to hurt you, but to help you evolve."

"You . . . *can't* be real!"

"I am.

She shook her head. "I don't want to evolve. Go away . . . *please!*"

"Everything is in a process of evolving, Claire. Including you. That is creation."

"To where?" she demanded, still not believing she was having this conversation with the nerd, the alien nerd. "*Where* am I going to evolve to?" she asked desperately, thinking he was going to abduct her. She felt her throat tighten with fear.

She had always made fun of those people!

"Wherever you desire. But you have so much to learn before contemplating that decision. That is why I have come here to help."

"Help me learn what?" She was actually doing this . . . participating in this crazy conversation!

"Help you learn the way your world operates, the way human beings are meant to operate. I would like to help you remember who you truly are."

She gulped down her fear. "Who am I?"

He chuckled, in a nice way that made her relax a bit. A tiny bit. Maybe he wasn't going to abduct her. Maybe he just wanted to talk. Knowing she was in the presence of *something* far more powerful than her, she would let him have his say and then maybe he would turn back into the lights and go back into the sky, or wherever he was from!

"You are a marvelous creation who, like the majority of humans, has forgotten your identity. You are a creator, and yet you give away your power and support others' creations whether they serve you or not. It is time, Claire, for you to clear your energy and begin to realize your purpose."

What? Some shred of reason slammed back into her brain.

"This . . . this is ridiculous!" she declared, trying to sit up straighter. "I can't be sitting here talking to you! I mean, I meet you in a video store and now you appear in my backyard after I've had . . . I don't know, maybe a ministroke or something, and then you try to tell me you are like this creator being from another planet who—"

"I didn't say I came from another planet," he gently interrupted. "There are many dimensions to this planet you are not even aware of yet. You can't even fathom the many possibilities available to you in this moment because your mind is struck in the third dimension. You could deny this is happening to you. You could jump up and call the police if you think they can help you, but they would be incapable of seeing me and supporting your claims. You could run to a hospital and check your nervous system to see if indeed your brain is short-circuiting. Or, you could believe me and realize you are blessed not to waste any more time in delusions of fear. There is work to be done, Claire, and I have come to assist you."

She simply blinked, breathing in, trying to make sense of what he'd just said. "Why me?" she whispered.

"Why not you? You are a marvelous being, Claire, and when we achieved union a few moments ago, I saw into your soul. It is most beautiful and yet there is fear that resides there as well. I have come to help you let go of that fear."

"I'm not afraid," she insisted, wishing she actually felt like that. "But I have to tell you . . . you see, you've come to the wrong person. I'm not holy or even a very good person. I'm selfish. I speak my mind. Sometimes I can be downright mean." She paused to catch her breath. "So you'd better take your lights and . . . and whatever is in them to someone else. You've made a mistake."

He smiled again. Patiently. Almost paternally, as though listening to a child's protestations. "I haven't made a mistake."

"You don't make mistakes?" she accused, wanting him to disappear, just go away. "Sounds a little arrogant."

"If I should make a mistake, I can change my course of action."

"Exactly!" she agreed, sitting up straight. "Change your course of action. Find the right person who will appreciate you barging into their well-organized life and turning it up-side down. The welcome mat has been pulled in here."

"Claire . . . Claire," he murmured, slightly shaking his head. "The longer you fight me on this, the longer it will take for you to begin your lessons."

Her shoulders tightened even more in defense. "Lessons? What are you talking about? I don't need any lessons."

"Now that could be interpreted as arrogant, don't you think?"

"My life . . . is not so bad. In fact, it's pretty damn good," she argued. "I have a great job, great friends, a terrific house and a fairly sizable portfolio to see me into retire-ment. And I'm healthy," she added, figuring she'd leave the vibrator off her list. "So you need to find someone whose life is falling apart. Maybe they'd listen to your lessons. I'm just fine."

"Are you . . . fine, Claire? Really?"

"Yes!" she insisted. "I'm perfectly fine. My life is per-fectly fine."

He continued to stare at her and Claire felt as though he was reading her thoughts again, probing her soul, seeing her life story.

"What about your family?" he asked in a low voice. "Are you also perfectly fine with that situation?"

Her jaw dropped and she tilted her head, completely shocked by his words. "How dare you pry into my past?" she whispered, feeling the anger nearly close off her throat. "I . . . don't know what you think you know, but—"

"I know everything about you, Claire. Ever since you came into this dimension. It is all written in your soul. It is the fear that you have denied that you need to examine now. Can't you feel the weight of it dragging on you and holding you back? You think you have put the past behind you, that you are done with the past, but perhaps the past isn't done with you."

"Look, you need to shut up now." She unclenched her teeth, less and less afraid of him, of whatever he was. "I don't care who you are or where you came from, but you and your lessons can take a flying leap right back to wherever dimension you call home. You need to get out of my life and leave me alone."

He stood up slowly. "You are upset again. It is understandable. I knew you would be a formidable challenge and I should have remembered and gone a bit more slowly." He looked down at her and smiled with kindness. "The point is I'm here now, Claire, and you cannot banish me. You gave away that power many years ago as a young girl, when you closed down a part of you that every creator needs to successfully manifest. I am here. We have achieved union. You are my assignment. The lessons will begin, whether they be as a whisper or a brick wall falling on your head. That choice, my beloved, is yours."

He bowed slightly and then, right in front of her, he began to transform into those marvelous swirling lights!

She sat, her mouth open, and watched the lights spiral upward and disappear into the dark night sky. Her breath seemed to leave her body in an abrupt gasp.

"I'll be damned," she whispered, suddenly aware of a chill as a slight wind touched her damp clothes. The sounds returned, the crickets chirping, the frogs croaking, the cicadas singing. Somewhere along the street a dog barked.

"What's happening here?" she muttered, bringing the towel over her shoulders as she fought for some sanity. How could any of this have happened? And what was with those lights? Why had they produced such an exquisite feeling that she had thought it was the best sex she'd ever experienced? With an alien? But he didn't say he was an alien. What then? An angel? A dimension traveler. That's what he said. He'd come from another dimension and he wanted to teach her some lessons about . . . being a creator?

She needed to get up, get inside, get some dry clothes on, get a bloody drink inside of her! Nothing like this had ever happened to her, never happened to anyone she knew. People just didn't have dimension travelers pop into their lives as teachers, she thought as she pushed herself upright. She felt dizzy for a moment and clung to the back of the chaise lounge to steady herself. Maybe it was all a dream? Maybe she really did pass out on the chaise after her laps? Okay, she didn't remember getting out of the pool on her own, or wrapping the towel around her, but it could have happened, right? She had been annoyed since the video store and . . . and that's why she'd gone swimming to tire her muscles and she had felt so sleepy floating in the water afterward and . . .

And none of it made sense.

It wasn't a dream. That fact kept all other explanations at bay.

How could he have known that stuff about her family? God, even the Gang didn't know about it. She'd told them her father had died when she was young, but she didn't want to discuss her family and had let them believe whatever they wanted. For all they knew her family could be dead. And they were dead, all of them, to her anyway—had been for almost twenty years now. She wanted nothing to do with her mother or stepfather, or his goddamned son. They could all rot in whatever hell their lives were. They had nothing to do with her or the person she had become.

Shaking her head to also shake out the anger she still felt, Claire pushed herself away from the chaise and walked up to the wide stone patio.

And to hell with *him,* whoever he was, for dragging that shit up again after a successful internment. How dare he or anyone else shake the foundation she had built her life upon? She may not be holy, or even as spiritual as Cristine or Isabel or any of the others in the Gang, but she was a decent person, which in itself was a minor miracle after surviving her beginnings.

And that's what she was . . . a survivor.

And screw anyone who tried to say she needed to *heal*.

She had healed and she refused to allow him to rip open old scar tissue.

Screw him and screw his lessons!

Chapter

4

SHE DIDN'T EVEN TURN AWAY FROM HER COMPUTER
screen when her phone rang. "Yes?" Focusing on a business
report, Claire waited for her assistant, Shelly, to speak.

"Claire, there's a man out here, a Mr. Clarke, asking to
see you."

"Does he have an appointment?" she asked, looking at
her calendar and not recognizing the name.

"No, he's a lawyer and he says he has important business
with you."

In a rush, her brain tried to compute who might be suing
her and for what, then deciding she had nothing to fear, she
said, "Okay, give me a few minutes to clear my desk."

"Right," Shelly replied and hung up.

Claire began putting papers back into the folder she was
working on while wondering what Mr. Clarke's business
might be. It couldn't be about the foundation. That had been
put together with three attending lawyers at her insistence.
Everything in the foundation's charter was airtight to protect Cristine and the Gang. Maybe it was a client of the firm
who was dissatisfied, or one of those she had handed over
for another to supervise when she had taken on the foundation. Being a financial advisor meant you were either a hero

or a villain, depending on the market and realistic expectations of the client. Realistic was the key word.

Well, she had nothing to hide. Her life was an open book, at least her business life. Her private life was fiercely guarded, or had been until that bizarre encounter at her pool two nights ago. *Stop thinking about it,* she mentally scolded. She'd lost count how many times she'd pushed thoughts of that crazy evening out of her head. It had been like when she was child and had a loose tooth. Her tongue couldn't seem to leave it alone.

A tooth. That was tangible. What did one do when it was the mind that seemed to be loose, becoming unhinged? She had managed at work to keep the whole crazy thing out of the office, convincing herself it had never happened as things resumed their normal routine. She'd had . . . an unexplainable episode. That's all it was. There was no explanation for it and maybe it hadn't even happened. Maybe she really did dream the whole thing. Maybe she was going into early menopause, or something was weird with her hormones or . . .

Running her hands through her shoulder-length hair, Claire sat up straighter and again pushed the insane evening out of her head. Now was not the time to remember her wet panties and sports bra she'd hung in the shower to dry.

She *had* gone swimming.

And something *had* happened.

Don't think about it, she again mentally commanded, as her office door opened and Shelly introduced Mr. Clarke to her.

Claire rose and held out her hand. "How do you do, Mr. Clarke? Won't you take a seat?"

The man was older, maybe in his sixties, and dressed impeccably in a dark gray suit and Ivy League school tie. "It's a pleasure to meet you, Mrs. Hutchinson," he said after shaking her hand and lowering himself onto one of the leather wing chairs opposite her desk. He appeared to be a bit uncomfortable as he sat with his briefcase on his lap.

"How may I help you?" Claire asked with a smile, sitting down and folding her hands in the lap of her navy blue suit. She tried not to look at the briefcase, instinct telling her she wasn't going to like whatever was inside.

Mr. Clarke cleared his throat and said, "I'm afraid I've come to report Eric Williams's death. Mr. Williams was your stepfather, is that correct?"

Claire felt as though someone had struck her stomach with a baseball bat.

"How did you find me?" she murmured, clutching the bottom button on her suit jacket. She'd kept her last name from her marriage, a marriage she'd believed her family knew nothing about.

"Your mother, Alicia Williams, hired our offices to locate you." He opened his briefcase and took out a folded paper. Handing it to her, he added, "You are requested to be at the reading of Eric Williams's will."

She took the paper and placed it on her desk, unread. "I don't want anything from that man."

"That isn't my business, Mrs. Hutchinson. I was to find you and inform you that you are named as a beneficiary in the will, and your presence is requested at the reading. As you will see it's on Monday of next week at the law offices of Whitman and Collier in Philadelphia."

"Can't I just sign something saying I don't want any money?"

"You would have to contact Whitman and Collier, Mrs. Hutchinson. Perhaps you'd like to think about it for a few days before making any decision."

"I don't need to think about it," she stated, realizing she'd spent decades not thinking about her family, denying she'd even had one, and by her definition of family she might have been better off if she had been an orphan.

"Perhaps you have a favorite charity," Mr. Clarke suggested with a sympathetic smile. "If not for yourself, maybe you could help others."

She immediately thought about the foundation. They were always trying to get grants and donations to help women in need. "I don't know," she answered. "All of this, your contacting me, is a shock, Mr. Clarke. I've had nothing to do with . . . any of them in many years."

"Yes, your mother explained."

Her head shot up and she laughed bitterly. "I'm sure she did. Her version of it." She tried to pull herself together. Straightening her shoulders, she said in her best professional voice, "I'm sorry for that outburst. Is there anything else?"

Mr. Clarke shook his head and closed his briefcase. "My business with you, Mrs. Hutchinson, is concluded."

Claire stood up and extended her hand across the desk. "Thank you, Mr. Clarke."

"May I report that you are at least thinking about attending?"

He seemed like a decent person. It wasn't his fault he was in the employ of liars and betrayers. "I will think about it, and I'll contact this other law firm before Monday."

Mr. Clarke shook her hand politely. "Thank you for your time."

She simply nodded and watched as he left her office.

When the door closed, Claire sank to her chair. She stared, unseeing, at her office, not seeing the mahogany bookshelves, the Persian rug under the leather furniture, the original watercolors on the walls. None of it seemed to exist as her mind grabbed hold of her and pulled her back in time, seeing them all together at the Chippendale dining room table, seated like the perfect little upper-middle-class family. Eric at the head of the table; Alicia, who'd sold out her soul for a wealthy second husband at the other end; David seated across from her, leering, knowing . . .

God, she hated them all and she wouldn't shed a tear for one of their passing.

Even though she didn't believe in hell, she hoped Eric's ass was held to the fire somewhere in the ethers. There had to be some kind of justice for people like him.

And like his son.

And then, as if lightning were striking her mind, she thought about the nerd.

Michael, that was his name.

He'd said even though she was done with the past, the past wasn't done with her. Had he known Eric had died? Had he known all along this was going to happen, that she'd be sucked back into the past like this? Had he been trying to warn her?

And just like that, her mind was accepting the unacceptable.

The nerd had been real?

She wanted to call out to him and demand answers, but she didn't dare do something so irrational at work. She cleared her desk, locked her files and picked up her purse. Opening the door to the outer office, Claire said, "Shelly, I'm going to take off. Call my appointment for this afternoon and reschedule, okay?"

Shelly, older and motherly, appeared confused. "Are you okay, Claire? You seem . . . I don't know, pale and sort of shocked."

"I'm fine," she lied, searching in her purse for her car keys. "Look, I'm sorry to make more work for you, but I have to leave. Oh, and tell Jim Doherty I had a family emergency and we'll have to meet tomorrow, or whenever it's convenient for him. Work it out with Maryanne, his assistant. I'll take him to lunch, whatever, and really apologize for me. It's a partners meeting and I can't afford to piss him off."

"You got it," Shelly said, taking notes. "Are you sure you're okay? Family emergency?"

Claire looked up and blew a strand of hair away from her eyes. Keys in hand, she shook her head. "I just need to go, Shelly. Tell them whatever you want." And she turned around and left the prestigious offices of Kellogg, Crainpool and Reingold Investments. It didn't matter that she had spent years building up her reputation and her clientele and was finally being considered for partnership. Nothing mattered in that moment, except getting away . . . running away.

She'd once been very good at that.

Fifteen minutes later she sat in her driveway, the air conditioner in the car running as she stared up at her house while thinking about the life she'd made for herself and how far she'd come from that withdrawn, sad child who had felt trapped inside a nightmare.

From the moment she'd first seen the long stucco white rancher, she'd known that with some paint and great landscaping she could make it into her home. Years ago she'd had it painted cream, the perfect backdrop for the green of her trees and shrubs. The double front doors were of carved teak wood and two huge urns of spiral evergreens flanked either side. It was simple, yet tasteful, and low maintenance.

The last thing she had wanted was maintenance.

In a flash she seemed to travel back to a time when her list of household chores had made her feel like Cinderella, only there were no evil stepsisters. Just David. Spoiled, manipulative, lying David. Three years older than her and stone evil. She didn't care what Isabel and Cristine said about there not being such a thing as evil. They hadn't lived her life. They didn't know what it was like . . . where you had to balance housework and schoolwork and lost innocence with a household where there were no boundaries for those around you. How many times had she run away before she was thirteen? Six? The police always found her before she got far enough and dragged her back. How could she tell them the truth? She was so ashamed. How many times had she wanted to run to someone, anyone, and beg for their help to escape? But she had kept her silence because of fear.

Sitting in the car, Claire hung her head as she felt that once familiar knot wrap around her belly and tighten.

Secrets.

Her childhood had been filled with them.

She had hated the secrets almost as much as she had hated the people who had caused her to keep them. It was as though she had enabled them with her silence, had been a part of the evil because she had lost her voice, her ability to shout out to the world that her family was a fake. To the rest of society they appeared normal, the typical American Dream fulfilled. Inside the house was a totally different story. And now she tried not to wonder what secrets were behind the white picket fences of the houses surrounding her own.

She had shut down after the first time, after David had threatened to harm her mother if Claire ever told on him. No eleven-year-old girl should ever have to carry the weight of that like a boulder attached to her heart. Her only escape had been in school. David had gone to a prep school and she had been free of him during the day, of his detached father whose only interest had been in accumulating more money and promoting his son to one day take his place as a pillar of the community. And then there had been Alicia, her mother . . . beautiful and greedy, willing to sacrifice her own flesh and blood to secure a lifestyle she had only dreamed of having.

She still could feel the pain of finally, desperately telling her mother about the abuse, sobbing and pleading with her mother to save her . . . and the jagged edge of betrayal that had sliced so deeply when her mother called her a liar, dragged her before Eric and demanded her stepfather beat the truth out of her. Nothing in her life could ever hurt as much as hearing her mother egg her husband to hit harder.

And Eric did, furious that his son's honor was being tarnished.

David's evil grin later that night as he had stuck his head into her bedroom where she had been curled into a ball, whimpering like a baby, silenced her for good.

No one was going to save her. The raised red welts from the beating would go away, but her heart had turned cold from her mother's betrayal. After three years of having her stepbrother sneak into her bedroom, hold his hand over her mouth as he took away her innocence and shoved himself inside her so brutally that even in her dazed, immature mind she knew it was about hate, not sex, Claire realized she was on her own.

She had been so alone in the nightmare of her young life.

Her only escape had to be in her head. She would use her mind and get out. She would go to college and never again need them for shelter or food or clothes or anything else to survive.

All she'd had to do was get through high school and secure a scholarship.

And she remembered stealing fifty dollars from her mother and going into a sporting goods store and buying a hunting knife. The next time David came into her room, he had found her prepared to kill rather than surrender.

The coward. He was nothing more than a bully, a protected bully who'd backed down when the tip of the shiny blade had pressed against his neck.

He never intruded into her bedroom again and that's when Claire realized she actually had the ability, the will, to take another's life. In her fragile mind, she knew something had turned inside of her. She would never again be sweet or nice, the daughter Alicia so wanted to show off to the country club crowd. She'd dyed her blond hair black. Painted her nails black. Rimmed her eyes in black pencil. Wore black clothes, all to show her complete disdain for her family's hypocrisy.

If she was the black sheep, she had thought, she might as well look the part.

Claire inhaled deeply, realizing her breathing had been shallow, and turned off the car. She had been one of a million victims of sexual abuse at a time when family secrets weren't televised on talk shows. It simply wasn't done. You just dealt with it and got on, the abusers safe by society's reluctance to look at the ugliness behind closed doors.

And now Eric was dead.

She felt nothing, except anger that his death was dragging all this shit up again. And his money? Her initial instinct was to take his money, however much it was, find out where he was buried and burn the lot on his grave. It would give her satisfaction, but not much more. Getting out of the car, she walked up to her house. Maybe she could donate the money, either to the foundation or to victims of abuse.

Sighing, Claire entered the air-conditioning of her house and felt her blood pressure lower. This was her sanctuary. Clean. Minimal, with gleaming hardwood floors, dark chocolate leather furniture, modern sculptures and colorful paintings. No muss. No fuss. And it looked like something right out of a designer's portfolio.

She dropped her purse onto the table by the front door and slipped out of her navy heels. The floor felt cool under her feet. Unbuttoning her suit jacket, she headed down the long hallway to her bedroom. The silence comforted her, the slight hum of the central air conditioner was like white noise, helping to empty her mind of the past. She entered her bedroom and began to undress slowly and methodically. Hanging up her suit, she knew where she wanted to be, so she stripped off all her clothes and pulled open the bottom drawer of her dresser.

Staring into the drawer, she blew her breath out in a rush.

No one needed so many bathing suits. All the tops and bottoms were thrown in together, making it look like a colorful tangled mass. Bikini. If it were night she would have turned off the pool lights and gone swimming nude. But it was the afternoon and a suit was required. She picked out a pale blue top and managed to find the skimpy bottom. Just enough to cover the bare essentials. She pulled the bottom on and adjusted it over her behind. She tied the top at the neck and her back, then shifted the small triangles of material over her breasts.

Not even looking in the mirror, Claire left her bedroom and stopped at the double linen closet in the hallway. She pulled out a white bath sheet and carried it out to the kitchen. From the wide glass doors she could see the pool, the blue water looking inviting and promising to cool her body and her mind. She filled a glass with ice water from the fridge, then picking up a pair of sunglasses from a bowl on the kitchen counter, she unlocked one of the glass doors and slid it open.The contrasting heat and humidity of the outdoors hit her like a wave enveloping her body. She quickly shut the door behind her and headed across the wide patio.

When she reached the second, smaller patio, Claire put her glass of water on a small table and threw the towel onto a chaise lounge along with her sunglasses. She barely noticed the blooming flowers in pots and urns scattered around the backyard. Paula and Cristine would know the names, but to her they were part of the backdrop that her landscaper had designed and maintained weekly. The pool was her main interest. She hurried to the deep end and dove cleanly into the water, intent on staying beneath the surface for as long as her lungs would allow. Under the water the silence was her friend, blocking out all thinking. The past didn't exist. Nothing was real, except the pure moment of swimming through the water like a frog, pushing everything out of her way, seeing if she could make it to the shallow end without surfacing.

Her lungs were near bursting when she saw the steps. Determined to make it, Claire sliced harder at the water around her. When her hand touched the cement step, she raised her head, breaking through the surface and gulping air back into her body.

"You are a very good swimmer."

She opened her eyes in shock and gasped. He was back. The alien nerd.

She blinked a few times and pulled herself to the first step. Kneeling on it, so her shoulders were almost covered in water, Claire ran her hands over her wet face.

"You're back," she muttered, trying not to act surprised. And she wasn't. Not really. Isn't that why she had come home early? Yes, she wanted to immerse herself into the pool, but she had also wanted to talk to him again, to see if he was really *real*. Had he picked up on that?

She held her nose and bent backward into the water so her hair would sleek back from her face and give her time to compose herself.

"I thought you might want to talk," he said with a smile as she slowly moved her arms under the water to keep herself upright and facing him.

What was the point of protesting another intrusion? Especially since he was right. She did want to talk to him. "I guess I shouldn't be surprised to have you pop into my life like this, huh?"

"You aren't delusional, Claire. I am real. *This* is real between us, no matter what you think or feel. I've come to help."

She took a deep shuddering breath and shook her head. "I don't know why I'm accepting all this without a fight. It's . . . not like me."

He grinned. "No, it's not. But I am grateful the fight is over. Now we can proceed more quickly."

"Do you know about it? About Eric?"

"I am interested in everything about you, Claire," he answered, sitting on the edge of the chaise, resting his forearms on his knees as his hands dangled between his legs.

"But did you know he had died when you . . . came the last time?" she asked, deciding to get the ground rules out in the open.

He simply nodded.

"And you didn't tell me?"

"You didn't seem willing to discuss much of anything at the time. You wanted me to leave."

"Right. Okay," she conceded. "But you have to understand this . . . this intrusion is not normal. If I spoke of it to anyone, they'd think I was crazy and in need of being institutionalized. I still don't know who you are or where you came from. You're *not* like an . . . alien, right?"

He chuckled and Claire felt a vague stirring of attraction, which *was* crazy.

"No, I'm not an alien. Not what humanity has labeled an alien. I am a sentient being, like you, who is from a different dimension. And I have come to you because the world, our world, yours and mine, is now threatened. What happens here in this dimension ripples through all dimensions and—"

"Hold it, hold it!" she interrupted. "You can't be serious. You can't think *I'm* going to try and save the world!" She couldn't help it. She laughed at his ridiculous suggestion.

He seemed confused by her laughter. "Well yes, Claire. That is exactly why I'm here."

"Hey, Dimension Man, take a good look. If you know anything about me, then you know I'm mouthy and selfish. I'm trying to save myself, thank you very much."

He didn't say anything for a few moments, then said in a low voice, "That's all you have to do, Claire. Save yourself. That is the only way . . . one self at a time healing the wounds and traumas that hold you back from your true potential. You have to begin to use your energy is a more productive way, for yourself and for the planet."

"Where are you *from*? And I still think you've got the wrong person. I can give you the names of a few other women I know who are much more suitable for the task than—"

"How many times must I tell you I haven't made a mistake?" he asked, running his fingers through his hair. "Why won't you accept you are the correct human to evolve at this time?"

She shook her head. "Well, have you at least *tried* any others?" she demanded, stepping out of the pool and grabbing her towel to wrap around herself. She sat down on the bottom of the opposite chaise. " 'Cause you want someone a little more knowledgeable and spiritual I think. I'm not religious at all," she added, running her hands over the soft cotton of her towel to dry them.

"Good. At this time in your culture, that is in your favor. You are not hampered by anyone's dogma. And we have tried others . . . many times. Unfortunately our messages got weaved into your religions and became rules that made humans rigid in their thinking."

Claire blinked, wishing she could reach behind him and grab her sunglasses so he couldn't see her eyes. What he was saying! Messages getting weaved into religions? "So you're . . . what? An angel?" Yes. She actually asked that question.

He simply smiled.

"Does that mean yes?"

"What else are you thinking?" he asked, looking deeply into her eyes.

Claire wanted to look away, but seemed frozen, staring back at him, remembering all that . . . that *stuff* he had done the other night. No normal human being could have accomplished that!

"You . . . you're not . . . *God*?" she barely whispered in a frightened voice, trying to make it sound like a joke.

"I'm not?" he asked with a grin. "Though we are getting a bit ahead of ourselves at this point."

She swallowed the lump of fear in her throat while her whole body seemed to tingle with some weird kind of energy. "This is crazy," she muttered. "And a lightning bolt might come down and strike us both."

He laughed.

Laughed!

"Rigid thinking," he said with an affectionate grin.

Claire felt like she wanted to cry. "God's a nerd? A *geek*?" she squeaked, feeling as if her entire world were being turned upside down. They put people away for stuff like this!

Shaking his head, the nerd looked at her as though she were a child. "Claire, does that label, nerd or geek, imply intelligence?"

She could only nod.

"Would you think of a divine being as intelligent?"

Another nod.

"So yes, God must be a nerd or a geek."

"Oh, *God*," she murmured and shook her head. "I was hoping God was female and . . . and I must be having a nervous breakdown to even be considering that what you're saying . . . any of it . . . has any basis in fact."

"But God *is* female," he answered.

"You just said . . ."

"I just agreed that God must be a nerd or a geek."

"God's a female nerd?" she asked stupidly. "Then how come you . . . you look like a male?" She wanted to dunk her head into the water and bring back the silence. Anything to wipe out this insane discussion!

"Claire, you asked if I was God."

She stared at him, unwilling to enter into the craziness any further.

"I am God," he answered softly, before adding, "I know that statement is shocking to you, considering the degree of indoctrination you have endured through your social systems. What you might consider even more shocking is that you are also God. And so is everyone, everything, every animal, every blade of grass. Wherever your vision focuses, you will find the divine. There cannot be a separation. You human beings in this third dimension are the only ones who forget your true identity. You are creators who have forgotten to create with responsibility and balance for all who inhabit this space you call the planet Earth. You are not alone here, and never have been."

"We're not?" she barely squeaked out, trying to resist that strange pulling toward him and what he was saying.

He shook his head. "Although you operate as though you are alone and give little or no consideration to other sentient beings, even the ones you see with your eyes, you are not alone. Your brain processes four hundred billion bits of information a second, but you are only aware of perhaps two thousand of those that concern your body, your surroundings or your time, those you have been programmed to see. That means true reality is happening in the brain all the time, yet you haven't integrated it."

He smiled patiently. "That is why when I say that I am God, but then so are you and every human being, every flowering plant, every animal, that *everything* is divinely connected, something inside of you beyond your programmed fears knows the truth of my words. There are many forms of life that you cannot see with your eyes yet you believe they exist. The atom is one, is it not? What about that which is creating so much fear in your world right now? Is it not termed the bird flu? Can you see the microbes mutating that cause this virus? No, but you believe they are real. There is much, Claire, that you cannot see right now that is real and alive and is happening all around you all the time."

"But . . . but I can't be God," she whispered in shock, not understanding half of what he'd said.

"Why not?" he challenged. "Remember, Claire, God is a term, a label given by man to explain what he couldn't understand. The abuse of that label is only partly written in your history because your history is written by the victors in the struggle. Men don't seem to learn from their past and now, in this time, they are once more using that label to destroy not only one another but the planet itself. Greed seems to be the new religion. If it were only your continual wars over the personality of the label God, then you would spend eternity in a self-made hell. But now that greed, combined with the misuse of knowledge, is threatening a planet you share, and if it is not healed will send ripples of imbalance throughout not just this universe but into infinity."

She swallowed the fear in her throat. "Are you saying that . . . we're nearing the end of the world?"

"Many would relish that thought, especially those who are so desperately attempting to engineer the fulfillment of a script written thousands of years ago. Let me tell you they are misinformed. The planet will continue. The human race may not."

"Religious fanatics," she murmured.

"Another label. My purpose in coming to this dimension— to you, Claire—is not to judge others or their beliefs. We have tried using men to stop erroneous behavior that affects all dimensions. It hasn't worked as we had hoped. Through evolution the male Y chromosome has been shedding genes for millions of years and is now a fraction of the size of the X, the female, chromosome. Males are predictable, while females are more changeable, better adapted to change. Women are now being asked to accept their rightful place as creators and bring their natural instincts to this dimension's world stage to help balance out this grievous misconception. Women, though they have been held back for thousands of years, know instinctively they are creators. They do it all the time."

Claire blinked a few times and then forced herself to stand. Her towel dropped away from her and she slowly walked to the pool. Step by step, she brought herself back into the water, until she could push herself off the last step and dive under the surface.

Silence.

She had to wipe his words out of her head. Because if she didn't, she would lose her fragile grasp on reality.

He wasn't God.

She wasn't God.

She was having some sort of breakdown, brought on by her past catching up to her.

When she surfaced he would be gone.

He had to be!

She so didn't want to be crazy . . .

Chapter

5

SHE REACHED THE DEEP END OF THE POOL AND CLUNG to the tiled edge for a moment to catch her breath. Still frightened, she slowly turned her head to look over her shoulder.

He was standing at the other end of the pool with her cup of ice water in his hand.

"Will you come back? I would like to show you something."

She didn't answer him. Maybe the problem was that she had entered into conversation. She had invited the insanity. If she shut up, he would go away . . . maybe.

"Claire?"

Don't answer him! Closing her eyes, she tried to empty her mind.

"Claire . . . ?"

The voice was much closer. She opened one eye and looked up. How the hell had he managed to run the length of the forty-foot pool in a matter of seconds?

"You're not going away?" she whined like a scared kid.

He smiled down to her and shook his head. "Not yet. I want to show you something." And he sat down on the side of the pool, right next to her arms, swinging his legs into the water, not caring that his jeans and sneakers were wet.

"You are frightened because I presented to you a concept you are unfamiliar with, so I would like to use something to better help you understand what I am saying."

"Listen . . . *Michael* . . . if that's really your name, I ain't alone in not understanding your God concept. Believe me. Most of the world would call what you're saying . . . blasphemy and . . . well, quite frankly, nuts. I can't be God, and if I am by some horribly insane mistake in the universe then the world is in even more trouble than I thought."

"Claire, first of all that term you use, that label, blasphemy . . ." He shook his head. "The only way you can disrespect or insult something sacred is to deny your own state of sacredness, to be moved out of your natural state by your fears. When you do, your ego is empowered, your separateness. You begin to believe that your thoughts and actions don't have consequences for you. What I am saying to you is not blasphemy. What has been done to the minds of humans by those ruled by ego is blasphemous. They took away your true identity as creators."

"But people don't know this!" she protested. "No one believes they're God. Everyone seems to be fighting for their own version of what you call a label."

"There are those who know this truth, have known it for many generations, and want to keep the knowledge to themselves. I am speaking about the misuse of power in religions, governments, any institution that wants to keep power among a chosen few and enslave others into forgetting their own power. Can you not see that some want you to believe you need an intermediary to connect with the divine? They want you to believe that you are not good enough or holy enough or enlightened enough to make that connection on your own. So you put another above you, lessening your own potential, give away your power and sometimes even pay them money to do it. You humans do the same thing with governments that are supposed to protect your liberties and then in their secret chambers devise ways to keep you enslaved while they become wealthy. There are enough natural resources for every single human being on this planet to live a good life. Why is it that babies are dying of hunger or thirst in their mothers' arms?"

"Greed?" she murmured, his words resonating inside of her. What he said about religions and governments rang true within her heart. "But I can't be God!" she protested.

He smiled again and a distant part of her felt a familiar attraction, as if she had known him all her life, which was crazier than what he was trying to get her to believe.

"I told you we were getting ahead of ourselves with this discussion. It isn't something I had intended to bring up so soon after connecting with you, but flexibility is an asset I try to cultivate whenever something unexpected presents itself. So . . . I am not saying you are *the* God, what your culture has come to worship."

"That's a relief," she mumbled, resting her head against the tile. "I knew that had to be a mistake."

"But you are divine. What else *could* you be?" Not waiting for her to answer, he took her glass and drank the ice water in one long sip. "That was very refreshing," he noted, then continued. "Now if you can, I would like you to imagine that this pool of water doesn't end with the walls that surround it. Picture it as an endless body of water than reaches into infinity. Think of it as divine. Can you do that? There is nothing but water."

"Why not? I've already gone beyond rational thinking." She turned her head and hung onto the wall with one arm. Looking out at her pool, she nodded. "Endless water."

"Nothing but water," he repeated.

She nodded.

"Good. Now, this glass I am holding. Can you think of it as yourself?"

She looked back at him and shrugged. "I guess."

He grinned as he bent down and scooped up water, filling the glass to the top. "What is in the glass, Claire?"

"Water," she answered stupidly. Any child could handle that one.

"Is it still the pool water?"

She nodded.

"What is the difference between this water and that?" He nodded to the pool.

"The glass."

"You, Claire. You are the glass, remember? You are the difference. Using this analogy, you come from water because you too are the water. The container, your body suit, is why you think you are separate from the source, from the divine. If God is divinely intelligent, creator of all you see, and you come from that source, how could you be anything else? Dear woman, you simply have forgotten your identity."

Her heart was pounding in her chest. Her mouth was dry. He made such sense, but . . . "So then everyone is god, with a small *g*? Not the big guy?"

"The big guy?" He chuckled. "Do you really think God is only male? Didn't you say you had hoped God was female?"

"So what is it?" she demanded.

"The better question would be, what is it not? And I will answer by saying nothing. No thing and everything. God, your label of God, simply *is all that is*. Nothing, not one single thing, exists that it is not. Giving a label to the source with a personality that comforts you doesn't make it so. If you could look closely at a blade of grass you would find God. When I look into your eyes, I see God, Claire. Can you simply try to see yourself as I see you?"

She bit her bottom lip. "See, maybe I could swallow all this if there were only decent people in the world. But there aren't. There are cruel, evil people, and I don't care what you say. If they're God, I don't want to claim the same space."

"You are thinking about your family," he whispered. "We need to discuss this."

"They aren't alone," she answered, not having the strength to even begin a discussion on her family. "The world is full of monsters. How can you say they are God? Because if they are, God is hateful."

"Let's concentrate on your family."

"Don't call them that!" she cried out, anger starting to replace her awe. "You have no idea what they're like, what they did and—"

Her words were stopped short when he slid into the pool next to her.

"What are you doing?"

"Joining you."

"But . . . you're dressed."

"Would you like me to be undressed?" And just like that his clothes disappeared!

He was naked. *Naked!* This . . . dimension traveler, or whatever he was, seemed unembarrassed by her shocked reaction.

"You have to put something on!" she protested. "I have neighbors."

"So you want me dressed? I am trying to please you, Claire."

"Well," she sputtered, "you can please me by putting on a swimming suit or shorts or *something!*"

"You humans are so attached to your body suits and yet display such embarrassment about them. It's very confusing." He closed his eyes, as though thinking of something.

She averted her gaze, though her mind did register a very nice upper body, lean and yet muscular. Again that attraction stirred. "Have you done it?"

"You can look now," he said. "I hope this is suitable. I accessed what you consider a bathing suit."

She looked down to the water and saw pale blue material covering his lower body. "Good. Now, those glasses. Do you really need them? Because nobody goes swimming with glasses on."

"Oh." He seemed surprised and removed them, placing them on the tiled edge of the pool. "And no, I don't really need them."

"Then why did you wear them?"

His smile seemed almost tender. "Because I wanted you to recognize the familiar."

"Familiar?"

He nodded. "Yes."

"I don't know you," she said, denying that feeling of familiarity she'd had before. She pushed off from the wall to create some distance between them.

He followed her. "You don't? Are you sure?"

"Listen, Michael, that is your name, right?"

"That is the name you can call me if you like."

"Okay, Michael. Something about you seems vaguely familiar, but I really don't recognize you."

"The name Michael might help to jar your memory," he suggested, treading water just like her and coming closer.

She moved farther away. "Michael? I don't know any Michaels . . ." Her voice trailed off as a picture entered her mind. "Except for Mike Murphy and he . . ."

"Died when you were thirteen."

And then she saw it clearly in her mind. The same blue eyes, looking deeply into her own. The smile, that same smile that had lifted her heart when she had withdrawn inside herself as a young girl. Mike had discovered a few months before he'd died that he had to wear glasses and he'd hated them, believing they made him look different. It had somehow bonded them. Two different, lonely kids. "You . . . you're my Mike?" Even to her, her voice sounded like a squeak.

His smile deepened with affection. "Hi, Claire. So good to be with you again."

It happened so suddenly, yet she felt as if it were taking place in slow motion. The buzzing in her ears became louder, filling her head as her vision narrowed and darkened at the edges. She knew she was going under the water, only this time the silence was going to be from fainting.

"Claire! *Claire!* Open your eyes!"

She heard the voice, felt herself wrapped in someone's arms and floating in peaceful comfort as wave after wave of pleasurable energy raced through her body. She didn't want to open her eyes. She wanted to stay right here, right in his arms, and just drift off to sleep . . . *wait a minute*!

Her eyelids fluttered and she saw his face before her, a look of concern in his expression.

"Are you all right?"

When she didn't answer, he added, "I shouldn't have revealed myself to you in the water like that. I am so sorry, Claire."

"Re . . . revealed yourself?" she muttered, wondering why she wasn't pushing him away from her. Selfishly, she didn't want the pleasurable feeling to end. Not yet. She felt . . . wonderful . . . peaceful, calm, almost happy. And she had no idea how he was keeping them afloat because they were still in the deep end.

None of it made sense.

If she wasn't so stunned she would have laughed at her last thought. Sense? That commodity had abandoned her last Friday when she'd gone into the video store. Nothing since then came even close to sensible.

"Are you really Mike Murphy?" she asked in awe.

"I am," he answered. "I am what Mike Murphy, age appropriate, would have looked like to you had that accident not happened."

She felt tears in her eyes as her throat tightened with emotion.

"But how . . . how can you be . . . Mike? He's . . . dead," she cried.

"Ahh, Claire, death of the body suit does not mean annihilation of what you term the soul, that inner voice trying to break through your fears and guide you. Your scientists will tell you energy cannot be destroyed. The energy of your friend Mike was transformed."

"So . . . you're not Mike? You're using his energy because you thought it was familiar to me?"

He looked so pleased. "Yes. I am Mike, but I am so much more."

She sniffled and blinked up at him. "Then who the hell *are* you?"

He sighed heavily, as though they were back at square one. "Claire, that night in the pool, remember the lights?"

She nodded.

"*That* is a more accurate description of who I am. I scanned your memory for someone you trusted as a child. You trusted Mike."

"But you're really the lights?"

"For you, right now, I am both the lights and the energy that was your friend."

She looked at her hand on his bare, wet shoulder, and felt that attraction intensify. She should push away from him, not want to wrap her arms around him and press her breasts against his chest.

"What are you thinking, Claire? Your energy has brightened."

She pushed away from him and said, "I need to get out of the pool before I burn." And she swam toward the steps, intent on squashing this insane attraction. She wasn't thirteen, some silly young girl, infatuated with a male who was kind to her, who listened to her and sympathized. God, she had to have some shred of dignity left!

When Claire got out of the pool she found Michael standing by the chaise lounge, dry and waiting for her. She ignored him and the fact he was still in that pale blue bathing suit and nothing else. *Don't look at his body, his firm lean body . . .* Wrapping the damp towel around her, covering herself, she said, "You should get dressed."

"I should?" he asked, looking down to himself as though not sure of the reason.

Nodding, she picked up her sunglasses from the chair and answered, "We're done swimming. I'm going into the house."

"Claire, we need to begin discussing your family," he said in a gentle voice.

Her head shot up, saw he was dressed in his jeans and blue shirt, and she couldn't suppress her anger. "How many times do I have to tell you they aren't my family? And they haven't been for twenty years!"

"I understand your anger. I would simply like us to examine the reasons behind it."

She shook her head in disbelief. "Do you honestly think I'm about to discuss that with *you*?"

"That is one of the main reasons I am here," he stated matter-of-factly.

She blew her breath out in frustration. "Well, then, I hate to ruin your trip from whatever dimension you came from, but I'm not doing it. I won't put myself through it again."

He reached out so suddenly she didn't have time to back away. His hand was on her shoulder and she felt that energy again seep into her pores, race through her bloodstream and produce a wave of peace.

"Don't you understand that you've been putting yourself through it every single day of your life for the last twenty years? Bitterness, Claire, is like an acid that destroys the container. You don't deserve to carry it around with you any longer. Eric's death is giving you the opportunity to be free."

"I can't go back there," she whispered pleadingly. "I can't."

He smiled with such tenderness that Claire wanted to weep with self-pity.

"Why don't we start by simply going into the your house? Small steps, Claire. At least for now."

She nodded. She could do that. Holding her sunglasses, she then walked with him up to the sliding glass doors. For some odd reason all the fight had gone out of her body. She didn't want to fight with him. Insanely, stupidly, *pathetically,* she wanted to be held in his arms again. Mike's arms. She wanted that feeling again so much that it frightened her. She entered the house first and left him to close the door. Strangely, she still felt peaceful, as if whatever he'd done to her had a residual effect. Standing in her kitchen, she asked, "Are you hungry? Have you had lunch?" She stopped with her hand on the refrigerator and looked at him. "Do you even eat?"

"Oh, yes," he answered, looking with anticipation at her fridge. "I have had ice cream, which is most delicious, is it not?"

She grinned at his formal use of language. "Yes it is. Have you had anything else?"

"Yes, during my exploration of this area I have had a Burger King, given to me by a very nice woman who I think believed I was homeless. And something peculiar named french fries and a Pepsi, that is what she called it."

"So your initiation to this world has been with junk food."

He looked puzzled. "Junk? It was . . . quite tasty in my mouth and it filled the aching in my middle." He touched his stomach area.

In spite of herself and the insane situation, Claire laughed. "Well, why don't I totally corrupt you and order pizza?"

"Pizza," he said, repeating the word as if trying to make it fit a definition.

"Take my word for it, it's good. Not good for you, necessarily," she added, picking up the phone and hitting the automatic dialing. "But I think you'll like it. Hi," she said into the phone. "This is Claire Hutchinson. You've got my address and phone number on file. I'd like to order a Marguerite pizza." She looked at Michael smiling at her. "With pepperoni on one half."

A few moments later she hung up and grinned. "It should come in about twenty minutes. Meanwhile, would you like a glass of wine?"

"Yes," he answered, watching her as she grabbed a bottle of Pinot Grigio and slid open a drawer for the corkscrew.

"Have you ever had wine before?"

"No, never. Is it as good as the Pepsi?"

How naïve and kinda cute. He may know all sorts of things about the universe, but there were certain areas in this world where she was the expert. A part of her wanted to tell him the truth, but the old Claire was beginning to resurface. "It's . . . different," she murmured, screwing into the cork stopper. "I hope you like it."

Maybe I could get him drunk and wrap myself up in his arms again! That's right, Claire, she told herself, pushing down on the corkscrew handles to lift the cork. *Take advantage of a dimension traveler!*

Hey, he'd invited himself into her life. It wasn't her fault he had some kind of magic in his hands and she hadn't had sex in over four years, six years if one counted good sex, and never if one counted great sex.

Grinning, she poured the wine into two glasses.

Maybe she could get something besides a lecture out of

this trip into bizarro world. She offered him the crystal wine-glass. "Here we are," she announced. "Drink up."

And a plan started forming as she watched his reaction to the wine.

She wanted that feeling again, that exquisite pleasure he seemed to exude.

Was it possible to take advantage of a . . . dimension traveler?

Chapter

6

EVEN BEFORE THE PIZZA ARRIVED CLAIRE COULD TELL the wine was having an effect on her guest. *Guest?* Who was she kidding? Uninvited bizarre guest was more like it. He had come into her life, *barged* into her life, uninvited and had made her question her sanity. He had brought up old memories, not just of her family, but of Mike Murphy. Sweet, cute Mike Murphy, who had recognized how unhappy she was and hadn't been put off by her adolescent imitation of Morticia Addams. Mike had thought her fashion rebellion brave for an honor student who'd refused to fit the popular mold, and she'd been devastated when he and his parents had died in a car accident while on vacation in Wyoming. She remembered wishing at the time it had been her family that had perished.

"Your energy . . . it just darkened," Michael said, tilting his head as he stared at her.

He had to remain Michael. She couldn't think of him as Mike. If she did, she'd throw herself into his arms, cry like a little girl, and that simply wouldn't do. At least not yet. Neither of them had consumed enough wine for that. "Just a fleeting thought," she murmured, refilling his glass.

"Now, Claire," he said, sitting at her kitchen table. "We

must begin to discuss the reason I am here. I only desire to help you through this difficult time."

She noticed that his speech was slower and he enunciated even more, as though it were an effort. Good sign. He probably hadn't eaten anything, so the wine was taking effect quickly. She hadn't eaten anything, either, and she'd have to watch herself until the pizza arrived. A distant part of her wondered if she could be committing some kind of sin or offense by getting him drunk. It was a distant thought and she shrugged it off. Might as well get some fun out of this insane mess. And wasn't she part of the Gang, women without rules? Besides, without the glasses, he was starting to look pretty attractive to her.

So this is what Mike would have looked like. Not bad . . . at all.

"Just relax, will you? The pizza should be here any moment. We can talk about all that stuff later." She sipped her wine and smiled at him.

"You seem much more . . . friendly, Claire," he observed, smiling back at her.

"Must be the wine."

"Then you should have more. Debating with you can be seriously draining."

She laughed. "So I drain you?"

He grinned. "You know it takes a great effort to stay here with you."

"How do you do it?"

"I have to compress my energy to fit into this body suit."

Hmm . . . interesting. "So, while we're waiting, let me ask you a few questions, okay?"

He nodded. "Certainly. Ask whatever you want."

Let's see . . . what did she want? "Okay. How old are you?"

"Old?" He seemed to ponder her question. "Age isn't something that is focused on, so I would have to answer that I am ageless."

"Must be nice not to get older, never having to worry."

"Worry is projecting yourself into the future, which isn't created yet, therefore not reality. A waste of creative energy by turning it into anxiety. Better to stay in reality, in the moment you are alive."

She knew that one from the Gang, but it was reassuring to hear him confirm it. "Right . . . okay, do you have a family?"

"Family . . . yes, an immense one. Since we all originated within the source I would have to say that all sentient beings in all universes are my family. And yours," he added.

She ignored his last words. "So since you have such an immense family, is there anyone in particular you are attached to?" *Let's hear this answer,* she told herself.

"Attached?"

She nodded. "Like a wife, or partner, or . . . I don't know, maybe a lover? Do you have such relationships?"

He chuckled and Claire noticed for the first time that he had dimples, slight ones, but they were there. Unexpectedly, another surge of attraction raced through her body.

She was attracted to this . . . this nerdy dimension traveler? Only he wasn't nerdy anymore.

It must be the wine. And then she realized she'd been attracted to him before she'd had a sip. This would not do. She could have fun with him, but there was no point in becoming attached.

"If I take your meaning correctly, then I would have to answer no. Marriage, as you know it, isn't necessary."

She brought her attention back to him. "So no lovers, no one to share your . . . energy with?" She was remembering being held in his arms and that night he first came to her as the lights. It had been like a mind-blowing orgasm. Her first mind-blowing one, and something inside of her felt like a junkie because she wanted to feel it again. How could she ask *that*?

"Energy is shared all the time, even in this dimension.

Have you ever walked into a room and instinctively felt a heaviness? Negativity?"

"Sure, but I'm talking about positive energy like . . . when you are the lights. It must be awesome to share that with . . . well, an equal."

He sat back and smiled, a little too fondly, she thought.

"It is. It's the highest form of communication. The unity is beautiful and memorable."

"But different with each person? Each sentient being?" she corrected.

"Of course."

"And you do it all the time . . . where you come from?"

"Not all the time, but it can be used as a greeting, a way of opening one's self to another for understanding and, of course, pure delight."

"Pure delight," she repeated. "That's a good way of putting it."

The doorbell rang and Claire jumped in surprise, sorry for the interruption in the conversation, but she was near starving. "Pizza's here!" she announced, running into the foyer for her purse and hurrying to the front door.

Not caring that she was still wrapped in a towel, she handed the staring young man a twenty-dollar bill and grabbed the large square box. "Thanks," she said and closed the door, her mouth salivating in anticipation.

"Here we are," she proclaimed, holding the box out in front of her. She placed it on the table and saw how Michael leaned into it slightly, as though to capture the aroma. "Smells great, huh?" she asked, opening a cabinet and taking out two plates. She put one in front of him and laid the other in front of the chair she'd been using. She went back into the kitchen and opened a drawer, taking out two cloth napkins.

"Okay," she said, pulling out her chair and throwing him a napkin. "Let's eat."

He caught the napkin and turned it over in his hand.

"For your mouth and fingers. This can be messy food. You eat it with your hands."

"My hands? Really?"

She grinned as she opened the large box. "Really. Now see, you take a piece, like this . . ." And she lifted a large triangle with cheese dripping, held it up to her mouth and took a big bite.

She nodded to him. "Go ahead," she mumbled, chewing happily on her pizza.

He pulled a piece away from the rest of the pie and fumbled with it a few seconds before putting it on his plate and staring at it. "It's so . . . soft,"

She giggled. "Kinda floppy, I know. I like the thin crust, so it's a bit of work. Pick it up and fold it like this down the middle, then bite off the end."

She watched him focus and do as she asked. "Now take a bite," she encouraged as he held the piece up to his mouth. "Go ahead before all the cheese falls off it."

He bit down and in a moment his eyes lit with pleasure.

"Good, huh?" she asked with a grin.

He grinned back at her and nodded several times as he chewed. Swallowing, he said, "It is very good, Claire. Thank you."

Claire was so ravenous she finished her first slice in less than a minute. She didn't want to appear gluttonous, but she couldn't resist reaching for another slice. "I don't cook very often; actually it's rare that I do."

Michael swallowed what was in his mouth, licked his lips and asked, "Why is that? Food seems to me to be one of the pleasures of this dimension."

"Oh, I agree. I just don't like to prepare it. I guess I'm just lazy.'

"I disagree. I think your reluctance to cook might come from when you were young."

She looked at him. "I said I don't want to discuss that with you."

"I'm simply remarking on the statement you made about not liking to prepare your own meals." He took another bite. "This is very, very tasty. Pizza. I must remember it."

"Okay, look, I am happy to share a pizza with you and some wine, but that doesn't mean we have to dissect my childhood right now, does it?"

He shook his head while chewing. When he swallowed, he said, "I can wait as long as it takes, Claire. My point would be that it is you who might want to get on with it, since you have a decision to make regarding Eric's will."

She put her slice down on her plate and stared at him. "Do you know *everything* about me?"

"I know enough to assist you in this challenge."

"What do you think you know?" she asked, feeling the muscles in her shoulders tighten with defense.

"Do you really want me to tell you now?" he asked with a smile before taking another bite.

He had her there. If he did know as much as she thought he did, then the discussion she had been avoiding would be out in the open. "Maybe not now," she answered, suddenly losing her appetite. Instead she picked up her wineglass and searched her mind for a distraction. "So where did you get your manners from? You don't speak with your mouth full. Someone must had taught you something of the cultural mores of this dimension."

This dimension?

And even saying that seemed ludicrous. Talking to someone who claimed to be from another dimension . . . like he was a normal guy sharing pizza with her!

Michael finished his slice of pizza and looked at the opened box.

"Go ahead. Have another slice. I did. Have as many as you want."

"Thank you," he murmured, reaching into the box. "Before entering this dimension there is a great deal of observation and what you would call studying. Manners are important, are they not? In some cultures touching another on the head is considered an insult. We aren't coming here to insult anyone."

Her attention was piqued. *"We?"*

"There are many of us coming to this dimension, all over the earth, to assist in the transition of energy."

"You've lost me. Transition of energy?"

"Yes. I thought we had discussed this. With males being so predictable and their chromosomes dying off, it is now up to the females to usher in this new era of raised consciousness where balance might once again be attained."

It wasn't the wine. She was confused. "You think women are going to save the planet?"

"Not the planet. That will survive. Save humanity before it destroys itself."

"We can't even get a woman elected president in this country," she complained, refilling his wineglass. "In the last two elections so many women voted against their own best interests and bought the lies of the ruling class and big business, or voted the way their husbands did. They thought they were voting for moral values—and considering who they put in office, with all the lies, betrayals and corruption, they got hoodwinked on that one too. I wouldn't count on women, unless they woke up and refused to be manipulated ever again."

"And *that* is what we're counting on, Claire. Waking up from centuries of indoctrination making women feel less powerful. Truthfully, it is your only hope now. The planet will not continue to take abuse."

She sighed. This was not going the way she had planned. "How did we get back to this discussion? It's depressing."

"I have given you too much information at one time."

She nodded. "I'm on overload, Michael. I don't want to

talk about saving the planet right now. I don't even want to talk about women taking their rightful place in the world."

"What do you want to talk about?"

"I want to talk about you."

"Me?" he asked with surprise. "I have already answered your questions."

"You've answered some of them."

"What else would you like to know?"

"Where do you come from? Really. What are those lights? Why do they make me . . . I don't know, feel so . . . good? What's in them?"

He sort of chuckled again, wiped his mouth and hands with his napkin and pushed back his chair a little bit. Picking up his wineglass, he sipped and then grinned at her. "So many questions. Let me begin with your first. Where do I come from? I come from a dimension that shares this planet with you. There are several. You live in the third. I normally exist in a higher one. In my dimension the need for a physical body is obsolete. We are pure energy and contained within that energy is information about us. You have that ability too, and you call it your aura. Even though you cannot see it all the time doesn't mean it isn't there surrounding you, giving off information about the state of your mind and your physiology. When I achieved unity with you as *those lights* you refer to, I was able to access your life history. The feeling you received while embraced by those lights is my complete and unconditional acceptance of all that you have been and all that you can become. Some might call it love."

Her head shot up and she almost dropped her wineglass. *"Love?"* she demanded in disbelief.

His eyes looked at her with tenderness. "Yes, Claire, love, the greatest form of energy in this universe and all others. What you felt from me when I was those lights was pure, no-holds-barred, unconditional love. I don't need to be loved back to love you or anyone else, though it is your natural state too. *That* is the transition of energy I am speaking about to balance out this dimension. And women, like you, Claire, are more open to it. Ask any mother about it. It isn't something she cultivates. It's there within her, springing to life when she connects with her beloved, be it a man or a child, when she sees herself, her own divinity, reflected back to her unconditionally."

"I could debate that statement about mothers from personal experience."

"Do you wish to discuss it now? I am more than happy to do so."

She scowled at him. "Okay, so you got me again. And no, I don't wish to discuss it now. We were speaking of the lights. Can you do it whenever you want?"

"Claire, it is my natural state."

"So you're more comfortable being the lights than being . . ." Her words trailed off as she looked at him.

"Than being Mike?"

She nodded.

"Yes, I am more comfortable being the lights. Think of it as if I asked you to be a tree all day long when you are used to walking and going wherever you desire."

"Must be restrictive."

He sipped his wine. "I am getting better and better the longer I am here."

Claire stared at his mouth, liking the shape of it, the fullness of his lips. "So how long are you planning on being here?" she murmured, feeling very mellow after the wine and pizza.

"As long as it takes."

"You mean you'd stick around until I . . . got whatever it is you're selling?"

"I'm not selling anything. What I am offering you cannot be bought, Claire. This isn't a tangible commodity, though it can produce tangible results."

He appeared slightly offended.

Without thinking she reached out her hand and touched his. "I didn't mean to insult you, Michael. Really, I know you're not trying to sell me; more like lecture me . . ." She stared at her hand over his and felt that tingling in her fingers race up her arm. Startled by the immediate sensation, she jumped up from her chair and her towel, which had been firmly tucked together, parted and fell to the floor.

Standing in her bathing suit, practically nude, Claire could only blink as she and Michael stared at each other in surprise.

"Perhaps this is enough for one visit," Michael said in a low voice, trying to stand.

Seeing how unsteady he was on his feet, Claire instinctively reached out to help him. "Whoa there," she said with an embarrassed giggle as she grabbed his upper arm.

His hand reached out and clasped onto her shoulder. "I don't know what's . . ."

"It's the wine," she whispered, as his head came up and he looked into her eyes.

He's going to kiss me, she thought. At least any other man, a human, would close the short space between them and bring his lips down on hers. But he wasn't human at all and he probably didn't have a clue.

Taking a deep breath, she thought she should show him.

Just as her lips grazed over his, she felt him pull back and stiffen in surprise.

"Claire, I don't think . . ."

"That's right, Michael, you aren't supposed to think right now. So please, don't talk," she breathed. "Just feel."

And then she kissed him.

No tongue. No great passion. Just a good kiss that left her so rattled she wasn't even surprised when she found herself falling forward and grabbing the back of his chair for balance. Exquisite, tiny, white dancing lights surrounded her and she reached out with her other hand and tried to capture one.

Just as quickly as they'd appeared, they disappeared. *He* disappeared.

Blinking, Claire couldn't help grinning.

Well, he'd stopped hounding her about her family so she'd accomplished that, but maybe, just maybe, she had something she could teach a being from another dimension.

As dumb as it might appear, she was actually looking forward to his next visit.

"Michael, Michael, Michael . . ." she breathed.

Who would have thought this surprise would've entered her life?

She could have her own playmate. He was perfect. Have fun and then he disappears. She didn't even have to tell him to leave.

No fuss, no sports or dirty laundry. No toilet seats left up. Did he even have to use a bathroom? Who knew? He didn't even care that she disliked cooking. She could do takeout for a month without repeating a meal and he'd probably be happy to experiment. He really was a perfect playmate. They could work on the kissing thing and she'd have to remember to limit his intake of wine if she wanted anything physical from him . . . and, weirdly enough, she found that she did.

She picked up another slice of pizza and sank into the chair he'd been using.

But she'd have to keep him secret.

No one could know about him, especially the Gang.

She then thought about Cristine and Daniel.

Suddenly a scene ran through her mind . . . of the day she and Isabel had found Cristine in bed after just learning she was pregnant. Cristine had said Daniel was different. And then Claire remembered seeing lights around Daniel's hand, first when he'd stopped that mugger outside the restaurant and then at the hospital when Cristine was in labor.

Dimension traveler!

She knew she should talk to Cristine, probably should run to her right now for advice. And the truth. Startled, as pieces of the puzzle began coming together, she remembered Cristine telling her and Isabel that Daniel was out there, enlightened, unlike the rest of men. And now she knew why. Daniel and Michael were probably alike. Of course! It made perfect sense.

Cristine's Daniel was like Michael! He had to be. All that traveling Daniel did was probably right out of this dimension! A part of her was itching to contact Cristine and demand the truth, but she knew why Cristine had kept Daniel a secret. Who would ever accept such a fantastic concept? No wonder Cristine had wanted to form a foundation for women! More pieces of the puzzle fell into place.

Suddenly Claire's fear for her sanity lightened considerably.

Cristine wasn't crazy. Cristine had a wonderful life. She was happy, happier than ever. Of course Cristine had made the error of falling in love with Daniel. That wouldn't do in her case. She simply desired a playmate.

In her heart she knew she didn't want to share Michael with anyone just yet. She didn't want to know the do's and don'ts of such a unique relationship. Cristine had thrived in it, right?

Besides, it had been a long time since she'd played with a man . . . or whatever he was.

And she was a woman without rules.

If she played it right . . . this could really be fun.

"WHAT IS *THAT* ON YOUR FINGER?" CLAIRE DE-manded, seated across from Tina and watching her friend push the hair out of her eyes for the third time. "Give me your hand," she insisted, grabbing Tina's fingers and inhaling with appreciation.

Tina giggled like a young girl. "Isn't it beautiful?" she cooed, now proudly showing off the stunning diamond ring on her fourth finger.

"Wow," Claire breathed, turning Tina's finger so the emerald-cut diamond flashed in the lights of the restaurant. "It's gorgeous."

"Two and a half carats. I told Louis he shouldn't have gotten me such a big stone but . . . I'm *thrilled*, Claire! He's such a sweetie. He said he wanted everyone to know how much he loves me."

Claire grinned widely. "And you deserve it. Good for the good doctor! So I take it by this gorgeous rock, you said yes to the man?"

Tina laughed. "I almost said *please*!"

Claire laughed along with her friend. "Well I couldn't be happier. So who else have you blinded with this stunner?"

"So far just Cristine. And I swore her to silence. I wanted to show you in person."

Claire picked up her glass of Chablis and grinned. "So, Miss Diamond Girl, I take it the wedding is about to be planned, thus the reason for this lunch meeting."

"Now look," Tina said, sitting up straighter and crossing her arms on the edge of the table, but making sure to leave her left hand visible. "I've decided we can hire a wedding planner if we have to, to make it easier on all of us. And I'm not even sure I want a big wedding. All that fuss for one day. I keep thinking maybe it should just be family and friends, something tasteful and small."

Claire swallowed her wine. "What? No storybook princess with a tiara and a ten-foot train?"

"See you're mocking me already and we haven't even gotten to the dress. Do you even *want* to be my maid of honor?"

"Hey, I'm sorry," Claire quickly answered. "Of course I want to be your maid of honor, though, technically, as has been pointed out to me by others, I am the matron of honor. Just tell me what to do."

"Well the first thing is to decide on the kind of wedding, and then the dress."

"Shouldn't the type of wedding be a discussion with your lover man? I mean, it's his wedding too."

"Of course," Tina answered. "But I want to get all the pros and cons straight in my head before I present anything to him. You're my support team, Claire, and that's the reason for this lunch meeting."

"Right . . ." Claire murmured, thinking a team might be more than one person. "Okay, have you got a month picked out?"

"Well that would depend on the type of wedding. A big wedding would take months to get the church and wherever we hold the reception. It's about availability and coordinating everything. That heads the con list because I don't know that I want to wait six months or longer to be a married lady."

"And a smaller wedding means you could get married sooner and take up residence with the resident."

Tina grinned. "We're already practically living together now, though with all the hours he works at the hospital I hardly see him. So time is precious. I want to present him with all the facts before we come to any decision. Make this as easy on him as possible."

Nodding, Claire said, "Okay, let's write all this down." She opened her purse and took out a pen and a grocery receipt she had shoved inside days ago. Straightening the long thin paper, she wrote the words *pros* and *cons* and separated the two words with a long line. "Large wedding takes six months to plan," she said as she wrote. "Church. Reception. Smaller wedding is more intimate, quicker, and you can begin married life sooner. What else?"

"Then there's the dress," Tina said as their salads were delivered to their table.

Claire moved her list to the side to make room for her plate. "It can't take too long to find the right dress."

After thanking their waiter and both getting fresh ground pepper on their salads, Tina and Claire dug into their lunch.

"A dress," Tina began, "for someone your size would be no problem. I've got more than a little junk in the proverbial trunk so—"

"Do not start that again," Claire interrupted with the pointing of her fork. "Louis loves you, remember? All of you."

Tina shook her head. "If the rest of the world was like Louis we wouldn't have a problem, but when sizes start at zero we've got our work laid out for us."

Claire blew her breath out with a rush. "Size zero. That means nothing, right? Zero equals nothing. Okay, I understand the petite problem for some women, but when zero is the goal for anyone, then does that mean they're focusing on disappearing?"

"You can make jokes. What size are you?" Tina asked, rolling her gaze to the ceiling. "A four?"

"I'm a six, and you know damn well it's got nothing to do with dieting."

"Good genes."

"In that sense, maybe," Claire answered. "Fast metabolism."

"You know you never talk about your family. Do you want to invite them?"

Claire's jaw dropped. "*No!* I would not. I . . . don't see my family."

Tina held up her hand. "Okay, I was just asking." She stabbed at a piece of spinach and murmured, "I can't imagine never seeing my father and brother."

"Well, you probably have a normal relationship with them. I don't with what tried to pass as my family."

"It's got to be hard, Claire . . . never to see them."

"It's quite easy," she replied, wondering how in the hell they'd gotten off track in the conversation. The last thing she wanted to talk about was her so-called family.

"I know you said your father died when you were young. But your mom, she's alive, right?"

Claire simply nodded and continued to chew. As soon as she swallowed, she needed to get them back to talking about the wedding.

"I wish my mother were alive," Tina said in a soft voice. "Especially now. I miss her so much."

Claire swallowed and quickly said, "I'm sure she would've loved Louis. What kind of dress would she have liked?" There. That ought to do it.

"Oh, she would have swooned over me marrying a doctor," Tina said with a grin, leaving her sad memories. "And she would have insisted that we have a huge wedding to announce it not just to the relatives, but to the entire state."

"But is that what you want, Tina? You need to figure this out. Big, or small and intimate?"

Tina sighed and dropped her fork onto the edge of her salad. "I don't know, Claire. A part of me, and don't you dare laugh, wants that big wedding, so, yes, I would feel like the storybook princess. But no tiara. And then another part of me says it's a waste of energy and money for one day. Louis would probably be thrilled if we eloped to Vegas."

"Don't you dare elope," Claire warned. "Unless the Gang does a road trip and goes with you."

Tina laughed. "God, I could just see that. Poor Louis with the Yellow Brick Road Gang tagging along. They'd probably have me married by an Elvis impersonator."

"Wise men say only fools rush in . . ." Claire sang in a hushed voice.

"I don't care if I'm a fool. I want to rush in, for the first time in my carefully planned life. Good marks in school. Better marks in college to get me into Wharton. Good job leads to real estate at the right time when property sales are through the roof. I've done everything with careful thought about the future. Now I just want to be a married lady and wake up every morning with the man I love."

Claire smiled with tenderness. "Then I think you've found your answer. A small and intimate exquisite wedding that can be planned quickly." A thought suddenly popped into her head. "Maybe you could have it at Isabel's. Think about it. Her backyard is gorgeous. It must be two or three acres, maybe more. You could have the gazebo decorated for the official ceremony. It would probably only take a month to plan everything."

Tina's eyes widened. "Do you think she'd do it? Give up her back lawn for a wedding party?"

"Honey, it's the summer and her backyard is in full bloom. It's like a private estate, surrounded by woods and even a stream. You know Isabel. She would love to have a party there so everyone could enjoy it. I think she'd even be flattered. Do you want me to ask her?"

"Shouldn't I do that?"

Claire shrugged. "I can find out how she really feels about it. I promise, if she has the slightest hesitation, I'll back off."

Grinning, Tina said, "See, you are a great maid of honor. Now, let's concentrate on the dress. Where should we start first? Philly or the Main Line?"

"The Main Line," Claire answered, though she felt her stomach muscles tightening with dread. "It's closer. If we don't find anything there, we can head into the city."

Tina sighed and her shoulders sagged. "I just want to look beautiful."

"You *are* beautiful," Claire said, and reached across the table for Tina's hand. "And we *are* going to find you the perfect dress. I promise as your wedding slave."

Tina smiled. "See . . . I knew you were the right one. You've accepted you're going to be my slave. Not every woman of color can make that statement today."

Shaking her head, Claire laughed. "So let's finish lunch and hit at least one store today. Thank God you chose small and intimate, or this could have gone on for months."

"Someday, Claire, you'll fall in love again and I'll gladly be your slave."

Her entire body stiffened at the suggestion. "Don't plan on that one, girlfriend. I don't think love is in my future."

Now why in the world did a mental picture of Michael pop into her mind?

Delete, delete, she thought as she focused on her salad.

She wanted a playmate, not a commitment.

"You never know, Claire, when love is going to show up and surprise you."

"I've had enough surprises, thank you very much."

"Just keep an open mind."

"Just finish your lunch, Miss I-Want-the-Whole-World-to-Be-in-Love-Along-with-Me. And leave the rest of us who like being alone, alone."

"I don't know. There's something different about you. The way you look . . . like an extra sparkle is in your eyes."

"You're seeing gratitude that you chose a small wedding. Now let's either eat or pay for this and start dress hunting."

Tina grinned. "Yes, ma'am."

Sparkle? How completely ridiculous.

They had no luck at the first bridal store and everything Tina had tried on made her look like an overdecorated cupcake. Glad to be home, Claire's shoulders sagged with relief. Poor Tina had almost burst into tears with the last dress and Claire had to unzip it fast and get them out of the place. This wedding dress might be a problem after all. She'd promised Tina they would continue looking next week. Enough time to recover. First she had to undress and then she'd call Isabel.

Please, please, let Isabel think it's a fantastic idea.

The very thought of a big splashy wedding was a six-month headache waiting to grab hold of everyone involved. She took off her suit jacket and gave thanks that it was Friday and she'd have the weekend to herself. She still needed to make a decision about Eric's will and call the Philly lawyers with her answer. She should do that today and put it behind her. It felt like a stone in her shoe that she'd been trying to ignore.

She pulled on a pair of soft workout pants with a drawstring and a plain white T-shirt. Walking back into the living room, she bit the inside of her cheek. Maybe a glass of wine . . . In the kitchen she brought down two glasses.

Might as well get it over with. Taking the opened bottle and the wineglasses with her, she placed them on the coffee table, turned on the smooth jazz radio station and sat on the leather sofa.

She opened her cell phone and dialed Isabel's number.

Hearing her friend's voice, Claire smiled. "Hey, you. It's Claire. How's everything on your end? That adorable little girl letting you get any sleep yet?"

Isabel laughed. "Yes, we're sleeping finally, all the way through the night. How are you?"

"Great. Just got back from bridal-dress shopping and my head's spinning."

"Oh . . . so Tina said yes. Good for her."

"She not only said yes, but is sporting a gorgeous diamond from Dr. Ramsey."

"I can't wait to see it," Isabel said. "We should have an engagement party for them."

Perfect opening. "Well, speaking of parties, Tina finally figured out she wants a small, intimate wedding. She still wants the fairy-tale stuff with the dress and flowers and everything, but doesn't want to wait six months to book a place for the wedding and reception. So anyway, I came up with an idea, and feel free to say no . . . I was thinking maybe—"

"Absolutely!" Isabel interrupted. "My backyard. It's summer. They could get married in the gazebo. We could have a tent and lay a floor for the tables and dancing. You should see all the flowers, Claire. Oh, it would be so lovely."

Grinning broadly, Claire breathed in relief. "I thought the same thing about your gazebo. Thank God we're on the same wave length, Issy. This saves us, me, so much time and legwork."

"When are they planning it?"

"That's just it. Tina is going to speak with Louis tonight and see if he agrees with a smaller wedding. Any man would, right? I just know she wants to be a married lady ASAP."

"She's waited a long time for him to come along, so I understand. Can I call her and tell her?"

Glad to be saved another phone call, Claire said, "Sure. She'd love to hear from you. She wanted to ask you herself, but I said I'd do it, wedding slave that I am, and feel you out."

"Well you felt me out and I'm thrilled. We'll all have to get together and plan this. Maybe sometime this weekend?"

"Just let me know."

"Okay, let me call her while Hope is quiet. I'll get back to you about a date for a meeting."

"Sure."

"Oh, won't this be fun, Claire? A wedding. I can almost picture it."

"Me too, Issy. Thanks."

"Talk to you soon."

She hung up the phone and sighed with satisfaction. Plans were solidifying for Tina. Now for her own.

Pouring herself a glass of wine to steel herself for her next discussion, she said out loud, "Okay, I don't know the proper protocol for this, but if you can hear me, Michael, I'd like you to come back. I . . . I'm ready to discuss my family." How bizarre talking out loud to thin air, anticipating a dimension traveler might hear her. Just how far had her once organized life veered off course? Isabel might tell her she was delusional and should seek professional help and serious medication. Cristine was the only one who would understand, but she wasn't ready to share Michael yet. No, not yet. There were a few things that she needed to take care of first.

She hoped she wasn't making a major mistake inviting him, but he did seem to know everything about her already. It wasn't like she would have to start at the beginning and—

Her thoughts ceased as she watched in wonder the swirling white lights appear before the fireplace. "Ahh . . ." Her breath left her in a rush of awe. She couldn't help it. They were so beautiful. Before she could concentrate on them to describe them in her mind, Michael started to appear.

Her Michael, she thought. He had come to her.

"Thank you for inviting me," he said, smiling down at her as his dimples appeared. He was dressed in those jeans and that blue shirt.

Didn't he have anything else to wear? Was that like his uniform, or something?

"Hi," she said with a smile, glad he was with her. "Thanks for coming."

"I have been waiting," he answered, coming to sit next to her on the sofa. "I didn't want to intrude any more than I already have."

Claire nodded, glad she'd had a couple of days to herself. "I appreciate you waiting for an invitation. Makes me feel like I've got some control over this thing. Would you like a glass of wine?"

"I don't think I should."

She almost giggled, knowing he was remembering his reaction to the wine. "It's okay to have one glass, Michael. I promise I won't get you drunk."

"It was a most peculiar feeling," he answered, shaking his head with wonder. "I couldn't seem to hold myself together."

"That's describes being drunk, all right. I'll be more careful."

"Then one glass, and I shall sip it as you had suggested."

She poured the wine into his glass and put it before him. Sitting back and taking her glass with her, Claire let out her breath. "So . . . how do we start? I just want to get this over with and put it behind me. I have to make a decision about Eric's will and, since you said that was the reason you came here, to me, I thought I might as well kill two birds with one stone and—"

"Kill two birds?"

She grinned at his worried appearance. "It's an expression, meaning take care of two things at one time."

"I see. Sometimes the verbiage can be confusing."

"Right. You take everything literally." She took another sip of her wine. "I'll try to be more clear." Again, a feeling of familiarity washed over her, which was nuts, since she was actually speaking with a being from another dimension! None of it seemed real.

"Thank you, Claire. Now, shall we begin?"

"Fine with me," she said, though it wasn't fine at all. She resented all these things coming into her life, bringing back painful memories. Sighing with resignation, she began. "You know I've spent years not thinking about those people and now it seems to be the focus of your visitations. I just don't know why Eric had to include me in his will and stir up all this forgotten dirt."

"But it was never really forgotten, Claire, was it? How many decisions have you made as an adult with the wounds of a child still influencing you?"

"My life isn't so bad, Michael," she said defensively. "In fact, it's pretty good."

"I didn't say your life was bad. May I ask why you married Brian Hutchinson?"

She blinked, surprised by his question. "I thought I loved him."

Michael nodded. "But your marriage to him didn't turn out as you had expected."

Claire almost laughed. "You could say that. Brian was a liar, a manipulator and a betrayer, so no . . . I didn't expect that in a husband."

"Did he remind you of anyone?"

Claire leaned her head back, as though stunned by the question. "No."

"Really? Who else in your life was a liar, a manipulator and betrayed you?"

She almost sputtered. "Are you . . . actually saying that I married Brian because he reminded me of my family? My mother and Eric and . . . David?" The last name felt like bile in her throat. "Because that's just crazy. If I'd thought that, I would have run for the hills."

"I know, Claire," Michael said in a sympathetic voice. "But why is it that you attracted someone with the same traits you so disliked in your family? Have you ever wondered about that?"

Not until now, she thought. Come to think of it, every single relationship, even in college, had resulted in the same thing. Betrayal. That's why she was done with relationships. They hurt too much.

"Have you?" Michael repeated, then sipped his wine.

She shrugged. "I suppose."

"Do you think, just possibly, that you might have been trying to heal your childhood wounds with others? Even on a subconscious level? That if you could do it with someone other than a member of your family, you might finally heal that deep wound that was inflicted upon you as a young girl?"

"But every single relationship ended the same way. I didn't heal anything."

"No, you didn't. You compounded the wound, until you built a wall around your heart so no one could ever hurt you again. It was survival, Claire, and you're not alone. Most of humanity does the same thing. Forgiveness really isn't about the other person. It's about yourself, releasing that negative energy behind that wall. It's about being free again."

Her jaw clenched. "You cannot be asking me to forgive them!"

"I know it's hard. You've been deeply wounded."

"Have you *any* idea what they did to me?" she demanded.

He slowly nodded and looked at her with compassion.

"They trespassed, and you were violated, emotionally, spiritually and physically."

Now she was angry. "Let's call it what it was, okay? No more fancy words. My stepbrother raped me, repeatedly. When I finally couldn't take it anymore and told my mother she dragged me in front of Eric, who beat me and called *me* the liar, and my mother kept telling him to hit me harder. I was her child, her own flesh and blood, and she incited him to hurt me even more. No one ever spoke of it again, but it was still there like the proverbial elephant in the room and I was frozen out. David became the victim of my so-called lies and played the injured party so well I was the one thrown away, betrayed by everyone in my family, so they could keep up the pretense of being pillars of the community. How can you possibly think I can forgive them for that?" Her hands were shaking so badly that she carefully placed her wineglass onto the coffee table.

"Claire, how can you not? It's for yourself, not them. You are still connected to them by threads of this negative energy until you find peace of mind."

"You ask too much," she muttered, wrapping her arms around her waist and staring into the darkened fireplace. "And I'd like to know how *they* could be god, even with the small *g*."

"They didn't know what they were doing."

"*What?*"

"Truly, Claire . . . your family . . . they suffer from a form of real insanity. They only believe in separation, the ego. They are lost from their souls, if you will. When you are insane, when you believe the outside physical world is more powerful, more real, than what is taking place inside of you, it is easier to violate another, inflict pain and betrayal. You think you can do whatever you wish to another, foolishly believing somehow you might get away with the violation.

You think you are hurting them, but in reality you are connected to the one you have injured. Cause and effect, Claire. It is a law of the universe. When you are sane and connected to your source, it physically hurts you to hurt another on any level."

She thought about his words and shook her head. "I'm sorry, Michael. I know you're trying to help me, but all I want to do is confront my mother and David and I'm just sorry Eric is dead and I can't beat him with a belt the way he beat me. I told you when you first came to me that I wasn't really spiritually evolved. I can't turn the other cheek so easily. They all got away with abuse. Criminal abuse. And I can't sweep it under the rug."

"Did I ask you to do that? To forget, or not confront?"

"Well, you make it sound as though I should."

"There is no should, Claire. This is about free will. Aren't you tired of this? Thirty years of pain isn't enough?"

"I can't make it all right," she muttered between clenched teeth. "I know if I see them I'll want to hurt them the way they've hurt me. It's why I've stayed away from them all these years. After everything they've done, I'll lose control and I'll be the one hauled away in handcuffs."

"You have a right to confront them, to tell them how they have trespassed. If you hurt them the way you have described, you will be the one who is ultimately hurt again and the cycle will continue. Because now you know about cause and effect. Once you know something, you can't pretend that you don't. You are held responsible for that knowledge. Can't you see that as long as you stay connected to them through this negative energy, they are still stealing your power from you? They don't even have to know about it. You're doing it for them by building that wall around your heart and carrying around the energy they placed there so long ago. Claire, dear, dear, soul . . . you don't deserve this. Can't you see that?"

She felt that familiar tightness around her chest, the burning of her throat, closing off her ability to speak. She would not cry! They didn't deserve her tears!

He reached out and touched her forearm. "Maybe you do, Claire," he whispered so tenderly that she felt the tears well up at her eyes.

She sniffled and bit the inside of her cheek. "You . . . you're reading my thoughts again," she accused in a hushed voice, trying to cover her embarrassment. And then she sniffled again.

"You are allowed to cry, to release that energy. It is a great gift you humans don't use enough. You think crying makes you weak, when in reality crying and releasing such intense emotions makes you stronger. It creates a space, free of negativity, to be filled with something new and fresh. Maybe even peace."

She pinched the bridge of her nose and hung her head. "You make it sound easy, and it's not. I'm afraid if I start, I'll never stop . . . I'll . . . disintegrate."

"You won't disintegrate. You will lose something you never needed and you will integrate something more deserving."

She felt the tears begin to fall down her cheeks and quickly wiped them away with the side of her hand. Her nose was stuffed and she breathed in through her mouth, trying not to give into what she felt was building inside of her. It was as if that wall was beginning to crack, little by little, and she was terrified of what would come rushing out.

"I can't do this!" she cried.

"Of course you can," he whispered, now stroking her forearm. "You can do it for yourself, Claire. You can release . . ."

His words trailed off as, crazily, instinctively, she crawled up next to him and buried her face in his shoulder. His touch had ignited something inside of her. She felt protected for the first time since she was a child with something genuine,

trusting and real. The sobs became deeper and longer and
she thought she might throw up at the wrenching of her
stomach. It was like expelling a monster that had buried itself deep within her heart. Clutching his shirt, as though it
were the only thing keeping her together, she cried like a little girl.

He held her in his arms, stroking her back, her hair, whis-
pering to her that it was all right, she was all right, it was
never her fault.

"I . . . I hate them!" she managed to spit out.

"I know," he answered softly. "But maybe what you actually hate is what they did to you. Remember they were pos-
sessed by their own fears. They were, and perhaps still are,
insane."

"How . . . how can I . . . *see* them again? I can't," she
wailed and felt him sigh deeply with concern.

"Claire," he said in a low, serious voice, "it takes great
courage to walk among the insane and still maintain your
balance. What do you think any conflict is about? Fear," he
added, answering his own question, "which is a form of
insanity. I will tell you that your stepbrother feared you
were taking away his father's attention from him and so he
violated you. Your mother's fear was that your accusation
would perhaps take away her security through her husband.
And your stepfather's fear was your accusation would take
away his reputation and that of his son, where he had placed
so much of his pride. In each circumstance, it was fear of
loss that drove them out of balance, into insanity. Each
time, each circumstance, each one of them had a choice.
And they chose madness instead of balance. They couldn't
see that their fears were truly about *themselves,* not about
you."

"But I'm the one that was punished," she answered
through her tears, starting to calm down. What he said made

some sort of sense, but still . . . "I was raped, Michael. Over and over!"

"I know," he said, holding her closer and tilting his head to rest upon hers. "And I am so sorry you experienced that violation. I am trying to get you to see that none of it was your fault, yet you subconsciously have been punishing yourself for the last thirty years. You were living in an unbalanced family, people who were programmed by their fears and sleepwalked through their lives. In each circumstance what was more important to them was the opinions of others, rather than what they thought of themselves. The only way they could ease their fears was to attack the one they believed threatened their place within the group."

"Like mad dogs in a pack," she muttered, sniffling and looking around for a tissue. She didn't want to leave the peace of his arms yet.

"Not unlike that behavior. Not evolved, still rooted in survival," he answered, holding his hand out to her. In it was a handkerchief. "When an animal is threatened, it doesn't think of consequences, it attacks."

She didn't even question how he made the handkerchief appear. Around him, the magical was becoming commonplace. She blew her nose and then rested her head back against his chest. "I'm exhausted," she murmured, feeling like she wanted to cry again, only this time not out of anger, but for how she had missed being held in the arms of someone who really cared about her. And she felt, maybe foolishly, that Michael did.

"I'm not surprised," he said, and placed his head back against hers.

"I don't know if I like what you've started," she breathed, still not able to inhale through her nose and feeling the burning at her eyes again.

"Healing?" he asked softly.

How could she say it was more than that?

Being held like this, by him, was bringing up a desire she had thought was lost to her forever. She didn't want to be hurt again, but she couldn't deny that for the first time since her father died, she felt safe, truly safe, in a man's arms.

Just her luck, Michael wasn't even a real man!

Chapter

8

"WHAT'S WITH YOU, CLAIRE? YOU SEEM DISTRACTED and tired."

She blinked and straightened in her chair. "Sorry," she answered, looking out of the gazebo to the flowering gardens. The last thing she wanted was to discuss what was rattling around inside her head since Michael's last visit. She turned her face and smiled at her friends. "You're right. I am tired."

Isabel's eyes narrowed as she stared across the table. "Not sleeping?"

Claire shrugged. "I have some things on my mind. Let's get back to the wedding planning. Really, Issy, your backyard is gorgeous. Breathtaking. Will all these flowers still be in bloom next month?"

Isabel nodded. "Most of them. The ones that fade will be replaced by others coming into bloom."

"Wow," Tina said, looking out to the expansive backyard. "It must have taken some time to plan all this so you'd always have flowers in the summer."

"It took years," Isabel answered with a smile. "Chuck and I did it together. We had a notebook with diagrams and we added to it with each growing season."

"What a tribute to him, to both of you," Tina whispered.

"I can't thank you enough for letting me hold my wedding here. It's going to be so beautiful."

Isabel waved off the gratitude. "Chuck would have loved it. A huge party in his backyard . . . he would have been in his element."

Claire thought about Isabel's late husband. "You're really okay now, Issy, aren't you?" Claire asked softly, picking up her glass of iced lemonade. "You seem so happy."

Isabel nodded. "We had our season together, a long, lovely season. Maybe it was spring or early summer. Now I'm into full summer, where everything seems to be thriving." She paused, then sort of giggled, which was odd for Isabel. "And I'm so grateful."

Tina grinned. "We're talking about Joshua and Hope now?"

Embarrassed, Issy nodded and said, "So what do you think of using the pale pink of the clematis as your decorating color? You could use it in the table arrangements and maybe Claire could have a satin ribbon on her dress. I'm just making suggestions since there's so much of it trailing up and over the gazebo."

Sipping her lemonade, Claire looked around them and couldn't argue that point. The big flowers were spectacular and growing everywhere on the outside of the gazebo. It was like sitting inside of a little house of flowers. "I agree, Tina. You can't ignore the statement this gazebo makes."

"You're right," Tina decided, looking around her. "I wouldn't have gone with pink as my first choice of color, but this is spectacular." She grinned at Claire. "Don't worry, I won't make you wear a pink dress. Issy's suggestion about the ribbon is fine."

Claire breathed a sigh of relief. "Thank you. I'll work pink into my outfit somehow, I promise."

"Okay, so we have a color scheme now," Tina said. "Pale pink, creamy white and we might as well include pale green. Let's talk about the tables. I'd like round ones that seat ten, and chair covers . . . oh, and flower arrangements in tall, thin, glass vases so that people can see one another. You've seen them, right? They look sort of like flower umbrellas."

Claire nodded. "That's going to be expensive, isn't it? How many tables are you talking about?"

"I think ten. Louis and I decided on a hundred people, and that's going to have to include everyone from family, friends and work. And we're both sticking to it, no matter what. And, thanks to Issy, since I'm saving so much in not renting a place, I can splurge on flowers and food. We have to find a really great caterer."

"I know of one in Philly, caters to all the movers and shakers in business and society. They're big on the Main Line too," Isabel added.

"What's the name?" Claire asked.

"Global Dish. Fantastic food and presentation. Because of the Victorian, I was invited to a sit-down dinner for the historical society, and I was very impressed."

"Write that down, Claire," Tina said. "I'll call on Monday."

"Have we set a date?" Claire asked, writing the name of the caterer under the reception heading.

"Well, really that's up to Isabel. What weekend is good for you in late August?"

Isabel shook her head. "Tina, *you* pick the date. We'll accommodate you."

"I was thinking about the weekend of the nineteenth, or twenty-sixth."

"Hey, I hate to bring this up," Claire said, "but what about the heat and humidity, or what if it rains?"

"I already looked into that online," Tina answered. "I think I should rent a tent with air conditioners. That takes care of any weather situation."

"Good idea," Claire murmured, glad they all wouldn't be

baking in the hot summer sun. "Okay, so now we have to think about music, photography and invitations. And there's the rehearsal dinner and the honeymoon."

Isabel laughed. "I'm impressed, Claire. Who knew you were such a detailed wedding planner?"

"Hey, I know how to go online too. Looked up all this wedding prep stuff this morning. If we're gonna do this, we might as well do it right."

Tina tilted her head and smiled across the table. "See, I knew you would be great, Claire."

"Yeah, well, let's get on with it, okay? It's so hot out here."

"It's not that hot," Tina said.

"It is to me."

"Why does the heat bother you so much?" Isabel asked. "It's only in the low eighties."

"I don't know. I've always hated the heat. So let's get back to business. We still have lots to do and—"

"And my wedding gown," Tina interrupted. "Don't forget that!"

Claire inwardly groaned. The wedding gown. Right . . . "That's for next week, Tina. We'll hit a few more places on the Main Line and then head to Philly if we have to continue the princess bride search."

"You promise we'll find it by next week?" Tina asked. "I'm so worried about it."

Nodding, Claire wanted to yell that it was a dress she would wear for *one* day, but knew that Tina still wanted the long white gown with all the trimmings. Even if her own wedding had been performed in the mayor's office and she'd worn a suit, Claire sympathized with Tina's anxiety. It was her day, and she'd waited a long time for it. "I can't promise all week, Tina. I have something coming up I need to attend, but we will work in a few good days of gown hunting."

Isabel turned to Claire. "Anything exciting?"

"Exciting?"

"Whatever you have coming up next week?"

Claire breathed deeply. "I wouldn't call it exciting. I have to go into Philly to be present at the reading of a will."

"A will?" Tina asked. "Did someone die and leave you something? A client?"

Even though Tina's tone was joking Claire bit her bottom lip, unsure how to answer. Finally she decided if that wall around her heart was beginning to fall down, she might as well add honesty and openness to her new inner self. "Actually, my stepfather died."

"Your stepfather?" Tina asked in a shocked voice, leaning into the table and forgetting her wedding plans. "Why didn't you say something before now?"

"Why? You didn't know him," Claire said, picking up her glass of lemonade and staring at the condensation running down the outside of it.

"I know, but you should have said something. We could have done this anytime."

"Tina's right, Claire. You should have said something."

"You two have the wrong idea," Claire answered. "I hadn't seen my stepfather in twenty years. I'm only going . . ." She couldn't tell them the real reason. Instead, she pasted a smile on her face and said, "Whatever is in the will, I thought the foundation could use it."

"You never talk about your family," Isabel said softly. "I didn't even know you had a stepfather."

"You wouldn't have liked him, Issy. Very pretentious. But he did have money, so I'm hoping whatever is in the will is enough to do some good for those who need it."

"Is your mother still alive?" Isabel asked.

Claire sighed. "We don't have to go through my family tree, do we?"

"She is," Tina said.

Claire looked up. "How would you know?"

"Because you said so the other day."

Claire forgot that conversation at lunch.

"You have a mother, Claire, and you never see her or talk about her?" Isabel asked in soft voice.

"This really isn't anyone's business," Claire protested. "I have my reasons."

"They must be good ones."

"They are. Now can we drop this subject and move this meeting into the house, because I'm melting out here in this heat."

"Must be the reason for your mood," Tina observed. "I only wish my mother could see me get married."

Claire closed her eyes briefly in frustration. "Tina, your mother and mine might as well have come from different planets."

Isabel reached across the table and placed her hand on Tina's. "Honey, your mother will be here with us in spirit."

"I wish I could believe that."

"Believe it," Issy said firmly. "I bet if you're open to it, you'll get a message on your wedding day that only she would give you."

Claire remembered feeling that intense love for her mother when she was a little girl. She had thought her mother was the most beautiful woman in the world and she'd loved to see her laugh. But the laughter ended when her father had died and left her mother worried about money. Then it was as if a different woman had come in and taken over her mother's body. She remembered the depression. The pills. The drinking. The nights alone when her mother got all dressed up and went out. She remembered the series of men coming to the house to take her mother out, until Eric arrived. By that time, her mother, the woman she had idolized, had disappeared.

"Claire? Are you coming?"

She brought herself back to the present and saw Tina and

Isabel standing with glasses of lemonade in their hands. "Sure. Let me get the list."

Together they walked out of the gazebo, Tina and Issy chattering about where to set the dance floor. Claire felt sick from the heat and dizzy from the memories she hadn't realized she remembered.

And she didn't want to remember.

Not anymore . . .

She was exhausted from the heat and after her shower, Claire crawled into bed. She had the central air set for sixty-five degrees and, with only a long T-shirt on, she kicked the lightweight down blanket to the bottom of the bed. *At last,* she thought, peace, cool peace. No one could fault her for taking a short nap on the weekend after the week she'd had. She wanted to curl up and fall asleep, but without warning memories started running across the screen in her mind.

She saw herself alone, scared during a thunderstorm, waiting for her mother to come home. How could she have been left alone at eight years old? What kind of mother went out on a date and didn't even come home or call during a thunderstorm? She remembered crying in fear for what had seemed like hours and finally falling asleep under the winding stairs . . . and her mother finding her, waking her, scolding her for hiding. And she remembered the sweet and distinctive smell of Manhattans on her mother's breath.

Her mother's wedding to Eric next flashed across her mind . . . The small group of adults gathered at the country club. The starched yellow dress her mother had made her wear. The headband decorated with tiny white flowers digging into her scalp. David pinching her arm when no one was looking, telling her she was nothing more than a stepsister, a poor stepsister, and she had better keep out of his way.

And she had tried to do just that as they all moved into that big white house with all its rooms, all that housework that became hers. Her mother and Eric had the master bedroom on the second floor and she and David had their bedrooms on the third floor. She had kept to herself as much as possible, not wanting to anger the older boy she had been forced to live with, the boy who seemed to be two different people . . . polite to the point of ingratiating in front of any adults and mean to the bone when they were alone.

Claire saw herself as a young adolescent, washing dishes and vacuuming rugs, polishing silver and dusting crystal, all because her mother didn't trust hired help, yet was incapable of running and cleaning the house herself. She hadn't even been paid an allowance. She could still recall her mother lecturing her, telling her how grateful she should be that they had a fine house and good things, that her father had left them without even insurance money to survive and what a good-for-nothing man he had been. A loser, she had called him. And every time she did, Claire had felt like a knife had been thrust into her belly.

Her father had been her hero. In the short time she'd had with him, she remembered him as handsome, tall, funny, affectionate. She used to run into his arms and he'd scoop her up and laugh into her cheek, saying she was his girl. His girl . . .

Claire felt her throat tighten with longing.

Maybe he'd died of stomach cancer to get away from the woman he'd married. Her mother couldn't have been much of a wife to talk about him like that after he'd died.

How many times had she wished her father was alive? She had foolishly, childishly, thought he would show up one day, telling them it had all been a terrible mistake. He would be alive and save her from her so-called family. Even though she had seen him in that coffin, looking all waxy and stiff, she'd still held the childish fantasy that he would somehow rescue her.

But he never did.

No one rescued her.

Maybe that's the way life really is and she'd learned that lesson young. No one comes riding in on a white horse and pulls you out of hell. You have to work your way out yourself. Not for the first time Claire wondered if life really was some kind of purgatory, a place where you played out different scenarios with different people, a kind of karmic playground where you were rewarded or paid for your transgressions sooner or later.

So what the hell had she ever done?

Maybe there was such a thing as past lives and, if there were, she must have been a horrid person and had paid for it this time around. It was the only thing that could explain what had happened to her as a child.

Realizing there wasn't an answer, she sighed and closed her eyes.

God, she was tired from spending the day outside with Tina.

It was the heat. It just seemed to suck all the energy right out of her. How she'd always hated it . . .

Within moments she suddenly saw herself playing in the sand with her father. It was down at the Jersey shore. She remembered the water, the seagulls, the boardwalk . . .

Blinking, Claire was surprised. So she didn't always hate the heat of summer? Was it because she'd been with her father? It didn't make sense . . .

And then, unexpectedly, she saw herself years later trying to fall asleep on the third floor of that big house. It had been before central air-conditioning was installed and the two windows in her bedroom didn't alleviate anything. The summer heat in the rest of the house had risen, making her bedroom an inferno, and she had flung off the sheet to find some relief.

Even as a grown woman, she could barely breathe, remembering . . .

That was the night David had first invaded her room and her body . . .

She became rigid with shock as she remembered her body burning with embarrassment and then horror and then pain. She hadn't even believed the stories the girls at school had been telling about what men did to women. Not until it was done to her, and then the nightmare lasted for almost three years.

It had been so hot, stifling hot, and she had thought she could taste the heavy humidity in the air as she'd drawn in her breath . . . and then the door slowly creaked open.

David.

Taller than her. Stronger than her. So much more clever than her.

She had thought she was going to die. She couldn't breathe with his hand over her mouth. The struggle. The threats. The ugly whispers. Her body's sweat mixing with his . . .

No wonder she hated the summer. The heat. The humidity. That feeling of not being able to breathe. Trapped . . .

"No!" she cried, turning over to her side and curling up into a ball for protection.

She wouldn't think about it!

She couldn't! She couldn't . . .

"It's all right, Claire."

She heard the whisper right behind her ear and gasped as she found herself wrapped in Michael's arms.

"You don't have to do this to yourself anymore. Let it go."

She felt . . . protected again within his arms. "Michael," she breathed, grabbing his wrist and bringing it closer around her waist. "Don't leave me. Please."

"It's all right, Claire. I'll stay as long as you need me."

"Promise?" Even to her own ears, her voice sounded like a little girl's. God, she hated being so weak, needing someone, a male someone, but recalling those memories was terrifying.

"I promise," he answered, resting his jaw against the side of her head.

She stayed still, relishing the feeling of peace that enveloped her. Whatever his magic was, she didn't want it to end. It had been so long since her muscles weren't tense, alert, ready to respond and fight.

Being in Michael's arms was like floating in the pool, all weight and stress removed, leaving nothing but thoughts she had pushed down so long ago that now seemed overwhelming.

And as much as she hated her weakness, Claire started crying, for herself, for a lost childhood, for all the other little girls everywhere around the world whose innocence had been cruelly ripped away from them. She heard it on the news and it sickened her. She read it in the papers and her blood boiled over in outrage. Children had a right to protection. They were born innocent, helpless, looking to the adults for safekeeping. No one had the right to violate them, ever, in any situation, but it was still happening in every country, on the Internet, in war zones and behind the closed doors of families all over the world.

So she cried for all the little girls, faceless, nameless innocents whose lives had been so altered by insanity.

They stayed together, spooning in silence, for over an hour, until Claire calmed down, sniffled and whispered, "I . . . think I'm damaged, Michael."

"I know," he whispered back and kissed the side of her head. "But you can heal, Claire. You don't have to live your life like this."

She sighed. "I don't think I've ever really given another male a chance to get close to me. Except now . . . with you," she added softly.

"And I am honored."

She sniffled again, trying to regain some control and not appear so weak. "Hey, it's not as if I'm doing any of this by choice, you know. You came into my life unexpectedly. I didn't plan to ever relive those memories."

"It is understandable why you felt you had to protect your heart."

"And my body," she murmured. "I've never really given another man my body, my whole self, without holding something back for protection. That's why . . ." Her words trailed off with embarrassment.

"That's why?" he asked, prodding her to continue.

How could she feel like this with someone she hardly knew? Yet deep within her she felt like she'd known him forever, that he knew everything about her, all her ugly secrets, and none of it mattered. She felt accepted, cherished, maybe even loved, even if that love was literally out of this world and more spiritual than physical.

Knowing she had to answer him, she waited a few moments, building up her courage. "That's why I was so floored with your lights," she finally admitted. "It felt . . . like nothing I'd ever experienced."

"We achieved unity, Claire."

She nodded. "It was beautiful."

"We can do it again . . . if you'd like."

His words, so close to her ear, made her shiver. Could she say what she really wanted to say? Maybe with him, someone she totally trusted . . . maybe with him she could do it, go beyond that wall of protection. Knowing she had to speak it aloud, she swallowed the fear in her throat and just said it.

"Michael, could we possibly achieve unity my way? Physically? I really want to know if . . . if I can make love with someone I trust. I . . . never have."

"Your way?" he asked, a note of hesitancy in his voice.

She arched her back slightly and snuggled deeper, her bottom fitting so perfectly against him as she took his hand up from her waist and placed it on her breast. "My way. The way humans achieve unity, only I've never really had real unity so I was thinking maybe . . ." She stopped speaking when she felt his arousal against her.

"Something's happening," Michael whispered, sounding a little worried.

Despite everything, Claire smiled. "Your body is responding to mine. It's the way unity begins . . . an attraction." She moved slightly, ever so slowly, against his arousal. "A body, Michael, can be used for pleasure, you know."

"I . . . I know that, Claire," he answered, his voice sounding lower, rougher, still unsure. "Intercourse. Sexual intercourse."

"Exactly. And what do you know of it?"

"Know of it?"

She nodded, becoming aroused by his arousal. "Have you ever experienced it?"

"No . . . I'm not sure if I should."

"Why? You wouldn't be breaking any rules, would you?"

"I don't think so . . . it's . . . just that I've never . . ."

She heard the uncertainty in his voice and quickly turned around, facing him. Wrapping her arms around him, she looked into his eyes and smiled as she lifted one leg over his hip, making contact with him again. "I can show you," she whispered. "I can't promise it will be better than your way of unity, but you can't come to this dimension and miss out on sex, Michael. It would be such a shame if you did. We don't have many things that can compete with your dimension, but I bet this is one of them."

He stared back at her, his eyes wide with wonder. "I don't know, Claire."

She felt his breath on her lips when he spoke and she knew by the way his hand was caressing her back, almost automatically, that his body was sending signals to his brain to continue. "Just follow your feelings," she said, stroking the thick, curly hair away from his temple. How could she have ever thought of him as a nerd? He really was handsome, not movie star handsome, but normal handsome with the most beautiful eyes and wonderful full lips . . .

"Don't turn into your lights or disintegrate on me, Michael," she breathed, gently holding his head and brushing her lips against his. "Stay here with me. I promise you won't regret it."

Her kiss seemed to ignite him and he kissed her back with passion.

It was all she needed.

Fueled by her own desire to connect with someone she trusted, to prove to herself that she could give herself completely, Claire took the lead. Hands became instruments of exploration, eliciting gasps of pleasure. Lips became sensors of desire as clothing was quickly shed. She watched his face light up with surprise and her own pleasure increased by giving it to him.

"Claire, you are so beautiful," he murmured, running his hands over her hip and down her thigh. "I want to touch you everywhere."

She almost giggled. "Go ahead. Be my guest."

He placed her on her back and leaned over her, exploring her body from her face down. Gently, ever so gently, almost reverently, he slid his fingers over her skin, marveling at her breast when his touch made her nipple erect. He explored further and, when she felt that old familiar tensing of warning as he approached her womanhood, she concentrated on letting go of the fear, of telling herself that Michael was trustworthy. He wouldn't hurt her. He would be loving and gentle and . . . and all thoughts ceased as Michael seemed to connect to something very human as his mouth came down on hers while his hand gently continued to explore her.

She was overwhelmed as he seemed to know exactly what she wanted. She didn't care if he was reading her mind, just as long as he didn't stop. Over and over again she felt herself building, gathering, as she clung to his shoulder with one hand and grabbed the sheet in her fist with the other. He kept kissing her, not giving her time to think, only to feel, and she wondered who was the teacher now and if she didn't say something soon they might well miss their chance . . .

"I want you inside of me," she pleaded into his mouth. "Please, Michael . . . now."

She guided him and when he filled her, he looked down on her with such surprise that his jaw dropped open and all he could say was her name.

"Claire . . ."

His hands grabbed hers and she started moving, positioning herself so he was still stroking her exactly where she wanted him. Over and over, he brought her back to where her legs were clinging to him, moaning, willing to give of herself completely.

"Claire?" His voice sounded shocked, as though never having felt himself physically before.

"Just . . . go with it, Michael," she gasped, so close to the edge herself. "Come with me."

Their hands were clasped together over her head. Their eyes were locked on each other, reading the power each was capable of giving. They moved as though they were one being, intent on their destination.

Never before had Claire known what this was truly like, to trust someone so much that all thought disappears, wiped out by pure desire. She moaned as she came closer to the edge again, each nerve ending alive with sexual energy. It was almost exquisitely unbearable.

"Claire?" Michael's voice sounded as desperate as she felt.

"I know," she breathed, clinging to his hands tightly as though they were the only things keeping her grounded. "Oh, God . . . oh, God . . ."

"Claire!"

"Mic—" She couldn't even get his name out as she exploded in sheer joy.

Together they leapt in faith over the edge, soaring out of the mundane and into the divine. Wave after wave of pleasure filled her body until she felt she could no longer contain it. It simply had to transcend the limits of her skin. And that's when it happened . . .

She felt herself leave herself, leaping out of her body and soaring like a star into the unknown. Michael was with her, mingling his own joy with hers in a vast darkness that was filled with breathtakingly beautiful lights. And she kept soaring, over and over, farther and farther . . .

"Claire! Open your eyes!"

From far away she heard a voice, but wanted to ignore it as she felt so weak even opening her eyelids would take effort.

"Claire! Open your eyes!"

She felt herself being shaken and reluctantly blinked.

Michael was above her and he seemed worried as he blew his breath out in relief.

"I . . . I'm okay," she muttered. "Dear God . . . *what was that?*"

Michael leaned his forehead against her chin and shook his head. "I believe, my love, that is what you humans call an orgasm."

She almost laughed as her body contracted around him again in after shocks. "I know that. I mean . . . out there . . . those lights. I felt like . . . like I was soaring."

He lifted his head. "You left your body. It can be dangerous when it's spontaneous. You lost consciousness for a few moments."

"You mean I . . . *fainted*? Again? Like in the pool?"

He nodded. "Yes, that is the term. Fainted. Are you all right now, Claire?"

She drew in her breath deeply. "I *fainted*? I'd never fainted in my life before I met you!"

He raised his head and smiled at her so tenderly she almost groaned.

"Have you ever experienced anything like that in your entire life?"

She shook her head. "Never. And if you're looking for compliments, like every other human male after sex, then you got it. You've certainly got it, Michael. My God, that was unbelievable!"

He brushed the hair back from her face. "You are better now?"

Nodding, she said, "I'm better. I won't faint on you again. I'm just a little dizzy and—"

"Claire, I can't stay here with you any longer. I'm sorry, so sorry . . ."

His words trailed off in a cloud of dancing lights and Claire was left with an emptiness that was nearly overwhelming. Breathing heavily, she looked up to the ceiling of her bedroom with frustration. "Hey, we're going to have to talk about the importance of cuddling afterward!"

Oh, well, it wasn't as if he'd fallen asleep on her.

Chapter

9

"CLAIRE, THERE'S A MICHAEL ON THE PHONE. DIDN'T give a last name. Says he'd like to speak with you."

Claire immediately said, "Put him through." Then she remembered to thank Shelly before punching the button for the second line. "Michael?"

"Hello, Claire."

It was Michael. Her Michael. Chastising herself for being so possessive, she said, "You're using a phone?"

"I wanted to speak with you and I didn't think it would be appropriate for me to appear in your office."

"No . . . no, you're right. You'd be hard to explain." She mentally shook herself. "*Why* are you calling me here?"

"Perhaps I miss you."

She blinked several times, then smiled. "You do, huh?"

"I do."

She was so pleased by his words and felt like a silly young girl. It was almost like speaking with a boyfriend, but Michael was no boy and he was much more than a friend. Now that she'd had sex with him, her body had been craving him like an addict who hadn't had a fix in days. Just thinking about them making love gave her shivers. "I miss you too," she admitted reluctantly. "And I shouldn't because I'm at work."

"Can you leave your work? There's something I want to show you."

Now that was intriguing. "I can't, Michael. I left early last week and I really should stay."

He didn't answer her and Claire worried he'd hung up. "Michael? Are you still there?"

"Yes. I was concentrating on the circuitry that is making this connection, as I didn't have the proper numbers to use or the coins required."

"Where are you?"

"I am in what you call a telephone booth, though there is no booth, simply a stand with a molecular composite you call plastic covering three sides."

"But where?"

"Outside your building."

She jerked her head to the window and slowly stood up. Leaning toward the glass she looked outside and down the street to the phone booth.

Michael waved.

Seeing him, she felt her heart melt and she yearned to be with him, to touch him, brush her skin against his. Waving back at him, she said, "Okay, don't move. Don't go away or disappear or anything. I'll be right there."

"What about your work, Claire? I do not wish to make things more difficult for you."

"Just . . . hang up and wait for me," she ordered and repeated, "I'll be right there."

She watched him hang up the phone and did the same with her own. Without thinking, she turned off her computer, cleared her desk, picked up her purse and walked out of her office. She stopped at Shelly's desk and said, "I have to run out for a little while. Cover for me, okay?"

Shelly's mouth opened in surprise. "What's going on, Claire? Are you okay? You look flushed."

She started nodding and stammering. "I . . . ah . . . I . . . I'm a little dizzy and I . . . think I should . . . you know, check it out."

Shelly started to rise. "Should I call your doctor and let him know you're coming?"

"No!" She lowered her voice and tried not to feel like a ten-year-old lying to her teacher about her homework. "Don't bother, Shelly. I'll call from the car. And don't worry about anything. Just shoot me an e-mail about whatever comes up. I can finish the day at home on my computer."

"So you're not coming back?"

"I don't know. No, probably not."

"Are you *sure* you're okay, Claire?" Shelly asked suspiciously, as though she wasn't buying her flimsy excuse.

Claire squared her shoulders as she headed for the door. "Now would I be leaving work in the middle of the day if everything was okay? I promise it's nothing serious. I just have to . . . you know, check it out." She pulled open the door that led into the lobby. "I'll see you tomorrow. Thanks, Shelly." Guess she wasn't coming back to work today.

Nodding to the receptionist, she walked past the tastefully decorated furniture that always reminded her of an exclusive men's club, all Ralph Lauren plaids and deep greens and burgundies. There was even a fireplace to complete the picture. She made sure not to make eye contact with any of the waiting clients and pushed open the outside door.

The heat seemed to take her breath away and she hurried to her car, thankful her parking space was next in line after the partners. Once inside, she started the car, lowered the windows, blew out the blast of hot air trapped under the hood and started the air conditioner. Already she could feel her scalp beginning to sweat. Not waiting for the full effect of the air conditioner, she shifted into reverse and backed out of her parking space before Shelly came after her calling her a liar.

She screeched to a stop in front of the phone booth and when Michael just stood there smiling, dimples and all, she reached over and opened the passenger door. "Get in," she called out, then blew her breath out between her teeth as Michael took his time coming to the car. It would be just her luck for Shelly to be watering that big plant she had on her windowsill. "Hurry up!"

He entered the car and Claire waved her hand. "Close the door, will you?"

"Why are you so upset?" he asked calmly, as if he had all the time in the world.

Her eyes widened until he shut the door beside him. She slammed her foot on the accelerator and they took off. "Because I just ditched work so you could show me something." She headed for the highway. "Now, what is it?"

"It's not here, Claire. What does that mean, *ditched*?"

Her fingers tightened on the steering wheel. "It means I told a lie and ran away from my work. Now what exactly do you have to show me?"

"You lied?"

Her shoulders sank in defeat. "Do not get all holier than thou on me, Michael. I had to say something to get out."

"But you're not a prisoner, are you?"

"Of course I'm not. It's just . . . I have responsibilities, and one cannot stop working and leave whenever one wants . . . unless one owns the business, which I don't."

From the corner of her eye she could see him shaking his head.

"Don't judge me," she commanded. Really, she'd done it for him!

"I wasn't judging you. It just seems unfair that you would have to tell a lie in order to play."

She blinked, sure she hadn't heard that correctly. "What did you say?"

"I said it seems unfair that—"

"Not that part, the next part. In order to . . . what?"

"Play."

She slammed her foot on the break, unprepared to see Michael lurch forward toward the windshield. She grabbed his blue shirt to protect him. "Did you drag me out of work to *play*?"

He sat back and looked at her. "I didn't drag you anywhere, Claire. I simply wanted to play."

Confused, she shook her head. *"Play?"* she repeated. "Like in . . . kid's play?"

"Exactly!" he answered, smoothing out the front of his shirt now that she'd let go of him. And he was smiling.

Smiling! Like he was some child who had discovered something great.

"Michael, I can't just up and *play* anytime you want! I have a job. I'm an adult."

"You're an unhappy adult who never really played when you were a child. I think it's time, don't you?"

She simply stared at him, unable to form words, until a horn blared from behind her. "Buckle your seat belt." Shaking her head, this time to bring some sense into it, Claire turned back to the steering wheel and began to drive aimlessly, following traffic, feeling like she was in a dream. She'd ditched work to play.

Play!

They drove in silence for a few minutes, until Claire sighed in surrender. It wasn't like she could go back to work now and explain to Shelly that she'd been mistaken. She wasn't dizzy, she was beyond dizzy and bordering on crazy because she'd hooked up with a dimension traveler.

Somewhere in the back of her mind she remembered thinking she'd thought Michael would be a great playmate. She just never thought it would be actual *playing*! She'd been thinking about something a little more adult.

"So . . . what exactly did you have in mind?" she finally asked.

"You will need to drive to the Pennsylvania Turnpike and proceed east."

She turned to him. "The turnpike? Where . . . ?"

"I will give you the directions, Claire. Don't worry. I researched it on your maps."

"So you're not going to tell me where we're going?"

"No. I would like to surprise you."

"We're not going to the shore, are we? Because I'm not a big fan of the shore, especially today when it's hot and—"

"We are not going to the seashore," he interrupted, seeming very pleased with himself.

She thought about it. "And no amusement parks like Great Adventure over in Jersey. We are heading to New Jersey, aren't we?"

"We are simply going to be traveling east for the time being."

She bit the inside of her cheek. "Well, just so you know, I'm not going to be standing in line or going on any rides that are going to make me sick. So if it's Great Adventure, you'd better change your plans."

He laughed. "You really don't know how to play, do you?"

She straightened her shoulders. "*This* doesn't feel like playing."

"Doesn't this vehicle have music?" he asked, as though ignoring her last statement.

Giving up the twenty questions, Claire turned on the stereo. The CD she'd been playing on her way into work suddenly filled the car.

Play that funky music white boy . . . play—

She immediately silenced the CD. "Sorry. Just like to listen to the old songs sometimes when I'm alone in the car."

"May I hear it?" Michael asked.

"Oh, c'mon, this is stuff from high school and college. You wouldn't like it. You probably would be happy with classical music."

"Now who is judging whom?"

"I just thought . . . you know, you being from another dimension you'd want classical or New Age stuff with harps and Native American flutes."

"What is your music called?"

"It isn't *my* music," she said, a bit too defensively.

"The music in this machine then. The music you listened to when you were younger."

She sighed heavily, knowing there was no way out. He'd just pester her until she told him. "Funk. It's called funk."

"Funk," Michael repeated. "Funk."

Claire almost burst out laughing. Hearing Michael, dimension traveler, try out the word *funk,* as if he was a scientist storing it for future knowledge, was funny.

"Yes . . . *funk,*" she said with a giggle as she pushed the CD back inside the player. It began playing from the beginning.

"*Early in the morning,*" she sang, then said, "the Gap Band."

Michael listened to the words and Claire watched him sporadically from the corner of her eye. Finally she said, "You have to feel it, Michael. The beat." And she began to move her head with the rhythm. She turned up the volume until the music filled the car. "Can you feel it?" she asked, unable to hide the big grin on her face.

Michael started nodding in time to the beat. "Yes. Yes, I can. Very . . . lively."

This time she did burst out laughing. "Lively. Good word. You're right."

Turning onto the turnpike, she got her ticket and headed east. "You know it's funny," she said, turning down the volume a little. "When I hear this kind of music, it takes me back in time to college and I feel young again, happy, free."

"See, you remember how to play."

"Now in college, when I played, it was usually with the help of that first subject we discussed."

"First subject?"

"In the video store."

She could almost hear him trying to access the information, like a hard drive whirring in a computer.

"Pot. Weed. Mary Jane," she said, giving him the answer.

"Ah, yes, marijuana, also known as grass."

"Right. Almost lost my scholarship because of it, until a young professor took me aside and told me I was . . ." She hesitated and decided to substitute the verb with something a little less graphic, "screwing up my life and I needed to get my priorities straight."

"One of your angels in disguise."

"Good way to put it, but I listened and got my act together." Smiling, she merged into the traffic heading east on the turnpike, set her cruise control to seventy-nine miles an hour, and when she was settled comfortably, she relaxed, finally let it all go—her guilt, her desperate need to control things around her—and just surrendered to the unknown.

"Oh, oh! This is a good one," she announced as the next song came on. *"She's a brick* house," she sang, getting in the mood and letting herself just *be* in the moment. *"She's mighty, mighty, lettin' it all hang out . . ."*

"What does that mean," he asked over the music. "Comparing a woman to a house?"

She laughed. "It means she's . . . stacked." She quickly glanced at his confused expression. Holding her hand before her breast about five more inches, she added, "Big, firm, buxom, full. Front and back. The opposite of me."

It finally dawned on him what she meant. "Ah . . . a brick *house*!"

Claire laughed. "Now you've got it."

She tapped the steering wheel with her fingers in time to the music and saw Michael tapping his knee, getting into it, nodding his head with the beat.

Hold on . . .

Unbelievably, she was having fun. It was like playing hooky, ditching class and all her responsibilities, and just letting the day carry her away.

How long *had* it been since she'd really played?

They listened to the rest of the CD as they sped across eastern Pennsylvania. Michael told her to get off on Route 1 and head toward the Delaware River. Still puzzled, Claire managed to shut up and do as he asked. Something in her didn't want to know until they arrived. And that was new. She wondered how much energy she had wasted in the last three decades trying to control things so she wouldn't be surprised or hurt. Had she forgotten how to really live?

Had her childhood robbed her of that?

A half hour later, after a really great ride where Michael was getting the hang of seat dancing, Claire sat in the car and stared out the windshield at the sign.

"You've got to be kidding." She said, after pulling the car into the gravel parking lot.

"I'm not kidding. This is what I wanted to show you. Let's do it."

"Tube rafting down the Delaware River?" she asked incredulously. "Michael, this is ridiculous."

"It is not. It will be fun. Trust me."

She blew her breath out so hard her lips fluttered in derision. "This is for kids and teenagers and—"

"And adults like you, Claire, who take yourself too seriously."

She wanted to argue that point with him, but quickly came up with a better one. "I am wearing Gucci, Michael.

Now that may not mean much to you, but I am not about to go tube rafting in Gucci."

He smiled. "I happen to know you have a bag in the rear compartment of this vehicle containing more appropriate clothes."

Damn! Damn his all knowing ability to sniff out her gym clothes!

She bit the inside of her cheek. "I have nowhere to change," she argued.

"Claire, stop fighting this. Change in the car."

"What about you? You seem to only have those jeans and that blue shirt, which, I must tell you, is starting to get a little dull. To go rafting you should have a bathing suit or shorts and T-shirt. We just aren't dressed for this, Michael."

"You are being childish," he answered and held up his hand, "which is different than being childlike and playing. Be more childlike, Claire. Change your clothes."

She left work to go tube rafting down the Delaware?

"Please?"

She pursed her mouth and stared at the big, fat, black inner tubes lined up in a rack. It was crazy. It was probably dangerous. She could catch some kind of virus from the water.

"It's perfectly safe," Michael whispered, reading her thoughts. "I promise I will keep you safe."

She turned her head and looked at him. "You are something else, you know that?"

He grinned. "Yes, Claire. I do know that. I have been telling you that since we met at that store."

She tried not to grin back at him. "You'd have to be. No ordinary man could get me to strip off Gucci for tube rafting."

"Then you will do it with me?"

He looked so pleased her heart melted again. "Do I have a choice?"

"Of course. You always have a choice, Claire. That is free will. But I am so happy you have chosen this."

She popped the trunk, opened the windows and turned off the car engine. "So you'd better put up some kind of Jedi shield around this car so no one will see me change," she said, yanking her arms out of her suit jacket. Throwing it onto the backseat, she added, "And you can get my bag from the trunk."

Nodding, he opened the door then hesitated. Turning to her, he asked, "What is a Jedi shield?"

She chuckled while unbuttoning her blouse. "I'll explain it on the river. And while you're out there at the back of the car, you might want to whip up some shorts for yourself."

Michael looked out the front window to a man walking his dog by the river. "Like that?"

Claire shrugged as she took in the tan shorts and the white Polo shirt. "Good enough," she pronounced, leaving her shirt unbuttoned and starting on her skirt.

Changing in a BMW proved to be a challenge as she pushed her seat all the way back and slid the skirt down her legs. Thank God she didn't wear panty hose. Instead, she kicked off her heels and was grateful for the self-tanning cream she applied every few days. At least she wouldn't be pale white.

Michael came back to the car door and opened it, putting the gym bag on the passenger seat. She noticed he was wearing the shorts and Polo shirt and her solar plexus sort of rippled in attraction. He looked so good. Again she wondered why she had ever thought of him as nerdy. He had great legs, muscular yet lean. His arms were covered in light hair and looked strong. Unwillingly, her brain ran a memory of being held in them, feeling so safe and protected. She wanted that again, that feeling of peace. He was very . . . male. Casually male. Comfortable in his own skin.

But it wasn't his skin, she reminded herself. It was what Mike Murphy's skin would have been had he lived.

Who cares anymore? She was more than attracted to him and, in that moment, realized she actually wished he was her boyfriend—which was stupid. Maybe for today she could pretend.

"Claire? Do you need help?"

She brought herself back to the present and shook her head. "I'm fine," she said, pulling open the gym bag and taking out shorts, sneakers and a sleeveless T-shirt. "Just make sure no one's looking," she added, while proceeding to change in broad daylight, in a parking lot, on the Delaware River . . . No one would believe it.

She paid the man for two tubes, locked her wallet in the car and listened to the directions for safety. Michael sat in his tube, which was connected to hers with a rope. The man held the tube for her and she finally managed to collapse back into it, gasping when the cool Delaware River enveloped her behind. "Are we havin' fun yet?" she yelled to Michael, who was looking very happy and relaxed.

"You will," the man answered. "Just chill out and let the water take you. You'll see where you're to get out about two miles downriver. Then someone will bring you back here to your car."

"Great," Claire muttered, using her hands to turn her tube toward Michael's. "So I take it you're the leader in this."

Grinning, Michael looked at the man. "Thank you for your assistance, sir."

Claire turned her head back to the shore. "Yes, thanks. How long will it take?"

The man kind of laughed. "Lady, you can't tell. It's a river. It has its own time. Usually it's about an hour or so."

Nodding, Claire again thanked him and turned her attention back to Michael who was about four feet ahead of her.

"Are you sure this is safe?" she asked, looking at the river water and picturing snakes biting her ass.

"I promised you, didn't I?"

"Just checking," she murmured, watching the bank of the river for anything sliding into the water. Pennsylvania had snakes that lived in water, didn't it? What did she know? She wasn't exactly the outdoorsy type; never had been. The thought of camping brought a shudder. She was a lady that needed a real bathroom.

"Will you please relax?" Michael called out. "Your thoughts are so chaotic it's impossible for you to enjoy anything. This is supposed to be fun."

"I know, I know," she called back, still worried about her behind dragging underwater. Anything could get at it. Fish don't bite, right? What if—

Suddenly she was pulled forward with a jerk and held onto the sides of the tube as tightly as she could. Michael was pulling her toward him. When their legs were touching, he said, "Let's stay together."

She let out her breath. "Good idea."

"Now, tell me about the Jedi shield."

"What?" she asked, still studying the shoreline for any varmint that might come sliding into the water.

"What you said in the car. You wanted me to put a Jedi shield around it so you could change your clothes."

She shook her head. "That was a joke. Like in *Stars Wars*. Do you know about *Star Wars*?"

She glanced at him as he briefly closed his eyes, obviously accessing something, and then smiled. "*Star Wars*. A futuristic series of motion pictures depicting the battle between good and evil."

"Close enough," she answered, starting to like being this close to Michael in the water. Maybe it wouldn't be so bad after all. "There's these knights, the good guys, and they've managed to figure out energy and harness it. They have these light sabers and stuff like that. I've only seen the first couple of movies when I was younger."

"What was your favorite part?"

She thought about it. "Besides the romance? Let's see . . ." She allowed her hand to drift in the water, feeling more relaxed. "I think it was at the end of the first movie, when Luke Skywalker is flying his plane into the Death Star so he can destroy it. He has to get it right and no one else had been able to do it."

"And what happens?"

"Well, he tries a couple of times but his aim is off. Finally, he makes another go of it and he pushes all his highly technical equipment out of the way and sort of flies by the seat of his pants, trusting himself, his inner voice. *The force,* they call it."

"And is he successful?"

She grinned. "Of course. That was the whole point of the movie."

"A powerful metaphor, is it not? When you realize your inner guidance system is all you really have, then the adventure truly begins."

Nodding, Claire said, "I remember thinking at the time that it made perfect sense. Of course that depends on one's definition of the force."

"You see, Claire, you have known about your own power for some time now. In many ways you have used it. In others, you've denied it."

"Hey, you think it's so easy when from the time a kid is able to understand, that power you talk about is slowly drained right out of him by his parents or the church or anyone that wants him to behave according to their wishes or their creed? It takes years to deprogram, to take back yourself."

"But you did it."

"Yes, and not many were happy about it. Society doesn't

want you to think outside the box. It wants you to give the force a personality and live your life by that personality's rules."

"It frightens them that they might be mistaken. They've spent their lives upholding those rules. They have institutions dedicated to those rules."

"But most of those rules were made up by man, not by God or the force or the source or whatever label you want to give it," she countered. "The Ten Commandments. Good rules to live by. Then Jesus added, love others as I have loved you. Better rule. Too bad most who claim to be his followers can't live by that one."

"Claire, you're speaking about a group of followers who are very vocal, not the whole. There are many who follow the Christ's teachings who try very hard not to judge."

"I know," she admitted reluctantly. "Those others just make me grit my teeth. No religion has a monopoly on God. They hijacked a religion and think God is an ignorant bigot. I swear, Michael, this whole thing about gay marriage confounds me. How does a committed partnership threaten anyone's family? And I have this sneaking suspicion that all those homophobic men who are so scared of it have had homosexual leanings and are terrified of themselves so they lash out at all gay people thinking it makes them look super straight. I mean, why else would they be so afraid?"

"You may be right," he answered. "People who live in fear do fearful things."

"Wouldn't it be funny if I was? If some respected research showed that?" She chuckled. "You'd get mowed down by all those men voting that a civil marriage was a civil right."

"You might want to consider politics, Claire."

Her head jerked toward him. "Are you kidding? Politics today? Where the lobbyists are writing the legislation for bills and their paid-off congressmen pass them? If I wanted to work in dirt, I'd rather be a gardener. At least something beautiful would grow. Besides, I don't think I'm diplomatic enough for politics. My mouth would get me in deep trouble. It's scary enough as it is to have to walk in two worlds, the one everyone expects and . . ."

"The real one," he supplied. "Where the only thing you really have any control over is yourself and your reactions?"

She nodded. "There's a whole lot of people who would argue that other world is real. Including me, until you showed up in my life."

"I am real, Claire."

"I know." She shook her head. "I can't believe I'm saying that, but you are real, Michael, at least to me."

He pulled the rope even closer until they were drifting down the river side by side. "I want to kiss you," he murmured. "Ever since . . . our unity, our physical unity, I have thought of little else. I . . . yearn for you. Is that the right word?"

She grinned, forgetting their political conversation. "Me, too."

He leaned over to her and she leaned into him.

Holding the back of her head, Michael kissed her. Deeply. Passionately.

Claire felt herself melt and she clung to his shirt with one hand. "Let's go home," she murmured against his lips.

Michael smiled into her eyes. "Let's finish our ride down the river. Hold my hand, Claire," he said, taking her hand in his as they parted. "I won't let you go."

His words repeated inside her head. How she wanted that to be true.

Never, ever, had she felt so right with another human being.

And just as quickly her mind told her Michael wasn't a human being at all and he would let her go one day, when whatever he'd come to do was accomplished.

How had it happened so fast? Finally, for the first time in her adult life she felt cherished.

The truth slammed into her brain with the force of a bullet between the eyes. She was falling in love with someone who belonged in another dimension.

Damn, it had happened without her permission.

She'd better have that talk with Cristine . . . soon.

Now she really needed to know.

Chapter

10

THE RECEPTION AREA OF THE LAW OFFICES OF WHIT-
man and Collier reminded her of her own office with that
look of catering to old money, Claire thought while sitting
in a leather wing chair after announcing herself to the receptionist. She wished she'd had a Valium or some kind of
drug to relax her, as her stomach was twisted in a knot and
her heart was pounding. It didn't help that she hadn't eaten
breakfast. She'd been too nervous for anything but coffee.

God, what was she doing here after all these years,
maybe twenty feet away from her mother and David who
were in some room down that hallway in front of her? And
why had Eric included her in his will? Was he laughing
from the grave by putting them all in the same room?

Just the thought made her want to throw up and she tried
to ignore the twisting of her stomach muscles, the sweat
that beaded along her hairline, the salivating that made her
continually swallow.

It would not do to have an anxiety attack now, especially
since she had to face her mother and David for the first time
in over two decades.

Calm down. Breathe deeply, she told herself, inhaling until her lungs were full and then slowly exhaling. At least she
was wearing her best Armani suit, so deep blue it almost

looked black. She wore no blouse underneath and hoped by the time this thing was over she didn't have huge perspiration stains under her arms.

She must look cool and collected. She couldn't let them see her sweat She suddenly wished she had a lawyer with her, or even a friend. Michael had volunteered, but she didn't want him involved in this. Besides, she was afraid of what he might say. Probably something deep and spiritual, and then they would think she was in some kind of cult. No, she had to do this alone. She had to walk into the lion's den and remain safe.

Michael had tried to prepare her, telling her to imagine a bubble of light surrounding her that no one could penetrate, not their thoughts or actions or words. She closed her eyes briefly and imagined the bubble. Surely, now that she had a dimension traveler as a lover such stuff would work.

And then her crazy mind immediately switched to her and Michael returning home after their tubing adventure. They'd been so hungry for each other, for the privacy to make love, they'd begun tearing off each other's clothes on the way into her bedroom. She closed her eyes, remembering his touch, his kisses, his body fusing with hers. God, it had been so long and never like that—

"Mrs. Hutchinson?"

Startled, she jerked her head up and opened her eyes. "Yes?"

"I'll show you to the conference room now."

She smiled at the professional woman and rose, bringing her small purse with her. *This is it,* she thought. This is what it's like to walk into a room of animals you know are capable of devouring you. What did that *Dog Whisperer* guy always say in retraining owners of aggressive, red zone animals? Remain calm and assertive. Don't make eye contact. Right. She had to be her own pack leader now. She squared her shoulders, raised her chin and took deep calming breaths as she followed the woman down a hall. When she opened a door, Claire barely smiled and murmured thank you before walking into the room.

The first thing she saw was a long table. At one end were two male lawyers in chairs. To their right was an old woman in a wheelchair and next to her was a man with salt-and-pepper hair and stooped shoulders. Next to him was a woman, middle-aged and a bit frumpy, and next to her was a child, a girl who looked to be about ten years old, her blond hair pulled back with a pink headband that matched the piping around the collar of her white sundress.

"Mrs. Hutchinson, thank you for joining us," the older of the lawyers said, standing and coming to meet her as she walked past the empty chairs on the left side of the table. "Ethan Collier," he added, holding out his hand.

Claire shook it. "How do you do?" she asked formally, still not acknowledging her relatives.

"This is Bruce Warrington, my associate."

Claire nodded to the younger man.

"Please, have a seat," Mr. Collier offered, pulling out a chair for her opposite the others.

She nodded and sat down, grateful the lawyer obviously understood the sticky relationships involved. Only then did she look at her mother and try not to show her surprise. What was she? Sixty-eight now? What had happened to her? Her face was deeply lined. Her blond hair was almost white. She looked old and sickly, as though she'd had a stroke or something.

"Claire."

Just a word of greeting. That was it.

She barely nodded to her mother and ignored David completely.

Calm and assertive, no matter what.

Surprisingly, David refused to be ignored. "You're look-ing well, Claire. You've never met my wife, Caroline, and my daughter, Elizabeth."

Claire turned her head and slightly smiled at the woman dressed in a boxy brown suit with a huge gold pin attached to the lapel. Her hair matched her suit, except for the strands of gray threaded throughout. Claire had a feeling she once might have been very attractive. "Hello," she said with barely a smile. And the girl hardly looked up from her lap. When she did, Claire thought she saw a deep sadness there. Maybe she had loved her grandfather and was still grieving. Eric could be very nice to those he cared about, like her mother and David. Maybe he had formed a close bond with his only grandchild.

Still, she refused to make eye contact with David. He was the most vicious of the pack, but she had to admit to some satisfaction that he had aged so poorly, looking far older than his years. He was only forty-six, but she would have thought him to be in his late fifties or older.

She turned her attention to the lawyers who were seated before two leather folders and waited while the one named Collier cleared his throat.

"I would like to thank everyone for being here today for the reading of Eric's will. We shall forgo with the legal reading of being of sound mind, etcetera, and proceed to the distribution of Eric's estate . . ."

She could feel David's eyes on her and raised her chin slightly as she tried to concentrate on the lawyer's voice . . . something about charities, about a codicil made shortly be-fore his death.

"And so half of the estate will go to Alicia, with the re-maining fifty percent evenly distributed between his son, David, and his stepdaughter, Claire."

"*What?*" David demanded. "Her? She isn't even blood related and she never saw him once she left for college!"

The man named Collier sighed deeply, as though he knew the reading was going to be unpleasant. "I am executor of your father's will, David. And I am bound by law to execute his last wishes. He wanted Mrs. Hutchinson to share equally with you."

"I'll fight it!" David pronounced, his face red with anger and looking around him for support from Alicia or his wife.

Her mother remained silent, pursing her lips and turning a large emerald ring over and over on her thin finger. Caroline Williams closed her eyes and lowered her head, as though even she didn't want to get involved.

Claire decided it was time to speak. "Just how much money are we talking about, Mr. Collier?"

"Well, since Congress has passed such a favorable estate tax reduction, you and David would share almost eight million dollars. David's share is dependant on the codicil, however."

Claire tried hard not to show her shock. Four million dollars!

"What's the codicil?" David demanded. "This entire thing is outrageous. The old man must have been senile!"

"Eric wasn't senile," Mr. Collier answered. "The codicil concerns your twenty-five percent of the inheritance, David. There are certain conditions that must be fulfilled and are outlined for you. There is also a trust fund established for Elizabeth of which I am the trustee. When she reaches twenty-one, she will inherit two million."

"I'm not in charge of that?" David demanded. "I'm her father!"

"Again, David, I am only executing *your* father's last wishes. Now, if you will be patient, I have a personal letter from Eric I am instructed to read after the formalities of the will."

Everyone sat in silence. It was going to be like hearing from the grave, Claire thought, still stunned by the amount of money left to her.

" 'My family,' it begins," Mr. Collier read. " 'I wish to thank my wife, Alicia, for her years of devotion and hope she will use her inheritance wisely and make her remaining years as comfortable as possible. I ask my son, David, not to contest this will and to build a legacy he can be proud to leave. I ask my stepdaughter, Claire, to accept my apology for doing her a great wrong and alienating her from her mother. I also ask Claire to find in her heart forgiveness for the past and to become acquainted with her niece, Elizabeth, who reminds me of her when we tried to be a family. I am so sorry we couldn't make that happen and hope the future will correct my errors of judgment.' Signed, Eric Steven Williams, II."

"What does that mean?" Caroline whispered. "I don't understand."

Claire felt like she had been hit with a baseball bat. What was Eric saying? He wanted her to know Elizabeth? She looked at the child, who still hung her head and stared at her hands in her lap.

Oh, God . . . please . . . don't do this to me, she mentally pleaded.

Eric knew something and he wanted her to know it too. That had to be what he meant!

It was as if her heart split open in that moment. She felt such pain that she automatically held her hand to her chest and gasped. Looking directly at David, she said, "I will be happy to get to know Elizabeth."

David stared back at her with hatred in his eyes. That same hatred she had seen when she was a child. Only now, this time, she wasn't afraid.

Calm and assertive, she told herself, amazed that she could sit across from the one person who'd had so much influence in shaping her life, and stare him down.

"There must be a reason Eric wants me to know your daughter," she stated in a crisp, clipped tone. "And I can only think of one."

She had the satisfaction of seeing his eyes widen with a flash of fear.

"You're insane," David muttered. "Aren't you a little late to be throwing around accusations?"

Not shifting her gaze from David, Claire found the strength to ask, "Mr. Collier, would you please have one of your assistants come and get Elizabeth? She can wait for her parents outside this room."

"Don't bother!" David declared, breaking the gaze and pushing back his chair. "We're leaving. Come, Caroline. Elizabeth, get up."

"Not so fast, David," Claire said, hearing Mr. Collier buzz an outside phone. "As you are an official of the court, Mr. Collier, I ask that you detain David Williams in the room without his daughter present."

"Claire, stop it," her mother said in a parental tone. "Don't do this now, in front of strangers."

"When, Mother?" Claire asked. "What better time?"

"I don't understand any of this," Caroline said, standing next to her husband.

"I know you don't," Claire answered. "Please, if you care about your daughter, have her wait outside."

That same professional woman who'd led Claire into the conference room opened the door and looked expectantly at Mr. Collier.

Claire looked at Elizabeth, who appeared to be on the verge of tears. Her heart went out to her and she wanted to grab her arm and race with her from the room, but she knew she didn't have any rights. The only thing she could do was get it out in the open.

"We're leaving," David declared.

"I want to know what's going on," his wife demanded. "If it concerns Elizabeth—"

"Will you just shut up and get out of here?" David grabbed his wife's arm.

"What are you afraid of, David?" Claire asked calmly.

He spun around like a cornered animal and bared his teeth.

Calm and assertive, she told herself. Years ago that look might have scared her, but now she wasn't fighting for herself. She was fighting for a little girl. A helpless little girl who had been betrayed by her own father. She had to be right, or David wouldn't be so scared!

"Elizabeth, go outside with this woman and wait for us, okay?" Caroline asked, seeming to get stronger since her husband's verbal attack on her.

The woman held out her hand and Elizabeth slowly walked up to her. When the two left the room and the door was closed behind them, Caroline said, "I want to hear what you have to say, Mrs. Hutchinson."

David looked furious at his wife's statement.

Claire swallowed and inhaled deeply. She nodded to Caroline and turned to Mr. Collier. "David repeatedly raped me as a child and I believe Eric was trying to tell me he's doing the same thing with Elizabeth."

"I told you, she's insane!" David yelled. "How dare you? What proof do you have?"

Claire ignored him as Caroline slowly sank to her seat.

"You are an officer of the court, Mr. Collier, are you not?"

Mr. Collier simply blinked, shocked by her words.

"Are you?" Claire repeated.

"Well yes, but . . ."

"And now you are aware of David Williams's crimes against me and, I believe, his daughter. You have to report this, don't you?"

"How *dare* you attempt to ruin my life, my reputation." David screamed. "You resent me for something that happened thirty years ago!"

Claire turned her head and saw him seething, becoming more and more angry. "It's happening now, isn't it?"

He turned to his shocked wife, still speechless after

hearing Claire's accusation. "Caroline, get up! We're leaving immediately!"

"David . . . ?" His wife looked up at him pleadingly.

"You *can't* believe this bitch! Get up, Caroline!"

The woman slowly rose to her feet, unable to look at Claire. "I . . ."

"You have nothing to say," David commanded, picking up her purse and slapping it into her stomach where she caught it. "We're going to our own lawyers right now!"

He held his wife's upper arm and led her out of the room like a master who was not used to anyone questioning him.

When the door slammed shut, Claire turned to the lawyer. "Mr. Collier, what do you intend to do?"

The older man conferred with his associate for a few moments and then said, "You are correct. As an officer of the court I will have to contact the authorities on this matter. You are aware, Mrs. Hutchinson, of the gravity of your accusation?"

"Mr. Collier, I have spent almost thirty years paying for the gravity. I am only asking what I believe your client, Eric Williams, wanted."

"But his son . . ."

"I don't know why Eric chose this way, but I believe he finally came to know David and was highly suspicious of what David was doing to his granddaughter. All I want is for the authorities to investigate it."

Mr. Collier stood and exhaled deeply. "If you ladies would excuse me? Eric said the reading would be difficult . . . I just never imagined."

"Thank you, Mr. Collier."

Alicia simply nodded as both men left the room. She looked up. "Are you satisfied?"

Claire stared at her mother. "Satisfied? You think I came here for *that*?"

"You obviously had an agenda," her mother said slowly.

She looked at her mother, dressed in a black pantsuit, her nearly white hair still styled in the same flip she'd been wearing since the last time she'd seen her. Her fingers were weathered and deeply veined and sparkled with rings, while a large line bracelet of diamonds hung from her thin wrist. "My only agenda was to be present for the reading of the will. You heard Eric's letter. He practically spelled it out."

"You've had a grudge all these years and now you think you've evened out the score. Not only David will be ruined. My name will be dragged into the dirt along with him."

Claire slowly rose and placed her hands on the table separating them. "After all these years, that's still all you care about? *Your* name? *Your* reputation with your country club crowd? What about that little girl? Is there any unselfish shred of decency left in you?"

"What do you want from me, Claire? I'm all alone now."

"What do I want from you? Oh, I don't know, maybe to admit you cared more about yourself than what was happening to your daughter?" No response. "What about finally taking responsibility for sacrificing me so you could have security? Other than that, I want nothing from you. You're a stranger to me."

"I'm your mother. You can run away again, but you can't deny that."

Claire felt her heart pounding inside her chest and she mentally repeated the words *calm* and *assertive* again. Standing across from her mother after all this time was more devastating than she could have imagined. There was no remorse, no asking of forgiveness or understanding. Again, she could be sacrificed so easily for her mother's greed. "You're my mother, but for the life of me I don't understand you."

"You couldn't understand me, unless you'd lived my life."

"Please . . ." Claire said, looking at all her jewels. "It's a little late for a pity party. You don't seem to have fared too badly. You got what you wanted. Now you're a rich woman in your own right."

Her mother kind of snorted with derision. "I earned every cent," she said, slowly running her hands over her thighs as though smoothing out invisible wrinkles. "Do you think it was easy being Eric's wife? He could be very demanding, even cruel. He only mellowed after he found out he was dying from cancer."

"Oh, I remember his cruelty. And I remember you egging him on, telling him to hit me harder."

Alicia looked up to her daughter. "You still hold that against me? It was over thirty years ago. If I had sided with you, both of us could have wound up on the street. I had no choice."

Claire unclenched her jaw. "You always have a choice. I was your child. I was being raped by David. But yours was the worst betrayal. The welts from the beating faded, but I'm still dealing with what happened to my mind and heart."

"Well, if that the worst that's happened to you, you've led a charmed life."

"You know nothing about my life," Claire answered, picking up her purse.

"I know you're unmarried. Divorced your first husband and you must have made a decent settlement from it because—"

"That is none of your business," Claire interrupted, walking around the front of the table. "You gave up the right to be my mother when you threw me to the wolves."

"Claire!" her mother said forcefully and Claire stopped walking toward the door.

"Eric's gone. David and his family won't be visiting after this fiasco. I'm all alone now. I thought . . . perhaps . . . after all this time . . ."

Claire slowly shook her head. "You really are unbelievable," she said. "You actually think you can manipulate me?

Hire someone, Mother. Get a companion or a nurse, because that's all you're looking for."

"I don't know why I should have expected anything less from you."

"No, I don't know why you should," Claire answered. "You're so afraid of being alone, aren't you? You need the diversion of other people around you so you won't have to deal with yourself. Well it's time you lived the life you created. Like I said, we always have a choice. And here's mine. Good-bye."

She walked to the door and left her mother behind. Still, her hands were shaking and her heart pounding. How *could* that woman be her mother? Never, not for one moment, had she even tried to say she was sorry.

Heartbroken and disappointed, Claire wondered why she had even expected it. Hadn't she learned her lesson all those years ago?

Some people never change.

Chapter

II

SHE SAT IN HER CAR AND LEANED HER HEAD AGAINST the steering wheel, feeling exhausted and nauseated. Her mother had been right about one thing. It'd been a fiasco. Why the hell had Eric left it up to her to do his dirty work? More convinced than ever that David was abusing his daughter, Claire felt weak with shock and loathing. At least she'd taken that dirty little secret out from under the rug and it had turned into the proverbial eight-hundred-pound gorilla in the room no one could ignore. She only hoped Mr. Collier and Caroline would do the right thing for Elizabeth.

Poor child. Her own father . . .

"What is wrong with this world?" she muttered in anger, hitting her fist on the dashboard.

"The majority of humans live in fear."

She heard his voice and should have been surprised to have him pop into her car, but she wasn't. Claire pushed herself off the steering wheel and leaned over the gear shift to him. Michael held her in his arms, stroking her hair, murmuring to her that she had made the appropriate choice.

"But will *anything* be done?" she demanded into the comfort of his shoulder while sniffling to stop the tears from coming. "David's probably at his lawyer's right now figuring out how to sue me."

"You can't control another's choice, only your own. Don't live your life in fear of the unknown, Claire. You did what you could."

"But was I right, Michael?" she demanded, raising her head and looking at him. "You would know. Is David violating his daughter?"

"You made the appropriate choice, Claire."

"Are you saying he is?"

He hesitated and then nodded.

"So I wasn't wrong," she murmured, sitting back in her seat and staring out the front window. "That poor little girl. God, I hope they haul his ass off to jail and he gets a taste of what he's been giving out."

Michael placed his hand upon hers. "You have a right to your anger. You may want to rethink your wishes for him, though. He is insane, Claire. What he has been doing is not sane thinking. He is ruled by his obsessions, his addictions."

"I don't care, Michael. He's a threat to society, especially his daughter."

"Cause and effect, Claire. You need not do or wish anything more. You brought the situation into the light and now the effect will manifest. Clear yourself of his energy. You were courageous today."

"I don't feel courageous. I feel sick. Even my mother tried to stop me."

Michael sighed and squeezed her hand. "You can't make her love you the way you want, or the way you think she should," he whispered with compassion.

She jerked her head toward him. "I didn't say that."

"Every child wants her parent to love her, even adult children."

She closed her eyes briefly. "She'll never change. She's still selfish and manipulative."

"She is ruled by her fears."

She almost laughed. "She actually thought she could get me to be in her life now. How crazy is that?"

"She fears the unknown. She has always looked outside herself to define who she is. She thinks if she is alone, she will die. She thinks having another person around her will validate her, keep her alive. Without that reflection from another, even a contentious reflection, she doesn't know who she is and that terrifies her."

"Well it's time she looked in the mirror then. I am so done with these people. Today just confirmed it."

He stroked her hair back from her face. "You are tired. Don't think about it now. Don't make decisions when your energy is depleted."

Sighing deeply, Claire shook her head. "It isn't even noon and I'm exhausted. Let's just go home."

"Yes," Michael murmured. "Let's go home."

She took a nap, which was unusual for her, and felt much better when she awakened. Michael appeared in her bedroom, carrying a tray filled with fruit, crackers and a cup of hot tea. He placed the tray on the bed and she scooted up the mattress until she was sitting against the pillows.

Smiling, she rubbed her eyes and said, "Now, *this* is the way a woman should wake up. Thanks, Michael."

"You are most welcome, Claire. I looked in a magazine and this seemed very appetizing."

"So you can . . . like . . . manifest whatever you want?"

"If it is material, physical, then most likely yes."

"Wow . . ." she remarked, picking up a strawberry and popping it into her mouth. She chewed and a burst of sweetness made her moan with appreciation. Swallowing the delicious fruit, she added, "Like the clothes at the river."

He only nodded, seemingly pleased that she was pleased with his offering of fruit.

"Hold on a sec," she said, leaning over the bed to her night table and picking up a glossy catalogue from an upscale department store. She thumbed through it until she found what she wanted in the back section. "Here," she said, laying out the catalogue on the bed. "Can you do that?"

She showed him a layout of men's clothing from Ralph Lauren and Armani.

"You want me to look like that?"

"Well, not look like that, but wear clothes like that. Aren't you tired of those jeans and that shirt?"

"I was informed that this clothing would be appropriate and nonthreatening."

She grinned. "It's more . . . uninteresting, Michael. You're . . . a handsome man," she admitted with embarrassment, not used to complimenting males. And he was handsome, good looking, and maybe she was just a little prejudiced since she was developing some deep feelings for him. "You would look great in any of these outfits."

"You would like it if I wore these?"

"Oh, yes," she answered like an eager audience member, waiting to see him perform magic. "Any one of them."

He looked down at the catalogue again and studied the open pages as she bit into another strawberry.

"This one?" he asked, pointing to the left side of the catalogue.

She leaned forward. "Oh, goody. The Armani."

And before she looked up at him, a swirl of lights began transforming him. In less time than it took to swallow the strawberry, Michael was dressed in dark tan trousers with an open-collar, cream-colored shirt tucked in at the waist He'd even completed the picture by adding the belt and the leather loafers without socks.

"Melt my heart," she barely breathed, staring up at him

with a mixture of awe and a strong sexual attraction. Okay, it was more sexual attraction than awe.

"You like it?" he asked, running his hand over the sleeve.

"I *love* it!" she exclaimed. "So much better than the jeans."

"It's very soft," he remarked.

"It's probably a silk blend. Let me feel."

She ran her hand over his arm, feeling the muscles underneath the soft material. "Definitely has some silk in it," she murmured as he sat on the side of the bed.

"You seem much better, Claire. I am glad you slept."

She didn't want to remove her hand, but felt silly running it up and down his arm when it appeared he wanted to simply talk to her. "I am . . . much better. It was a difficult morning."

"Yes, but you got through it," he said, staring into her eyes and smiling.

She nodded. "I don't want to talk about it now, okay?"

"Okay," he murmured, squinting as he continued to stare into her eyes. "There is something . . . different about you," he added, as if trying to place what it was."

"Really?"

"Yes. Perhaps it is because you faced a situation you were fearing, but . . ." His eyes widened.

"What?" she demanded, thinking this was more like it. He was staring into her eyes with almost wonder, or something close to it. What if he said he loved her, like really loved her? Made some kind of declaration? What would she answer? Did she love him? If felt like love, more than lust surely, but still . . . was she capable of loving anyone, truly loving without condition? Impatient to hear his answer, she said, "C'mon, Michael. What were you going to say?"

He swallowed, as though even he was a bit shaken. "I see something in your eyes and your aura confirms it."

"What do you see?" she whispered, hoping it sounded sexy.

"Your eyes . . . they sparkle with . . ."

"With what?" she demanded, grinning. Sparkle, huh? Let's just see if he says what she's thinking.

"With life, Claire."

"Okay." Not what she was expecting to hear. "Anything else?" Like maybe sexual need, or major attraction? Might even be sort of, kind of, love?

"Claire, did you understand me?"

She nodded. "My eyes sparkle with life. I heard you. You've done that to me, Michael. I've never felt more alive than when I'm around you."

"Then you are pleased?" he asked in a hesitant voice.

She studied his face, wondering why he was unsure of her reaction. Hadn't she let him know how she felt around him? This wasn't her strong suit, admitting her feelings, but she figured she might as well come clean, especially with him. He'd know if she was lying.

"Michael, look . . . I'm not used to speaking about my feelings. You must know I thoroughly enjoy your company." No, that sounded like she was talking about a pet or something. "What I mean to say is that I am becoming attached to you. I miss you when we're apart and . . . I like you." Damn, she wasn't in high school! "I more than like you," she amended. "I may even sort of lo—" She couldn't say it.

"What was that?" he asked, grinning. "You may even sort of what?"

Her shoulders sank. "You know what I mean."

"I'm not sure. I think I would like to hear you say it."

"I don't say it easily."

"I'm sure you don't."

She blew her breath out in surrender. "Okay, so maybe I kind of love you. I mean, I know we've only known each other a few short weeks and it's sudden and all, but—"

"I have known you a very long time, Claire."

"Well, I haven't known you a very long time, Michael, so you'll have to be patient with me. I didn't believe this . . . us . . . could happen. Especially happen with someone like you. You know, from another dimension. Of course, I was so guarded that it would have to be someone from out of this world for me to—"

"Claire," he interrupted her rambling. "I understand what you are saying."

"You do?"

He nodded. "I do."

"Good."

He sat there smiling at her and Claire wondered when it was going to be his turn. It was kinda required stuff here. "Ah . . . Michael?"

"Yes?"

"Now it's your turn."

"My turn?"

Okay, loving a dimension traveler had its drawbacks. One of them was him not knowing when it was time to reciprocate declarations. "Yes, now you tell me how you feel. About me," she added, to make it more clear.

"Oh."

He got it, she noted with relief.

"I love you, Claire, beyond measure. I admire so much about you, your strength, your resilience, your compassion, your beauty, the way you surrender, the feel of your body when we make love. You will be a most beautiful mother."

She was getting all dreamy there with the compliments, until the end. Swallowing, she asked, "What did you say? A mother? Who said anything about being a mother?"

He seemed confused. "But you said you understood me when I told you that you sparkled with life."

"I thought you meant . . ." Her words trailed off.

"New life, Claire. You are with child. Our child."

She couldn't speak. She continued to stare at him like he was just released from an asylum. "I can't be pregnant!" she rattled off in a quick mumble of denial.

"But you are," he answered and looked confused. "You are not happy about this?"

Her jaw dropped. "Happy? *Happy*?"

"Claire, I don't understand your reaction. I sense fear and—"

"I'm not pregnant," she interrupted, sitting up straighter. "I can't be pregnant. You . . . you're not even human!"

"But I was using a human body when we achieved unity."

And then it crashed into her, the possibility that he might be right. Just her luck to have been in a sexual desert for years and then as soon as a male releases his little swimmers, her egg thinks it's manna from heaven! Okay, so none of it made sense, but then again *nothing* was making sense in her life anymore.

She pushed the tray of fruit to the side and got up.

"What are you doing?" Michael asked in a concerned voice.

"Getting dressed," she muttered, not caring that he was watching. She pulled on a pair of jeans under the worn, long T-shirt she'd used for sleeping.

"Are you going outside the house?"

"Yes," she answered, opening her closet and slipping her feet into a pair of sandals. "I'll be back."

She felt as though she were on autopilot as she left him in the bedroom and walked down the hall and into the foyer. Picking up her purse and her keys she opened the front door and headed for her car.

It was time to talk to Cristine.

Ten minutes later she parked the car in Cristine's driveway and marched up to her front door as though in a daze. She rang the bell while trying to calm down, but there was no answer. "C'mon, Cristine, be home!" she muttered, ring-ing the bell again, this time longer.

No answer.

Blowing her breath out in frustration, she looked around the house and then noticed a truck parked at the curb. Land-scaping. The backyard? Marching around the house, Claire noticed the side of the lawn was torn up with tire marks and she carefully tried to walk where there was still grass. Com-ing into the backyard, she breathed a sigh of relief to find her friend watching men roll out long strips of sod around a rectangular pool. It was then she remembered Cristine hav-ing mentioned it at the last meeting of the Yellow Brick Road Gang.

"Cris!" Claire called out.

Cristine turned her head and grinned broadly. "Claire! What do you think?" she asked, waving her hand out to the pool.

"Great," Claire answered, coming closer and seeing the intricate tile work of the pool and the wide interlocking stones surrounding it.

"We're almost done," Cristine said with excitement. "I was thinking about having a meeting here this weekend. We can combine business and celebrate Tina's engagement. I saw the ring and it's gorgeous, isn't it?"

Claire nodded. "Beautiful ring. Listen, Cristine, I need to talk to you."

Cristine immediately sobered. "What's wrong?"

She tilted her head toward the house. "It's private."

Cristine looked at the three men laying out her backyard grass and nodded. "Let's get a Coke."

Claire followed her friend into the house and was re-lieved by the wave of air-conditioning that washed over her. She followed Cristine into the kitchen and sat at the granite counter. Cristine opened the refrigerator and took out two cans of Diet Coke, filled two glasses with ice and put them on the counter.

"I haven't seen you in a while. You look . . . good."

Claire watched Cristine pop open a can and pour the soda into the glass closest to her. "Don't lie. I must look like I've walked away from a car wreck," she said, running her fingers through her hair.

"What's going on? What's so private? Are you okay?"

"I don't know," Claire answered honestly, touching the glass filled with soda.

"Claire, what's wrong?" Cristine asked, popping the other can and pouring herself a glass of soda. "You do look . . . rattled."

Claire snorted. "That's an understatement. I'm beyond rattled, my friend."

"Are you going to tell me?" Cristine asked, a note of real worry entering her tone.

Claire inhaled, filling her lungs with air, then just said it.

"I have a dimension traveler, Cris. Like Daniel and, I imagine, Joshua."

Cristine's jaw dropped as she simply stared across the granite.

"Say something," Claire demanded. "You aren't going to deny it, are you? I connected all the dancing lights and came up with an insane picture. Daniel and Joshua are dimension travelers."

Cristine shook her head. "I . . . I'm shocked, though I shouldn't be."

"Why shouldn't you be?"

Cristine closed her mouth, swallowed deeply and then said, "Issy and I were talking about it. We said since Tina has Louis now and Kelly has been dating John Lawson ever since Hope was born, that it was your turn."

"So I'm right, about Joshua? That's why she was finally able to get pregnant?"

Cristine nodded. "Should I call Issy and have her come over?"

Shaking her head, Claire muttered, "I can't handle another person right now. You have to tell me everything, Cris, because . . ."

"I know, sweetie," Cristine murmured soothingly while touching Claire's hand. "It's a lot to take in, isn't it? Dimension travelers? Spontaneous manifestation, the disappearing into a swirl of light."

"You sound like this, any of this, is even close to normal!"

"Claire, I've been living with it for some time. Don't forget my pregnancy. You all thought I was crazy. I just didn't know how to tell you, any of you, at the time. It's like nothing else any of us have ever experienced." She paused for a moment. "I guess I should be surprised, but after Isabel and Joshua, I suppose I'm ready to accept almost anything. What's his name?"

"Michael, at least that's the name he's using. Mike Murphy was a boyfriend of mine in junior high school who died. Not even a boyfriend really, just a friend. We only kissed once, but now Michael says he's using his body suit, he calls it, because he had hoped I would find it familiar. And I did."

"Daniel said he was like my guardian angel. Joshua told Issy he was her imaginary friend. Now yours is the ghost of your childhood friend . . ."

"He's not a ghost!" Claire protested. "A ghost couldn't have gotten me pregnant."

Cristine's hand came up to cover the surprised smile creeping into her expression. "Wow. You. Pregnant."

Hearing Cristine say it like that, as though she was some odd species of female she couldn't imagine having a single maternal instinct, made Claire wince. "At least he said I'm pregnant. *Sparkling with new life* is the way he put it! This can't be, Cristine! I only wanted a playmate, someone to have some fun with for a little while! I did not intend for this to happen, if it *has* happened!"

Cristine came around the counter and wrapped her arm around Claire's shoulders. "I hate to say this, but they're always right, Claire. The biggest drawback is they know everything you're thinking and feeling. There's no hiding anything. It's like you're forced to be *you*, the real you."

Claire's shoulders dropped. "Great! Now what do I do?"

Sighing, Cristine said, "I've got a pregnancy kit in my bathroom."

"You just so happen to have a pregnancy kit?"

"Daniel and I have been talking about having another child so, yes, I have a pregnancy kit. C'mon upstairs and we'll see."

Claire shook her head. "How did this happen? Any of it? And why? Why *me*?"

"There are no answers for why it happened. Issy and I have given up on that. But as for how you got pregnant . . . you made love to him when he was in the physical form, right?"

"I thought it would be . . . different, fun, something for me to show him that he hadn't experienced yet."

Cristine nodded. "Same here. And Angelique was conceived."

Claire felt desperate. "Cris, none of this can be possible! I meet some strange man who does strange things, seems to know everything about me, who makes me rethink the way I've looked at . . . at everything in my life and then *this*!"

Cristine chuckled. "I don't mean to laugh, hon, but since I've already been where you are right now I can tell you it's the absolute best thing that has ever happened to me. I know you're scared, maybe terrified, but I promise you something really wonderful is happening in your life."

"I liked my life," Claire murmured, staring down to the

granite counter. "I thought I had it all under control. Who *are* these men with their dancing lights and hypnotizing words?"

"He hasn't told you?"

"He said he was from another dimension and, from what I gather, he's here to help humanity from destroying itself, though what *that* has to do with me is another mystery."

Cristine leaned down and whispered in Claire's ear. "It has to do with our children."

Blinking a few times, Claire turned her head and looked at her friend. "What do you mean?"

"I mean that Angelique is gifted somehow. I think she's going to be a healer in some way. Hope is already showing signs of it. Isabel said wherever she takes her, everyone becomes calm, even dogs stop barking. Hasn't Michael told you that they've tried using the males but they are too predictable and—"

"Something about losing chromosomes," Claire interrupted.

"Right. So now they are hoping the females will take back their innate power and help raise the world's consciousness. Think of what gifted females like Angelique and Hope can do when they are women, and they won't be alone. Daniel said this is happening all over the planet. Women are giving birth to gifted children in every country."

"There's more of them?" Claire asked, feeling like her life had been taken over without her permission. "I didn't ask for this. They have no right . . ."

Cristine tilted her head as she stared at her friend. "Are you sure? Somewhere, at some time, you put out a wish, a desire, and it's been answered."

"I only wanted a playmate!" Claire nearly yelled while holding back tears.

"Shh, the baby is napping," Cristine whispered. "Let's go

upstairs and take the test, okay? Let's at least find out if you really are pregnant."

Claire slid off the stool and followed Cristine out of the kitchen, down the hallway and past the living room to the stairs. With each step, Claire felt as though she were sinking deeper and deeper into quicksand. This, whatever *this* was, was going to devour her, take her down and swallow her up.

She couldn't be pregnant! She simply couldn't!

Fifteen minutes later, she and Cristine were sitting on the side of her bed, both women staring at the stick in Claire's hand.

"I can't be pregnant," Claire whispered. "This wasn't part of my plan."

Cristine began stroking Claire's shoulders in comfort. "It wasn't part of mine, either, at least not the way it happened, but it was perfect without me realizing it at the time."

"It's too soon for a test to work. Don't you have to be late?"

"Not anymore, not with these new tests. They can tell days after conception. Besides, if you are pregnant, measuring time is meaningless. You could go to a doctor and he'd tell you you're at least three months. That's what happened to me. The father of your baby is . . . timeless."

Claire stared at the little window on the stick. *Please let it say not pregnant! Please!* It would just be too much, especially after this morning at the lawyer's office. Motherhood . . . the females in her family obviously didn't have a clue.

"So just be prepared if you are, Claire, for everything to proceed much faster than normal. Remember you guys thought I was pregnant with Charlie's baby because I hadn't know Daniel long enough to be full term with his?"

Claire could only nod. She felt like her body was frozen until she read the result of the test.

"Issy's pregnancy was shorter than mine and she gave

birth to a full-term baby. Everything seems to be speeding up and—"

Both women put their heads together and stretched their necks as a word began appearing in the window.

Claire watched in shock as the blue letters spelled out a word, one word, that would change her life.

Pregnant

"Well . . ." Cristine whispered. "I guess we know now."

Claire couldn't speak. She could barely breathe as she stared at the stick, though her hand started to shake.

"Claire? Honey, are you okay?"

She simply couldn't believe it! This couldn't have happened to her, not her! She was smart, a professional. She had a great job. A great house. She lived alone. She liked living alone. Most of the time anyway. "This was not supposed to happen," she whispered in shock.

"I know how you feel, Claire. I swear I do. I felt the same way. Remember you found me in bed, you and Isabel, right after I found out I was pregnant? Remember my shock, my disbelief? None of it was in my plans."

Claire nodded.

"Listen, the best thing I can tell you is . . . what is, is. And sometimes what is, is better than what you've planned or thought was supposed to be. Just be careful not to miss it because it's not the picture you painted with your expectations."

"I can't believe it," Claire muttered, still staring at the stick.

Cristine tried to take it out of her hand, finally prying her fingers open. "You're pregnant, Claire," Cristine said, standing up and walking into the bathroom.

Claire heard the plastic hitting the metal wastebasket. Cristine had thrown the stick away. Again, her life had altered without her permission.

"You have to face it," Cristine said, coming back to sit

next to her on the bed. "Look, I can't tell you what to do. You have a decision to make, but . . . well, you are forty-three, Claire. If you were ever going to have a child, this is it."

Claire turned her head and looked at Cristine. "Something's growing in me?"

Smiling slightly, Cristine nodded. "It can be a precious gift, if you can get your head wrapped around it."

"But the father . . . ! He's not even *normal*!"

Cristine laughed. "Honey, since Michael appeared in your life, *nothing* in it is ever going to seem normal again. You've got to get used to that."

Claire began shaking her head. "But I liked my life! This . . . this seems out of control!"

They both looked toward the doorway and saw Angelique standing there.

"Hi, sweetie," Cristine called out, holding out her arms. "Did you have a good nap?"

The toddler walked over to her mother and climbed onto her lap. She hugged Cristine and snuggled against her mother's shoulder, looking at Claire.

"Hi," Claire whispered, feeling her chest tighten and trying not to look into the child's big blue eyes.

Without warning, Angelique leaned toward her, holding out her arms. Not wanting to reject the child, Claire allowed her to climb onto her lap. Angelique then wrapped her arms around Claire's neck and murmured sleepily, softly, "It's okay."

Her eyes filling with tears, Claire gave Cristine a traitorous look as if she'd planned the whole thing and muttered, "You know this is totally unfair."

Cristine smiled with compassion and shrugged. "You ain't in control, kiddo. That's just the illusion. Surrender, Dorothy. Remember the answer is probably in your own backyard."

Holding the little girl in her arms, Claire felt a strange tugging at her heart, in her breasts, in her arms. There was something about the child's softness, her scent, her complete trust, her innocence.

Claire's eyes widened with surprise.

Good God, was that like . . . a *maternal instinct*?

Chapter

12

CLAIRE SAT ON THE SECOND STEP INTO THE POOL AND watched the twinkling of light upon the water. It wasn't Michael. It was the reflection of the backyard electrical lighting installed in the garden, backlighting trees and adding interest in shrubbery. She didn't have many flowering plants, but after seeing Cristine's backyard, she just might add more color. And maybe she'd buy an inside plant too. If she could keep it alive, she might consider extending her responsibilities.

Turning her attention to her house, she felt a rush of satisfaction. It never failed to amaze her. She'd bought a house all by herself. Furnished it herself too, without the help of a friend or a decorator. Looking at the back of her home and the play of shadows and light, Claire could honestly admit it was lovely.

She didn't use that word very often, especially about anything she'd accomplished, but it was lovely . . . and sometimes lonely.

That's what living alone is, she thought. An intersection of loveliness and loneliness. It's lovely to have your own space, your own peace. Everything is where you put it. The only one you clean up after is yourself. She didn't have to prepare a meal if she didn't feel like it and could order out as often as she wanted. She could walk around naked after a shower until she decided to get dressed. She was guilt-free to wear old clothes that were soft and comforting, even if some were nightshirts from college and nearly see-through and held together with frayed thread and memories. There was no one to answer to, no one who made demands on her, no one's opinion mattered more than her own. She could do whatever she wanted and not check in with anyone. It was lovely.

She sighed and reluctantly examined the other side of the coin.

She had to admit, at least to herself, at times she wished for a companion, someone with whom to discuss the news of day, visit an art gallery, go to the theater. And it might be nice to actually show up at Guiseppe's with a man once in a while. When she did cook and it turned out edible, she sometimes wished there was another to share her success. Sometimes at night, when she turned off the lights in the house on her way into the bedroom, she thought it might be nice if someone else shared her gratitude when she looked back at the living room and the light over the sculpture cast a low glow to the room. And, even though she relished sleeping alone, sometimes she just wanted to be held, especially if she was sick. It could be lonely. And then there was the sex . . . making love. Real love.

Until Michael had showed up in her life, she hadn't questioned it. She'd just gone on, day by day, thinking she'd made the only sensible choice. Marriage, relationships, just don't last—at least most don't. The averages were against it. Something always happens, someone loses a piece of themselves in order to keep the peace and, since it's such a disposable society, divorce or walking away is an accepted option. She'd been the child of a single parent and later a blended family. Both had been disastrous.

She'd seen a mirror once in New Hope. Around the edge

of the wooden frame someone had burned the words: *Mirror, mirror on the wall, you are your mother after all.*

It had terrified her, staring at her reflection in that small shop, and she'd immediately turned away. She didn't want to be her mother. Ever. That was her greatest fear.

She admitted she could be selfish with her time. She had a smart mouth on her and had little patience for ignorance. But she wasn't cruel or manipulative. She'd never betrayed anyone that she could remember.

She couldn't be like her mother.

Yet it was that very fear that had her sitting in the pool, contemplating a choice that would alter her life—no matter what the decision.

She thought of Cristine's words about being forty-three and if she was ever going to have a child, now was the time.

She hadn't seriously thought about children, hadn't ever truly felt like her biological clock was ticking away. She had no burning desire to replicate herself and repopulate the planet. She hadn't played with dolls since she'd entered grade school, preferring books and reading about others' adventures. Maybe something was missing in her that came naturally to other females. Just like her mother.

"Nothing is missing in you, Claire."

Startled out of her contemplation, she looked up at him standing at the edge of the pool. "So now you're reading my thoughts again?"

He shrugged and gave her a smile of apology.

"If you're coming in, then put on a bathing suit. Don't ruin those clothes."

Still smiling, he stepped into the water. "Do you think I care about that when you are so alone?" Sitting next to her, he put his arm around her waist and brought her closer to him. "Besides, I can dry them immediately."

Shaking her head, she answered, "You're more than a little

eccentric, Michael. If anyone saw you, they'd think you were nuts sitting in the water like that."

"And do you think their opinion would make me change?"

"No. I don't think anyone's opinion matters to you."

"That's not true, Claire. I value your opinion of me."

"Well, I think you're a bit eccentric. At least take off your shoes. That's Italian leather."

"Would it make you happy?"

"Yes."

She watched as he removed his shoes, emptied them of water and placed them behind them on the cement.

"There. Happy?"

She nodded.

He leaned down to look at her face. "That's not really true, is it? You are still upset by the news I gave you."

"Of course I'm upset. I'm pregnant. I never thought this would happen!"

"Never?"

She thought about it. "Once when I was married I had a scare, but I was only late . . ." Wanting to explain, she added, "I was wrong. I wasn't pregnant."

"You called it a scare. Being pregnant is frightening to you?"

"Yes, Michael, it is."

"I will tell you that I know you will be fine. You and the baby. It is a girl, Claire. A female." His voice held a hint of wonder.

She pulled out of his embrace. "Why did you tell me that? I don't want to know!"

"You don't?" he asked, confused by her reaction. "I thought it would be reassuring."

"Reassuring to whom?" she demanded, feeling hot tears burn her eyes and hating that she was so emotional. "To you, so you can join the dimension fraternity club, or should I call it the paternity club? Isn't that what all of you are really up to? Getting women pregnant so they can have your extraordinary female children? Isn't all this just part of your grand plan to help the planet?" She tried to calm down, but couldn't. "So what does that make me? I'm no different than a brood mare!"

A part of her hated to see him hurt, but another part was glad she had said aloud what she'd been thinking.

"I don't know why you would say that," he finally answered. "If you do not want this child, I will stop it from growing inside of you."

She felt suddenly very protective of whatever was in her womb. "You've done enough, and it isn't your decision. It isn't your body that is being taken over, your life that is being turned upside down. And besides, I've talked to Cristine. I know about Daniel and Joshua. What happened, huh? The three of you get together and decided poor Claire needed to grow up and be a woman and you drew the losing straw?"

"What are you talking about?"

"You don't know about Daniel or Joshua, the fathers of Cristine and Isabel's little girls?" she asked in a disbelieving tone.

"Ah . . . I know of them, I didn't until now know those were the names they were using."

"Great. So what *is* your name? I think I have the right to know since you did get me pregnant."

"First, in my dimension there is no need for such labels. You are known by your thoughts and deeds and each is unique. Second, I was not alone when the pregnancy occurred. You were there, Claire. It was your choice to show me physical intimacy. This child was conceived in love. There was no thought of poor Claire, only beautiful, exquisite Claire who shared her soul with me and left the bounds of the physical world and traveled with me as one into infinity."

"And look what happened," she retorted, not yet ready to let him off the hook.

"Yes, look what happened. Look what we created. A miracle. A blessing. It is up to you how you decide to look at it." He stood up, the back of his pants as wet as the bottom of his legs. "As for me, I find it impossible to remain here in this negativity. I will say good night."

And he left her, so suddenly that his lights seems like an arrow that shot through space and disappeared.

She closed her mouth and muttered, "I was the one who should have left."

Pushing herself off the step, she slid the rest of the way into the pool and began swimming. So he was offended, maybe hurt. Well how could he possibly think she *wouldn't* be rattled? Finding out she's pregnant the very same day after confronting her mother and David? Michael had come into her life and had shaken it up so much that it was hard to remember a normal day.

Again, Cristine's words sounded inside her head.

Nothing is ever again going to seem normal. You have to accept that and get used to it.

Cristine was happy.

Isabel was happy.

Both of them were thrilled with their lives. Cristine was even thinking about having another child. *With a dimension traveler?*

She reached the end of the pool and clung to the side. But then again, Daniel and Joshua weren't always there. Cristine said he traveled. Did interventions. Hah! Now she really understood.

Maybe it was like being married part time and single part time?

Cristine and Issy had all the benefits of a partner, a lover, a father to their children, and then they had time alone. It seemed to be working out just fine for them.

Then there was that feeling she'd had with little Angelique. The child had felt so good. Those tiny arms wrapped around her neck in total acceptance.

Love.

Was she ready for love? Real love?

At forty-three, was it finally time for her to grow up? Leave behind her ugly childhood and open herself to another? Become vulnerable? Give of herself totally and without fear?

Could she do it?

Wiping her face, Claire turned around and swam back to the steps.

Maybe she could start with a child, an extraordinary baby girl.

And then she'd see about the father.

But how could she be sure? What if she was wrong? What if she screwed it all up, and that bit of maternal instinct she'd felt with Angelique was simply a blip on the radar screen?

God . . . what if she was more like her mother than she'd ever thought?

She spent the next morning and afternoon at her desk catching up, even eating her lunch sitting in front of her computer. Shelly had gone out to pick up lunch and Claire's stomach was roiling in rebellion of the BLT she'd practically inhaled as though she hadn't had a meal in a week. She'd been so hungry and now she was feeling nauseated.

Pregnancy.

Did morning sickness start this soon? And it was past morning, so did pregnant women get sick in the afternoons too? She didn't even have a *Rolaid* on her or in her desk. Maybe she should ask Jim Doherty. He was always popping something into his mouth for his stomach problems.

Come to think of it, almost everyone at the office had digestion problems—gastric reflux, ulcers, IBS. What was it about investing other people's money that caused such ill-nesses?

Stress.

The answer came to her and she sighed deeply. It really could be a stressful environment, especially when the market fluctuated or the prime rate increased. And she suddenly wondered if it could harm the baby.

The baby.

Closing her eyes briefly, Claire realized she was identifying with whatever was happening in her womb. She pictured Angelique and Hope, two adorable, healthy babies.

Could she really do it? If she was super conscious of her mother's failings and swore never to repeat them, could she make at least a decent mother? Someone a tiny, helpless infant could depend on for . . . damn, for *everything*?

She couldn't work here. She'd have to quit her job, or work part time from home if the partners agreed. Would they allow her to work part time? She could forget making partner. Was it worth it to alter her plan, her career, her life?

And then she thought of Eric's bequest. Mr. Collier had said it would be around four million. She could invest half and donate the rest to the foundation. Maybe Cristine could include children, both boys and girls, who been abused. If she worked part time, she could still have a pretty good life and a decent portfolio.

The thought of working from home, being at home, was appealing. She could easily take care of a child and part-time work. Well, maybe not easily, but she could learn how to do it. The Yellow Brick Road Gang would help her.

Shelly buzzed, interrupting Claire's daydreaming.

"Yes?"

"Claire," Shelly said, her voice sounding cautious. "There's a woman on line two who says she's your mother?"

A wash of cold shivers made her stiffen in shock. "My mother?"

"That's what she says. And she sounds upset."

Angry that her mother had intruded upon her workplace, and wanting to avoid a scene, even a telephone scene, Claire said, "Give me a few seconds and then put her through."

"Okay . . ." Shelly answered hesitantly, as though she had questions she didn't know if she should ask.

"Thanks," Claire said and hung up the phone. She would read her mother the riot act about phoning her at work, or anywhere else for that matter. She was done with that bunch of manipulators. Michael had been right. They were insane.

She looked at the blinking light on the second line and punched it. "How dare you call me at work?" she demanded, not giving her mother the chance to speak. "And how did you get this number?"

"Have you forgotten Mr. Clarke who visited you in your office?"

Claire sighed. She had forgotten the man who'd told her about Eric's death. "What do you want? I happen to be busy right now."

"I thought you might like to know how successful you've been."

Claire closed her eyes briefly with impatience. "I don't know what you're talking about."

"The police just left my home."

Claire stared at the seat of the leather wing chair before her desk. "The police?"

"Yes, it seems they opened an investigation into David's life and they found some incriminating evidence in his home and on his computer. He then—"

"I don't want to hear about this," Claire interrupted.

"Well, you need to hear about what you've caused," her mother retorted with anger. "David obviously panicked and he tried to get away to JFK airport with Caroline and Elizabeth. They found the airline tickets for Mexico. He must have been driving erratically because there was an accident. A bad one. He's in surgery right now and the prognosis isn't good. Caroline has a broken arm, but from what I've been able to gather is in the midst of a nervous breakdown."

"Oh, my God," Claire whispered in horror. "And Elizabeth?"

"She was the only one wearing her seat belt. She says her parents were arguing when the accident happened. She has some bruises, but the police had her checked at the hospital and she's here with me now."

Claire let out her breath, thankful the child was alive. "I don't know what to say . . . Thank God, the child wasn't hurt."

"That's *all* you can say?" her mother demanded. "Your stepbrother is fighting for his life. His wife is fighting for her sanity, and I'm expected to care for a child who's deeply troubled! I hope you're satisfied, Claire."

She felt like her mother had slapped her in the face. Gathering up her strength, she tried to keep her voice calm. "David was a train wreck waiting to happen. I am truly sorry for his wife and for Elizabeth, but this is not my fault. I didn't drag Caroline or Elizabeth into that car. David did. I didn't drive it. David did. You can't blame this one on me. All I did was bring to the light what was happening. Don't you even *care* that your granddaughter was being violated by her father?"

"You have no conception of what this has done to the family name. It will be in the papers tomorrow. I've even had two reporters calling here; their audacity is beyond words." Alicia paused slightly. "And how am I expected to take care of a child when I'm in a wheelchair? I think the least you can do is take this child until one of her parents comes out of the hospital."

"Are you kidding me?" Claire asked in disbelief. "She doesn't even know me. *You're* her grandmother."

"Not by blood. Caroline's parents are older than I am and the maternal grandmother has a bad heart. There's no one else on Caroline's side to take the child. I'm not well enough for all this after Eric's death."

Claire didn't say anything, still fuming at her mother's selfishness.

"Or, I can always contact the state and have Elizabeth placed in a foster home temporarily."

"You're unbelievable," Claire muttered after unclenching her jaw. "Talk about a master manipulator. And you'd do it too, so you wouldn't have to take responsibility. I wonder how your country club crowd would view that?"

"Anyone who has taken the time in the last few years to know what has taken place with Eric's illness and my own would certainly understand my dilemma."

"You don't have a dilemma. You're just too selfish to give of yourself to a frightened child where you might have to answer some unpleasant questions. Still clinging to the illusion, aren't you? That everything is fine and normal, when in reality you're at the center of what has always been a highly dysfunctional family. If anyone needs to take a closer look at herself and the damage she's done to the people around her, it's you, Mother."

"Does that make you feel better? Regardless, Claire, I can't take care of the child. She's up in your old bedroom crying and I can't even get up to the third floor."

"I'll be there tonight. Have her ready at the front door. There will be no visiting. You and I have nothing more to discuss."

"She'll be ready. I took your advice and hired a nurse part time. The woman will come later this afternoon for the first time. She'll get Elizabeth ready and handle everything."

"I'm doing this for Elizabeth, not you. The poor kid has had enough damage done to her."

"Yes, dear. Well, I must run now. Elizabeth will be ready by six-thirty."

She hung up the phone.

Claire actually took the receiver away from her ear and stared at it in shock. Her mother had hung up on her! After she'd gotten exactly what she'd wanted!

But really, she thought, replacing the receiver, what else could she do? She couldn't leave that child in her mother's care. Hah! That was a laugh. What kind of care did Alicia ever give to anyone, save herself? She'd have poor Elizabeth washing dishes and vacuuming and waiting on her hand and foot like an indentured servant. And it could only be for a short while. Surely, Caroline would calm down with medical help. She didn't want to think about David.

There was such a thing as karma.

Feeling a bit desperate, she wanted to call out to Michael for help, but after the way they'd last parted she thought it better if she handled everything herself. Realizing she would probably be away from the office for a while, Claire got back to work. It would help take her mind off everything and she needed to really clear up anything outstanding.

How was she ever going to explain this to the partners?

It seemed as if she was easing her way out sooner than she had expected.

Looking around her office, she wondered how much longer she would be working at Kellogg, Crainpool and Reingold.

Was this it?

At five o'clock, she zipped up her leather portfolio and stood up. She looked at her desk, her watercolor paintings, the small personal things in her bookcases and felt a sense of sadness. She'd spent so much time working here and networking outside the office that her profession had become a big part of her life. Bigger than most people who have families and a real social life.

How would she function without the challenge?

She pressed the intercom button on her desk phone. "Shelly, would you come in here, please?"

"Sure. Do you need anything?"

"No, nothing."

"Okay."

She waited until the older woman walked through the door that connected them. "Have a seat," she said with a smile.

When Shelly sat down, Claire took the chair next to her, thinking it would be less formal that way.

"Are you okay, Claire?"

Claire grinned and shrugged. "I don't know about okay, but I do have to speak with you."

"Anything wrong? This sounds serious."

"I'm leaving," she said matter-of-factly. "I thought you had the right to know as soon as I had decided."

Shelly look stunned. "You . . . you mean really leaving the company, not just leaving for the day?"

Claire nodded. "I'm leaving the company, at least as a full-time employee. I don't know if the partners will want me working part time from home. That's another discussion for another day."

"But why, Claire? You're up for partnership. Is it a family problem? Is there anything I can do to change your mind? Damn, I loved working for you and now . . . what?"

Claire reached out and took Shelly's hand. "I've loved working with you too. You're a fantastic PA and if you don't decide to stay in the company, I'll write you a glowing letter of recommendation. I'll write it anyway to keep with your résumé. There's a family problem and I won't be in the office for a few days. It may be longer, I don't know yet. I have some vacation time so I'll use that until I know for sure when I can return. But I'll only be coming back to talk to the partners about leaving." She paused, seeing the disappointment on Shelly's face. Should she just say it? Tell the truth? "I . . . I'm pregnant, Shelly, and I'd like you to keep that to yourself for the time being. I just thought you deserved to know why I won't be working here full time."

Shelly looked shocked and Claire almost giggled at her expression.

"It's okay, you can speak if you want."

Shelly swallowed. "Pregnant . . . I'm stunned."

"That makes two of us."

"I didn't even now you were seeing someone."

"Things happen," Claire said evasively. "I've decided I want to change my priorities. I don't know how I'm going to do it, but I'm going to give a try."

"Congratulations, Claire."

Claire blinked. Someone seemed happy about this startling news. "Thanks," she muttered and stood up. "Now, I've got to run. An emergency in a different direction."

Shelly stood and shook her head in amazement. "I'm sad at losing you as a boss, but I'm really happy for you, Claire. You deserve happiness."

"Do me a favor, if you can? Start packing up my personal things in here? See if you can do it on the QT? I don't want anyone to get a hint of my plans until I speak with the partners."

"You've got it," Shelly said, looking around the office. "If anyone catches me I'll say I'm doing some reorganizing."

"Good woman," Claire answered with a grin, then touched Shelly's arm. "Thanks for everything, Shelly."

The older woman nodded. "You take care, Claire."

"We'll talk more in a few days."

She picked up her portfolio and left Shelly in her office—what used to be her office. Now that she'd made it official, actually told someone she was leaving, Claire felt a lightness enter her step.

She was pregnant. She was freeing herself from work. She had a whole new adventure opening up to her.

But first she had to pick up a terrified little girl.

Chapter

13

THE DRIVE ON I-76, THE SCHUYLKILL EXPRESSWAY, was nearly bumper to bumper with rush-hour traffic. Commuters returning to Philadelphia vied for position in whatever lane they thought would move faster than thirty-five miles an hour. Claire was stuck behind a truck and couldn't see around it. She glanced at the clock on the dash. Six fifteen. And she didn't even have a phone number to call to say she was running late. How odd, for the first time in many years she wanted to call her mother. Not to speak to her, but to ease Elizabeth's mind that someone was coming to help her.

She got off at the exit for Conshohocken, unwilling to go down memory lane as she neared the place where she'd grown up. All she wanted was to pick up the child and for both of them to make their escape. She tried not to think about David and his wife, both hurt in an accident. She kept telling herself it wasn't her fault, that she shouldn't feel guilty. David was responsible for the choices he'd made and the consequences. But still . . . there was this small part of her that said if she'd never confronted him, if she'd swallowed the truth like she'd done for twenty years, none of this would have happened.

It was Elizabeth that really made her speak up. After

hearing Eric's written words and then seeing the girl, some-how it all made sense. *And I'd been right,* she told herself. The police had found evidence in David's home and Michael had confirmed it.

Now if Caroline could just get some help and calm down, Elizabeth would have her mother and together maybe the two of them could start over, with or without David in their lives. What did she know? She didn't know Caroline or what the state of the marriage was. Best to keep out of everything at this point and just take care of the child until her mother was released from the hospital.

She turned left onto Matsonford Road heading toward Bryn Mawr and blew her breath out. She was almost there, the place that held so many bad memories. She followed the road that seemed smaller to her, more built up. She felt like she was on automatic pilot as she made turns on Montgomery Avenue, New Gulf Road, all leading her closer and closer.

After fifteen minutes she slowed the car and stared out the window.

There it was. The trees were much bigger and the land-scaping more elaborate, but in some ways it was the same. Lovely and at the same time forbidding, as though no one was welcomed who hadn't been invited. It was typical Bryn Mawr, the Main Line, home to the wealthy and the social elite. Three wide stories of white brick with multiple fire-place chimneys and a long circular drive leading up to the front door was only the main house. As she entered the driveway, she could see another outer building had been added. It was still light outside so the big glass lanterns on either side of the front door weren't turned on. Slowly, she stopped the car by the entrance, hoping Elizabeth would come running out and she wouldn't have to get out of the car and enter the house.

No such luck.

Swallowing to bring moisture back into her mouth, Claire

left the car and started walking to the front door. A feeling of heaviness descended upon her shoulders. It was like going back into prison. The last time she'd been here had been the day she'd left for college. All her summers had been spent with friends she'd made at school or she'd taken extra courses during the summer semesters to keep her away from the very place she now was about to enter.

So much time and energy had gone into avoiding this place, the people who lived here, and now she found herself coming back.

She watched her hand come up and her finger pressing the doorbell. It seemed surreal, like it wasn't really her doing it. Then, somewhere in the back of her head, she remembered what she'd done before going to the lawyer's office in Philly. Claire quickly imagined herself surrounded in a bubble of white light that no matter what her mother said or did, she wouldn't be able to penetrate.

She'd made it through that meeting and had managed to not to attack her mother. Maybe it would keep her safe again. She stiffened involuntarily when she heard the door opening.

Prepared to face her mother, Claire was surprised to see a stranger wearing a nurse's uniform. Then she remembered her mother saying that she had hired someone. "Hello. I'm Claire and I'm picking up Elizabeth," she said as politely as possible. "Is she ready?"

The woman nodded. "Come in and I'll get her."

So much for staying outside. Claire steeled herself for the entrance and walked into the large square foyer. She saw the black-and-white marble tiles and wondered who kept them shining now. In the center of the foyer was a round table with a huge arrangement of white calla lilies. She hated to admit that they were lovely.

"I've been instructed to tell you that Mr. Willams has . . . passed," the woman said uncomfortably, glancing up the staircase to check if anyone might overhear.

Confused, Claire said, "Yes. I had heard."

"Oh, you did." The woman looked relieved. Strangely relieved. "The hospital contacted you?"

Claire nearly squinted at the woman. "We are speaking of Eric Williams, correct?"

"I'm afraid I wasn't told his first name. The girl's father, I believe."

"Oh my God," Claire muttered, wishing she were closer to the stairs because suddenly her legs felt like Jell-O. David? *Dead?*

How many times had she wished it? Wanted to do it herself?

Quickly she asked for forgiveness and didn't know to whom she was making the plea. Dear God, dear God, David was dead!

"Mrs. Williams was told her stepson didn't make it through surgery."

Claire could only nod stupidly.

"Mrs. Williams also said to tell you the girl hasn't been told. She said you were to do it."

"Me?" Claire asked in horror.

The nurse simply nodded. "I'll go get her."

Left in the foyer, Claire sat on the second stair in shock. What did her mother think? That telling Elizabeth was some kind of extra punishment? Damn her. The girl should be told by someone she knew, like a grandmother, not by a stranger! How fucking manipulative and selfish can one woman be to use an innocent child like that?

Still, how *do* you tell a child who's been violated by her father that he's now dead? Would she be secretly relieved and then feel guilty? Or would she think it was all her fault? That once the truth came out, everything fell apart and now her father, whom maybe she loved, was taken from her? The kid could be screwed up for life!

This was too hard. She didn't know how to proceed, what she should say or do.

Michael, somebody, please help me, she mentally pleaded.

She didn't expect him to show up in her mother's foyer, and he didn't, but she thought maybe he could work some kind of magic and make things right, make sure she did or said the right thing.

Be yourself.

She heard the words inside her head as clearly as if they were said aloud.

That's it? That's the help? Be herself?

"C'mon," she muttered under her breath. A little more guidance would be highly appreciated!

Just be yourself.

Great! She blew her breath out in frustration and fear and stood up as she heard footsteps on the upper staircase. Holding onto the railing for strength, Claire looked up and watched the nurse lead Elizabeth down the stairs.

The poor kid was dressed in shorts and a T-shirt. White sandals were on her feet. Her hair looked messy and her face swollen, probably from the accident and crying.

Claire's heart melted and she smiled slightly.

"Hi, Elizabeth," she whispered as the child came closer.

Big, blue frightened eyes just stared at her.

"I don't know if you remember me. I'm Claire . . . your . . . your aunt, I guess," she added, fumbling with the words. Legally, she figured she was the stepaunt, if such a thing was correct. "You're coming to stay with me for a little while. Did your grandmother explain?"

"Mrs. Williams had me explain," the nurse said, obviously not approving of the way Alicia was handling the situation.

That made two of them, Claire thought. "Do you have a bag, or some clothes?"

Elizabeth shook her head slightly.

"The police brought her here from the hospital," the nurse filled in.

"Okay, no problem," Claire said softly. She figured there was no way to get into Elizabeth's home to retrieve clothes. Who had a key? She wasn't about to ask her mother.

Holding out her hand to the child, Claire said, "Shall we go? I bet you're tired."

The nurse put her hand on Elizabeth's shoulder and led her closer to Claire.

Without asking again, Claire took the child's hand and walked her to the front door. Before she left, Claire turned back to the nurse. "What hospital is her mother in?"

"Abington Memorial. It was the closest to the turnpike where the . . ." Her words trailed off as though she didn't know how much to say.

"Thank you," Claire quickly added and led Elizabeth out of the house.

She felt the child's hand tighten the closer they got to the car. "It's okay, Elizabeth," she murmured. "You can sit up front with me."

The little girl seemed to wrap her silence around her like a cloak of protection.

Claire opened the passenger door and Elizabeth got in. She fastened the seat belt and made sure it was secure against the child's lap and chest. "There we go," she said reassuringly. "It's only about an hour's drive. We'll be fine. I promise."

She closed the door and walked around the front of the car, not looking up at the house to see if her mother was watching. She wouldn't give her that satisfaction. Getting into the driver's side, she put her own seat belt on and glanced at her young passenger as she started the car. "Even though I'm a really great driver and this car has air bags in the front and side, I'm going to imagine the whole car and you and me inside it in a protective bubble of light that nothing can penetrate. You can do it with me if you want, a big beautiful bubble surrounding us and the car, keeping us totally safe."

She didn't know if Elizabeth did it, but Claire felt she had to say something to reassure the child. "Okay, we're off now." She shifted the car into drive and slowly left that house and its occupants behind them.

Neither of them spoke until Claire turned onto the turnpike, but she'd glanced over at the child and had seen bruises on her legs when her shorts rode up. She had no idea what the poor kid had been through and her heart felt heavy with compassion. Figuring she had to say something so Elizabeth wouldn't feel so isolated with a complete stranger, she said, "Maybe we could go to Target tomorrow and get you a few things. Tonight you can wear a T-shirt of mine to sleep in. I do it all the time."

No response.

"Do you swim? I have a pool in the backyard."

No answer.

"I love to swim. We can pick up a bathing suit too."

Nothing.

Finally, Claire said in a soft voice, "I know you're scared, Elizabeth. I am too. We don't know each other and I'm sure you're worried about . . . your mother. When we get to my house I'll call the hospital and we'll check on her, okay?"

Elizabeth nodded.

A good sign. At least the child was listening and not blocking her out completely. And she didn't ask about David. Claire decided in that moment not to say anything to her until tomorrow. Elizabeth had had enough of a shock for one day. A cowardly part of her was relieved by the decision, for she really had no idea how to break the news. Maybe Michael would help.

She set the cruise control to sixty-five miles an hour, the speed limit, far lower than her normal speed for the turnpike, and drove in the slow lane, letting all the other cars whiz past her. This trip was about safety, about getting a terrified child to an unknown destination as peacefully as possible.

Less than a half hour on the turnpike and Claire saw that Elizabeth had fallen asleep. Instinctively, she wanted to run her hand over the child's head, but didn't want to frighten her. She'd probably been too frightened for too long.

Even though Elizabeth was ten years old, asleep she looked like a baby. Her complexion appeared pale and Claire could see a purple bruise on her cheekbone. Turning her attention back to the road, she could feel a surge of protectiveness swell in her breast and had to swallow down the tightness in her throat.

This was not the time for self-indulgence, even though her emotions were so close to the surface. Probably being pregnant didn't help.

Pregnant.

She'd actually forgotten about it since leaving the office.

Keeping one hand on the steering wheel, she placed her other hand on her flat abdomen and thought, *Okay, I'm going to try and do this, kiddo. It'll probably be just you and me in the long run, so how about we make a deal? You ease up on the morning sickness that I seem to experience in the afternoon, and I'll take better care of myself. Not so much takeout or wine. I'll try to eat healthy stuff, like vegetables and those fruit smoothie things. I'll give you the best start I can, if you make this easy on me.*

She thought that was fair.

Oh, and you don't turn into one of those colicy babies and I don't get that postpartum depression thing that makes mothers want to throw their babies out the window.

She sighed. Maybe that was too much information too soon.

*Well you might as well know up front I won't be your typ-
ical mom,* she added. *But I'll try to be the best mom I can.
So . . . welcome to my crazy world, kiddo. And if you've got
a seat belt in there, you'd better buckle it. I think this is
gonna be one heck of ride . . . for both of us.*

She put her hand back on the steering wheel and unexpectedly felt a tiny flutter that rippled up to her solar plexus.

Shocked, she wondered if that was an answer.

Nah . . . it was way too soon, right?

Probably just gas.

She had no more time to consider the strange fluttering as
her exit came up. Putting on her turn signal, she reached for
her purse on the floor by Elizabeth's feet. Her hand acci-
dentally brushed the girl's ankle as she brought it up and
Elizabeth was so startled, her legs immediately tightened
together and she woke up murmuring, "Don't! Please!"

Stunned, Claire said, "I'm so sorry. I was just getting my
purse to pay for the toll."

Elizabeth grabbed hold of the seat belt at her chest,
breathing heavily, as though trying to get her bearings.

Not yet ready to deal with the child's reaction to being
touched and what it might really mean, Claire handed her
the purse. "Could you go in my wallet and take out two dollars? The toll booth is coming up fast," she added, though
she really had the time to do it herself. She just thought it
might be best to occupy Elizabeth and divert her attention
from what had just happened.

Claire was happy to see Elizabeth open her purse and
take out her wallet.

"There's bills in that back part, after the credit cards."

Claire's Coach wallet was soft lime green with a pale aqua
leather flap that closed it, and she could tell the child was
surprised that it wasn't a typical adult wallet by the way she
was handling it. "I got it at Peddler's Village, at the Coach
outlet store. We might go there too. Some great shops," she

said, taking the two one-dollar bills from the girl's fingers and then grabbing her exit ticket from the visor.

Elizabeth didn't answer her, but Claire was encouraged by the child's willingness to do as she'd been asked. It was a start.

She paid her toll and they left the turnpike. The rest of the way was much slower driving as they passed towns in typical Pennsylvania suburbia . . . lots of trees left over from farms now separated by large shopping centers and developments of new Mcmansions, huge homes with identical immature landscaping built close together with no real property. Fortunately, Haverton was a much older town and if it wasn't the Main Line, it was still a charming community where the houses were different from each other and some of the trees were over a hundred years old. It reminded her of Princeton, across the river in New Jersey. Big old homes with character. Of course hers didn't exactly fit the bill. It was on a quiet side street, off Main Street, where the historical society made sure nothing modern was ever built. She turned onto her street, glad it was still dusk and Elizabeth would be able to see the house and know where she was staying.

"Here we are," Claire pronounced, pulling into her driveway. She unbuckled her seat belt and turned off the car. Looking at Elizabeth, she added, "I hope we can be friends."

When the child still didn't respond, Claire unbuckled her seat belt for her.

"Shall we go in?" she asked.

Elizabeth's answer was to open the car door.

Blowing out her breath in gratitude for making it home without traumatizing the child, Claire opened her car door and joined Elizabeth as she walked up to the front doors. She got out her keys and unlocked one door.

The air immediately changed as the air-conditioning hit her. "If it's too cold I can give you a T-shirt with long sleeves or a sweater. Or I could turn the temperature up," she added, not sure what to say to the child.

Elizabeth walked into the house and stopped in the foyer. It was like she'd been properly trained how to behave in a stranger's home, as if she were waiting for instructions.

Claire smiled. "You can explore," she said. "I have a guest bedroom with a door that leads outside to the pool."

"Can we . . . call my mother?"

"Absolutely," Claire answered, thrilled to have heard the child's voice. "Though I don't know if we can actually speak to your mother tonight, but I'll call the hospital and find out how she's doing."

Elizabeth looked up her expectantly and Claire realized she wanted her to call immediately. Dropping her purse onto the narrow table against the wall, she placed her hand on Elizabeth's shoulder and led her into the kitchen.

"Do you want something to drink?" she asked, opening her refrigerator and wondering what she had for a child. A soda maybe? She didn't keep milk in the house and realized she needed to go food shopping for healthy stuff.

Elizabeth shook her head and Claire closed the fridge, then picked up the phone and dialed information. "Abington, Pennsylvania," she answered the automated questions. "Abington Hospital."

She smiled down at Elizabeth's worried face and let the phone company connect her to the hospital. "Yes, hello. I'm calling for information on one of your patients who was admitted today. Caroline Williams. If it's possible, may I be connected to her or to the nurse's station on her floor?"

She nodded to the child and smiled again. Covering the lower part of the phone, she whispered, "They're connecting me to the nurse's station."

Elizabeth simply continued to stare up at her, waiting to hear something about her mother.

"Yes, I'm wondering if you could give me any information about Caroline Williams. I believe she's on your floor."

"And I'm speaking to . . . ?" the nurse answering the phone asked.

"I'm Claire Hutchinson and I'm taking care of her ten-year-old daughter while her parents, while Caroline is hospitalized," she replied. "Her daughter is very worried about her mother and I told her we'd call to check."

"Mrs. Williams is resting comfortably. Her physical condition is stable. However, she's been sedated and is scheduled to be transferred to another floor that can better monitor her emotional state."

Claire forced herself to keep smiling. "I'm wondering if you wouldn't mind telling her daughter that her mother is resting comfortably. She's had quite a difficult day and I think she would be reassured to hear that from a nurse."

"Just that she's resting comfortably?"

"Yes. She's ten years old and I think that's all she needs to hear tonight so she can get a good night's sleep."

"Sure. I'll do it."

"Thank you so much. Her name is Elizabeth."

She handed the phone to the child.

Elizabeth took it and said quietly, "Hello?"

She watched the girl's facial muscles relax as she listened to the nurse and Claire knew she'd done the right thing. "Ask if we can call tomorrow," she whispered.

"Can we call tomorrow?"

Elizabeth looked at Claire and nodded.

"Good," Claire murmured when she was handed back the phone.

"Thank you so much," she said, even though the phone had already been disconnected.

"Great news, huh? Your mom just has to get stronger."

"How long . . . when is she coming home?"

Claire slowly shook her head. "I don't know, Elizabeth.

I was told she broke an arm, so that might take some time, you know? Maybe we should just take it day by day. Today we found out she's resting comfortably. I think that's great news. And we can call tomorrow and see how she's doing."

"When can I see her?"

Claire swallowed. "I don't know that answer, either. I'm sorry. I'll try and find out who her doctor is and see if I can talk to him tomorrow, okay?"

Disappointed, Elizabeth only nodded.

"Do you want to take a bath or a shower? Or just jump in the pool?"

The girl shrugged.

"How about a shower then? Let me show you your room. You'll have your own bathroom," she added, leading her out of the kitchen. "I want you to feel free to do whatever you want, Elizabeth—"

She stopping speaking and turned around. Looking down, she grinned. "Are you always called Elizabeth? Do you have a nickname? Liz or Beth?"

"Beth."

"Can I call you Beth?"

She nodded.

"Good. So, Beth, like I was saying, I want you to consider this your place while you're here." She led her out of the living room and into the hallway. Stopping at the first bedroom, she flipped on the light and added, "You don't have to ask if you can get something to eat or if you can watch television. Stuff like that."

She watched Beth look around the bedroom. Like the rest of the house, it was decorated in clean contemporary lines. Probably not very comforting to a little girl. "You know, I've been thinking about changing the look in here. Maybe tomorrow you can help me pick out some sheets and a comforter."

"Okay," Beth answered, staring at the queen-size bed.

Claire walked over to a door and opened it. "Here's your bathroom."

Beth looked inside. "It's big."

"Not too big. You should see mine. I guess I like big bathrooms. Hey," she said, nodding out the door. "Come see my bedroom and we can try and find you some underwear. It might be big," she added, walking out of the room, "but we can tie a knot in it to make it smaller or something."

She turned on the light in her bedroom and headed for the long dresser. Opening up the top drawer, she looked inside. "What do you think?" she asked, holding up a pair of white bikini panties.

Beth shrugged.

"You're right. Too dull. You don't want to try a thong, do you? Nah . . . never mind. Even I think they can get uncomfortable. How about these?" She brought out a pair of pale blue panties with a tiny ruffle in the front.

"Okay," Beth said, and Claire could see the girl's eyes lighten with interest.

So she's a girly girl, Claire thought. Best to remember that when they went shopping. She closed the drawer and opened another, the one containing folded nightgowns. "What do you think about this to sleep in?" she asked, bringing out a short white nightgown with short sleeves. It had been a gift one Christmas and Claire hadn't returned it, thinking she might need it if she stayed over at someone's house. It was prim and proper, with tiny lace ruffles at the neckline and the end of the sleeves. She held it up to Beth and saw that it would come down to her calves. "Might just do until we get you something better in your size."

Beth accepted the nightgown and held it with the panties.

"There's shampoo and conditioner in your bathtub," she said leading Beth back into the guest bedroom. She turned around. "Do you know how to shampoo your hair?" she asked, realizing she was treating the girl like an equal.

"My mom . . ." Beth stopped speaking and her bottom lip trembled.

"That's okay, honey," Claire quickly said. "I can shampoo your hair for you, if you don't mind."

Beth tried to shake her head and start over. "My mom showed me."

"Oh, good. Well, I'll show you how to turn on the shower and then I thought I'd order some spaghetti and meatballs for dinner. I'm starved."

Beth simply blinked.

"Do you like spaghetti?" Claire asked, pulling back the white shower curtain.

The young girl nodded and put the panties and nightgown down carefully on the long vanity.

"Okay, then, that's settled. Here, I'll show you how the shower works. It's really easy. And you can use the towels in here for your hair and to dry yourself."

A few minutes later, giving Beth some privacy, Claire rested her shoulder against the wall outside the bathroom, listening to the child get out of her clothes and into the shower.

She closed her eyes and sighed.

So she'd start the less takeout part of the promise tomorrow.

They still had to get through tonight.

Chapter

14

SHE MUST HAVE WOKEN UP FOUR TIMES DURING THE night to check on Beth. The child was so drained she'd slept right through. Claire's internal alarm clock had her wide awake at seven-thirty . . . only she didn't have to get up for work anymore. How odd—she'd spent decades ruled by her ambition.

The reality of what she'd done yesterday hit her between the eyes. She'd made public her intentions to have a baby, work part time, even if it was just for the foundation, picked up David's child and tucked her in for the night. Good reason to feel like she hadn't slept, and they had a full day ahead of them. She wondered how late she should let Beth sleep. It was summer, after all.

When she was Beth's age, her mother had treated summer like any other season and would come in at eight o'clock, pull the sheets down to the foot of the bed and tell her to get up. There was always a list of chores waiting to be done. So much for the lazy days of childhood summers. Claire decided to let Beth awake naturally. All they had to do today was shopping.

And then she realized she'd have to tell the child about her father.

Immediately, Claire felt sick to her stomach at the thought.

She didn't know what to say, how to say it or how to deal with whatever the child's reactions might be. Maybe she could call Isabel. She was wise—she might know how to break such news. But then she'd have to explain everything and she wasn't prepared for that yet.

Michael.

He would know what to say.

Claire remembered the last time they'd been together out at the pool. He'd been so eager to get away from her that he'd raced like a rocket out of her presence. Feeling even more nauseated, she sat up and wondered if it was her nerves or morning sickness.

Hey, I thought we had a deal, she mentally chided, rubbing her belly, which, if she wasn't mistaken, was now swollen. She pulled up her T-shirt and looked at the rounded bump.

That couldn't be!

Just yesterday she was flat!

She hurried out of bed and stood before her mirror. Grabbing the shirt up to her breasts she studied her reflection. There it was. The bump. She turned sideways, marveling at how quickly her body was changing. Cristine had said the pregnancy was going to be fast, but *this* fast?

Was it because she had accepted it and—the baby . . . how weird to even think a baby was growing inside of her . . . and now the baby was taking over her body, draining it of nutrients, depending on her for everything to survive. The responsibility was overwhelming. Again a wave of nausea rushed over her and she headed for the bathroom. She sank to her knees before the toilet and held back her hair. Good God, this had better stop soon because she had too much to do to be spending time kneeling at a toilet.

She started to get dry heaves and her stomach wrenched painfully as she clutched her hair. "Please," she pleaded in a hoarse voice, "make this go away." Again she heaved.

After ten minutes of it, now sitting on the floor and hugging the toilet like it was her lover, Claire finally felt like she might be able to get up. She flushed the toilet and dragged her sorry behind off the floor, then headed to the sink and turned on the cold water. Cupping it in her hands, she rinsed out her mouth and lifted her head. It was then, from the mirror, she saw Beth at the doorway, looking puffy-eyed and worried.

"Hey, good morning," Claire called out, trying to smile.

"Are you sick?"

Shrugging, she said, "Just a little bit. I hope that was it for the day."

Beth still looked worried.

"How about some breakfast?" Claire asked, wiping her hands on a towel. The very thought of food was dangerous at the moment. "We can get dressed and stop at IHOP. It's right around Target. And after Target we can go food shopping. I'm afraid I don't keep much food in the house."

Beth shrugged. "Can we call the hospital first?"

Poor kid. "Sure. We'll call after we get dressed." She looked at Beth's narrow straight hips. "I have a top you could wear, but I don't think my shorts would fit you. Do you mind wearing the ones you had on yesterday?"

Beth shook her head and headed out of Claire's bedroom.

Damn, she should have washed them for the child. Why didn't she think of that? Anyone with any sense of child care would have known not to put dirty clothes back on the kid. Especially since those clothes were the ones she'd worn when she'd been in a tragic accident.

Taking a deep breath, Claire vowed she would try and do better.

They called the hospital and found out there was no change with Caroline and Claire learned the name and number of her attending physician. Beth ate waffles at IHOP and drank orange juice while Claire was satisfied with wheat toast and tea. In Target Beth picked out a few outfits, shorts and tops, and Claire kept filling the cart with more shorts and tops, sundresses and bathing suits and underwear and nightgowns. In the shoe department they found flip-flops and another pair of sandals, a pair of white sneakers with pink laces and a pair of ballerina flats.

Satisfied that the child had enough clothes to last a week or more, they headed to the housewares department. There Claire let Beth pick out new sheets and a comforter to match in the palest of blush colors, barely pink. Obviously pink was a favorite color for Beth. Claire only cared that the sheets be at least four-hundred-thread count. She was sort of a thread-count snob, but since she'd be keeping them she didn't feel it was an unreasonable request. She let Beth have free rein in picking out throw pillows and the ones she decided on were actually in good taste, with only minor frills and lace. Next she headed for the toy department.

"Okay, Beth, do your thing. What do you want? Do you like dolls?"

The girl shrugged, still shy whenever Claire threw something extra into the carts. They now had two carts since the first was filled to capacity.

"Well you should go exploring and find something to play with," Claire encouraged. "I can't help you here."

Beth started to slowly walk up and down the aisles, but to Claire it looked like she just being obedient. There was no real interest. Grabbing her purse, she left the carts in the larger aisle and walked up to the child. "You don't have to get anything if you don't want. Do you like books?"

Beth's eyes lit up and she said, "I like to read."

Claire grinned. "Then we're in the wrong department, girl. Grab your cart and let's go."

The two of them left the toys and entered the books and CDs. "How about music?"

"I have Clay Aiken at home."

Claire swallowed. "Clay Aiken?" God, she was *so* out of it if Clay Aiken was the new heartthrob for little girls. "Okay, let's find his CD."

They ended up getting three CDs, an inexpensive Walkman and five books.

Feeling like the kid was set, Claire herded them to the long bank of checkout aisles. After everything was put into big bags, Claire wondered if they should stop at home and get rid of it before going to the grocery store. This was hard work and she still had to find stuff Beth liked to eat!

It took over an hour to go up and down each aisle at Genardi's. Beth seemed to realize Claire didn't know too much about food and she slowly took over, telling Claire that 2 percent milk was better than whole milk and the bread should have whole grains in it instead of plain white bread. Claire wanted to take notes, realizing that all this nutritious stuff was old hat to the kids now. They didn't expect white bread because they'd grown up with mothers who knew whole grain was better for them. She guessed you didn't miss what you never had. And Beth had been taught right, thanks to Caroline.

She made one decision on her own. Ben and Jerry's ice cream. Chocolate chip cookie dough. Heck, she was pregnant. She could have a craving. She mentally brushed off the fact that this particular craving had begun years ago.

Although she was so tired that she thought she needed a nap, Claire wanted to prolong the grocery shopping because she knew that when they got home and put everything away, she was going to have to get to the next thing on her list.

And she was dreading it.

She knew she had to tell Beth today, even if she wanted to hide the truth from her. God forbid she should see a newspaper or turn on the TV and hear about the accident and that her father had never made it out of surgery.

During the day she had tried to see David in Beth, but couldn't. David had dark hair and brown eyes. He'd *had* dark hair and brown eyes. Beth must take after her mother's side of the family, for which Claire was grateful. It would have been painful to see the person she had resented for so long in this precious child.

It took four trips to empty the trunk and the backseat of the BMW and it took almost two hours to put away the groceries, put Beth's new clothes in the washer, along with her sheets, and fold all the empty bags. She let Beth put on a bathing suit and use one of her T-shirts until her own clothes were dry.

Finally they were done and Beth looked as tired as Claire felt.

"It's been a long day already, huh?"

Beth nodded.

"Do you want to go out to the pool?"

"Okay," Beth answered. "Can I bring the Walkman?"

"Sure. But first let me change. Don't go in the water without me. There's some sunblock in that bowl with the sunglasses. Make sure you put it on, all right?"

Nodding, Beth walked over to the bowl on the counter.

"I'll be right back."

This time Claire put on a one-piece black suit, thinking it would hide her bump. It didn't. She shrugged at her reflection and headed back to the kitchen. Putting two towels on the counter, she then poured them both glasses of cranberry juice and added ice. Might as well bring the box of Triscuits that Beth had pointed out was whole grain and had zero trans fat. Claire opened the box and tried one.

It was like chewing on salty cardboard, she thought, picking up the cranberry juice and taking a sip. Damn, was *this* what she was going to have to do for her own kid? Teach her about nutrition, like Beth? She could see herself keeping salty cardboard crackers for her child and then sneaking off to the garage to scarf down greasy potato chips and cheese steaks. Something with some *flavor*!

She knew she was dragging her behind, playing for time, and looked out the kitchen window. She could see Beth rubbing sunblock onto her legs.

Oh, God . . .

How was she ever going to do this?

Taking a deep breath, she reached into the bowl and got a pair of sunglasses. Putting them on, she closed the box of crackers, stuck them under her arms with the towels and picked up the drinks.

Somebody, somewhere had better be watching and helping her out on this one.

Right before she opened the front door, she thought, *Michael, I know you're pissed at me, but I could use your help on this. It's too much to ask me to do it alone.*

She didn't expect an answer and none came.

Walking toward the lower patio, Claire plastered a smile on her face. "I brought some juice and crackers," she called out. "Could you wipe your hands and help me with this stuff?"

Beth immediately wiped her hands on a towel she took from under Claire's arm, along with the other towel and the box of crackers. That left Claire free to place the drinks on the table separating the chaise lounges.

"It's hot out here," she declared, walking over to the pool and dipping her toes. The water felt cool and inviting. "You know how to swim, right?"

The girl nodded and picked up a glass of juice. Claire watched as she took a long drink. She was so well behaved, Claire kinda wished that was the way they came, but she knew Caroline deserved the credit.

Sitting on the first step into the pool, Claire watched the water lap against her shins and said, "Beth, would you come and sit with me for a little while?"

She felt the child move toward her and didn't turn her head as Beth stepped into the pool and sat next to her in her two-piece pink-and-green floral bathing suit.

Beth didn't say anything, but reached down and ran her hand under the water.

"I have something I have to tell you, honey, and I'm a little scared because I'm not sure how to say it. It's about your father."

Beth's hand stilled and she brought it up to lay on her thigh.

"You know he was hurt pretty bad in the accident, right?"

Beth nodded, staring out to the pool.

"They operated on him and . . . well, I'm so very sorry, Beth, but he didn't make it out of the operating room." She took off her sunglasses and placed them on the cement. Looking down at the child next to her, she asked, "Do you know what that means?"

Beth didn't say or do anything. She kept looking out over the water.

"Honey, your father died from his injuries and . . . I'm so sorry," she murmured, wrapping her arm around Beth's shoulders and feeling the child's muscles stiffen. "I wish I could say it better, or make it less painful for you, but I thought you should know. And I'm sorry you have to hear it from me, someone you hardly know . . ."

"May I go swimming now?"

Startled, Claire said, "Sure. But, Beth, are there any questions you want to ask? Anything at all . . ."

Shaking her head, Beth walked down the rest of the steps and left Claire staring after her.

That didn't go well. She may not know a whole lot about children, but Claire knew Beth should have had some reaction. Anger or tears or confusion. Something. Maybe she was in shock. Maybe she couldn't comprehend the gravity of it all. Unsure what to say or do, Claire entered the pool and began to swim toward Beth who was now at the deep end, holding onto the metal stepladder.

When she reached the child, Claire asked softly, "Are you all right?"

Another nod.

"Maybe it's not my place to say this, Beth, but I want you to understand that accident wasn't your fault. It was your father's. He was driving the car, not you."

Beth was staring at the tiles on the side of the pool.

Claire bit the inside of her cheek, wondering how far she should go. There were things that Beth needed to hear and understand. Deciding she wasn't getting help from anyone, or anywhere, she cautiously proceeded on her own.

"I know your parents were arguing in the car, but you must understand, Beth, is wasn't about you. Not really. It was about your father and . . . and his behavior, what he had been doing."

Beth turned her face away from Claire, as though she was embarrassed.

"Look, I know being here with me is uncomfortable and strange. I know this kind of talk should be with your mother or someone you at least know, but this is the way things turned out, at least for now. I just want you to know that I understand how you feel. My father died when I was young."

"Did he have an accident?" Beth asked, still not looking at her.

"No. He was sick, suddenly very sick, and then he was gone."

Beth didn't respond.

Claire took a deep breath, keenly aware of what she had to say. "And I know how you feel about what was being done to you by your father . . . because it was done to me too, when I was about your age," she hurried to add when Beth started to swim away. She caught her arm and brought her back to the ladder. " I know how scary it is, how bad you feel, how alone you think you are and you don't know how to stop it."

Beth turned her head slightly and stared at her hands on the metal railing. "Was it your father?"

"No, but it was someone close to me, someone who never should have touched me like that. I was so scared it took me two years before I told someone."

The girl didn't say anything, just continued to stare at her hands clutching the railing.

"I'm telling you this, Beth, because I was just like you. I want you know you aren't alone, and that none of this is your fault, not one single thing. And I know that for a fact. You didn't do anything wrong, no matter what you were told or what you felt. You're a little girl and someone who was supposed to protect you didn't do that." Claire paused and prayed she was saying the right thing. "Your father, Beth? He was sick. In his head. He wasn't thinking right, like other fathers do. Something was wrong with *him,* not you. It wasn't your fault. Not what he did to you. The arguing in the car. The accident. None of it was your fault. He was scared because he was found out and he knew it was wrong and he was going to be punished, so he tried to run away and take you and your mother with him. Your father was driving that car. He caused that accident. Everything that happened was because he made the wrong choices."

"Because he was sick?"

"Yes. Something happened inside of him that made him sick. If he wasn't sick, he would have done everything he could to protect you. That's what a father does. He protects his little girl. He doesn't hurt her."

Beth turned her head even more and stared at Claire's throat, as if she couldn't yet look her in the eye. "My mom said he was a monster," she whispered. "And she hated him."

Claire could see tears forming in the child's eyes and felt the heaviness in her own chest increase. Her throat was tight, matching the burning in her eyes. She had to keep it together for Beth's sake, so she took a deep breath to steady herself. "Maybe what your mom meant was that she hated the things he'd done to your family, especially to you. It wasn't right, Beth. It was never right. You deserved to be protected and loved the right way, the way fathers who aren't sick in their minds love their daughters."

"Is . . . my mom going die too?"

Claire reached out and wrapped her arm around the girl's thin shoulders. "No, honey. She has a broken arm and . . . and maybe a broken heart right now. I think maybe she feels bad because she didn't know what was happening to you. But she isn't going to die in the hospital. Do you believe me?"

Beth nodded. "Maybe I could go see her and tell her that daddy was sick in his head."

"Maybe you can," Claire answered, not having the strength to stop the tears from rolling down her cheeks. She gently kissed the top of Beth's damp head. "When I call the doctor before dinner I'll ask when you can visit. I'm sure she wants to see you and wrap you in her arms. Well, at least her good arm."

Beth's sweet young face looked up at Claire. "Don't cry," she whispered, looking worried. "It wasn't your fault."

Claire, on the verge of blubbering, grabbed Beth and held her close to her chest. "You are one terrific girl, you know that?" she mumbled, wishing she could protect the child from being hurt ever again, by anyone. But then again, that was part of life. She would form attachments and be disappointed. It seemed to be the human condition. Hopefully, Caroline would get her some professional help, some counseling, and Beth wouldn't have to be screwed up for almost thirty years and unable to form a real relationship with a male.

She thought of Michael, someone else she was going to have to check off her to-do list. This time with an apology.

Sniffling, Claire said, "Can I tell you a secret?"

Beth, holding onto Claire's shoulders, nodded into her chest.

"I'm going to have a baby. Maybe that's why I'm crying so much lately."

Beth looked up at her. "Really?"

Grinning, Claire nodded. "Hardly anybody knows, just one of my friends. You know, I think you'd be like cousins, or something."

"I would?"

"I think so. I'm sort of your aunt because your grandfather Eric married my mother, Alicia."

"Granmama Alicia is your mother?" the child asked in surprise.

Sighing, Claire nodded. "We don't get along all that well, I'm afraid."

Beth looked relieved. "Me, either."

Claire laughed and kissed Beth's forehead. "I knew I liked you, kid, right away."

"She always corrects me and then makes me dust her furniture."

Claire shook her head. "She did the same thing to me. Well, I promise you won't have to work around here, except to make your own bed."

"I would help you . . . Aunt Claire," she added shyly.

"Look, you don't have to call me that. You can call me Claire, if you want."

"I . . . don't have any aunts," she said hesitantly.

Sniffling, Claire said, "Well, ya got one now, Beth." She grinned down at the girl. "Hey, I've never been anyone's aunt before. You think I can do it?"

Grinning slightly, Beth nodded.

Deciding that they'd had *the* discussion and Beth seemed to accept everything she'd said, Claire asked, "Can you float?"

Beth shrugged. "I try and then I start to sink."

"Well, lets go back to the shallow end and I'll teach you."

Together they swam toward the steps. Before they reached them, Claire stood up and held out her arms. "Now you have to trust me. Do you think you could do that?"

Beth, bobbing in the water that came to her shoulders, nodded.

Within minutes Claire was holding Beth by only a finger at the small of her back. "You have to relax and tilt your chin up. Just enjoy the feeling of being held by the water."

She watched the thin young girl in front of her floating so calmly and felt something deep and emotional grab hold of her. Was it love? Could she possibly love this child that she didn't even know existed last week? Or was it the pregnancy that made her so emotional?

"Do you think my father is in heaven?"

Blinking rapidly, Claire was startled by the question and didn't know what to say. "I don't know, Beth."

"I hope so," Beth answered with her eyes still closed. "I don't think it would be fair if God didn't let him in . . . because he was sick."

Claire felt that tightness return with a vengeance, threatening her composure. Swallowing deeply, she tried to concentrate on the child, yet it was as if something was breaking up inside of her, something she'd thought was vital, that had kept her safe since she was a little girl.

Dear God, she still cared about him, even after all he'd done to her!

Claire managed to force the words out of her tight throat. "So you . . . forgive him, Beth?"

The child nodded. "You said he was sick."

But he was also a bully, a manipulator, a liar, and . . . she suddenly thought of Michael's words. David was insane. Not thinking sanely. She'd used a less scary word with Beth, sick, but that was the truth of it. Strip away all the symptoms and the root cause, the disease, was insanity.

How could this little girl do something I had found impossible?

The years of anger and resentment that turned into hatred bubbled up inside of her and Claire had to stop helping Beth. "Honey, that's enough for now," she was able to get out. When Beth was standing in the water, Claire added, "I don't feel too well. Maybe it's still morning sickness." She couldn't look the child in the eye.

She turned and walked up the steps to the towels. Wrapping one around her, Claire turned toward the house, wishing she could go inside and bawl her eyes out . . . for herself, for Beth, for everyone who had ever been betrayed by another's insanity.

"Aunt Claire? Did I say something wrong?"

Wiping her face on the towel, Claire turned toward the pool and shook her head. Sniffling and smiling, she said, "Beth, you said everything right. Sometimes children are far more wise than the adults around them. I'm very proud to be your aunt."

Beth looked pleased by her words and pushed off the steps to swim.

Claire sat on the bottom of the chaise lounge and stared at the little girl swimming to the deep end.

How very odd that it took David's child to show her how to forgive.

Chapter

15

SHE HELD BETH'S HAND AS THEY WALKED OUT OF the elevator and onto the sixth floor where Caroline was hospitalized. Beth, dressed in her new pale blue sundress, looked adorable carrying a bouquet of summer flowers for her mother.

Claire leaned down as they approached the nurse's station. "Now remember, your mom may have a broken heart and be very sad, and she might not seem the same right now. You have to be strong for her, okay?"

Beth nodded, a tense look on her face.

A broken heart seemed the best way to describe to a child that her mother may be in shock and not herself. Claire looked at the room numbers on the wall by the wide doors and counted down two more doors. *Please let this go okay,* she prayed. Beth needed some reassurance. The doctor said Caroline was sedated and she wanted to see her daughter. He also said he wasn't transferring her to the psych ward as Claire had been told a few days ago. He thought Caroline was suffering from shock and given perhaps a week of rest, counseling and medication, she should make a full recovery. It had been great news and they'd been allowed a visit.

"Here we are," Claire whispered at the doorway. "Do you want to go in by yourself?"

Beth looked up at her and shook her head. "You come with me."

It wasn't a question. Claire nodded and together they walked into the room.

Caroline looked like she had shrunk. She appeared smaller as she lay in the hospital bed, her right arm in a cast, looking out the window.

"Mommy?"

Slowly Caroline turned her head and when she saw her daughter she burst into tears, holding her hand over her mouth.

Beth began to cry and even Claire felt like she might join them.

"Beth, why don't you give your mother the flowers?"

She watched as Beth slowly walked up to her mother and held the bouquet out to her, as though afraid she wasn't doing something right.

Caroline, her face showing signs of bruising, took the flowers and nodded her head, still trying to stop crying.

"I'm so sorry," Caroline mumbled, her eyes swollen and red. She dropped the flowers to the bed while reaching with her good arm for Beth.

Claire watched as Beth hurried to her mother's side and wrapped her little arms around Caroline's neck.

"It's okay, Mommy," she said, sniffling. "It wasn't your fault."

Hearing that, Claire clutched at the buttons of her white shirt and quietly backed out of the room. This should be a private time for them. It wasn't her place to intrude. And, truthfully, hearing Beth tell her mother that was way too painful. Claire knew she would be blubbering again if she stayed and, quite frankly, didn't know yet how Caroline felt about her. She might blame her for accusing David and turning all their lives inside out.

Blame the messenger.

She'd done it herself with Michael. Accusing him of ruining her life and a half dozen other things that had caused him to leave her presence. He couldn't stay in her negativity, that's what he'd said. *Her negativity.* It sounded so awful and she didn't blame him for leaving her alone. Leaning against the hospital wall outside the room, she could hear Caroline crying and trying to talk to her daughter.

Her daughter . . .

She touched the waistband of her tan skirt under the blouse she'd left out over it. *Her daughter.* Her own daughter was growing inside of her. Suddenly, with people all around her in the corridor, Claire started crying, not in sadness, but in gratitude, in awe.

She was going to have a baby. A little girl!

She'd managed okay with Beth under the most stressful circumstances. She now knew she could do it. Beth had shown her that. She wouldn't be perfect, but she'd learn every day. She wasn't like her mother at all. She really did have maternal instincts and, if she could love David's child, she must be okay in the heart department too.

Nothing was wrong with her or missing in her.

It had been her own self-doubts, her own crushing disappointment in her childhood that had made her think she was incapable of real love or family relationships. Suddenly she wanted Michael with such urgency that she had to press on her solar plexus to stop her from calling out to him. She wanted to feel his arms around her, tell him she was happy and she knew now she was blessed, just like he'd said.

It was a miracle.

She was going to be somebody's *mother*!

Finally, after thirty years of fear, she could come out from behind that thick wall she'd built around her heart. She could give herself permission to love again.

"Aunt Claire?"

She wiped her face and looked down at the child standing in the doorway.

"My mommy wants to talk to you."

Claire reached for Beth's hand. Sniffling, she said, "Okay, let's go back in."

Beth shook her head. "She said I was supposed to wait out here for a little while."

"Oh." Claire let go of the child's hand. "Right."

She tried to smile as she passed the child and walked back into the room. Her stomach clenched almost painfully and she didn't think it was morning sickness. Not this time. It was fear. What was Caroline going to say? Steeling herself for anything, Claire squared her shoulders and walked to the bed closest to the window.

Caroline was watching her and Claire felt she had to say something as she stopped at the foot of the bed. "I am so very sorry, Caroline."

The woman nodded slowly. "You can't be sorrier than I am," she answered, her words slightly slurred from her medication. She reached for the flat box of tissues on the sliding tray over the bed. Blowing her nose, she dropped her hand with the crumbled tissue to her side and blew her breath out roughly. "Thank you for taking care of Beth. She said you've been very good to her. She . . . likes you a lot."

"I like her a lot," Claire murmured. "You've done a terrific job, Caroline. She's a wonderful child."

Caroline burst into tears. "I . . . I didn't do a . . . a terrific job!" she protested through her sobs. "I should have known! I should have *known*!"

Startled by the abrupt change, Claire hurried to the side of the bed and clasped Caroline's hand, crumbled tissue and all. "Don't do this to yourself," she whispered. "It wasn't your fault. I know how Beth felt. When you're little like that, you think you have to keep this dirty secret to protect yourself and . . . and those around you. The important thing is, Caroline, when you *did* know you tried to do something about it. You confronted David."

"The bastard. He was always cold and a bully, but this! This is unconscionable. His own daughter . . ." Her words trailed off into fresh tears until she wiped at her nose and again repeated, "I should have known. I should have known . . ."

Claire could now see in Caroline's eyes a faraway tortured look, a disconnection with something so horrible she could only mourn her own guilt.

"The important thing now, Caroline, is for you to get better. Beth needs you."

Caroline turned her head so quickly that Claire was startled by the look of anger. "Do you know what they found? The police? *Things!* Magazines of young girls, children! They took away his computer. There were Web sites . . . children . . . My God, where was I? I should have known . . ."

"Caroline, you need to concentrate on Beth now," Claire said, trying to redirect the woman's mind. Should she call a doctor to come in, someone to give her shot of something to calm down?

"He was going to take us away to Mexico because he said they couldn't extradite him. Mexico! He said he was taking us the long way to JFK because the police might be looking for him at the Philadelphia airport. So he was going to go in the opposite direction, through New Jersey. He was supposed to show up at the police station with his lawyer in the morning, but he was insane with anger and he blamed me for believing you, for questioning Beth, for allowing the police in the house."

Claire listened to the slurred words and saw Caroline was getting more agitated speaking about David. She didn't know what to say to the woman to calm her down.

Suddenly, Caroline grabbed Claire's wrist tightly.

"He was a monster!" Caroline whispered, her eyes wide with fear. "I had to do it," she whispered even lower. "I told Beth to put her head down and cover her face."

Claire could hardly breathe as she stared back into eyes that really weren't connecting with hers. She couldn't even get the moisture into her mouth to ask the question burning inside her head.

Caroline looked around the room, then leaned her head up, closer to Claire's. "You would understand, after what he did to you. I had to do it, don't you see?"

"What?" Claire asked, hardly breathing.

"I grabbed the wheel."

Oh, God . . . Claire swallowed down her fear.

"I stopped him," Caroline whispered and let her head fall back to the pillows.

"Yes," Claire whispered back and was relieved when Caroline's fingers let go of her wrist. It seemed that the woman had used up all of her energy in her confession.

What am I supposed to do with that information?

The room was silent for a good thirty seconds, until Claire said, "Caroline, you have to get strong. Beth can stay with me as long as it takes for you to heal, but you owe it now to your daughter to make that happen as quickly as possible. The two of you need to make a life together."

She didn't respond, just continued to stare out the window.

Claire rose. "I'll get Beth now and you can say good-bye. We'll be back for a visit as soon as the doctor tells us it's okay." She squeezed Caroline's hand, lying limply on the sheet by her side. "Please get better, Caroline. Your daughter really needs you now."

She brought Beth back in and whispered, "Your mom's very tired. Give her a kiss and tell her we'll be back as soon as the doctor lets us."

Watching Beth kiss her mother, Claire felt protective of

them both. How strange that she spent so many years without acknowledging family and now it appeared she had one, even though they weren't related by blood. Still, she felt she had to help Caroline too. The guilt the woman was feeling must be unbearable.

Beth walked back up to her and said with trembling lips, "She didn't say anything."

She took Beth's hand and led her out of the room. "It must be the medication, the medicine, they're giving her. It can make you very sleepy. Don't worry, she'll get better soon."

Claire prayed her words were true.

Now she had to call Caroline's doctor and discuss what had been revealed. If Caroline had a chance of recovery, she had to deal with her guilt, not just about Beth, but for grabbing that steering wheel and causing an accident that killed her husband.

As they waited for the elevator, she held Beth's hand even tighter. She knew that had she been in Caroline's position she might have done the same. David had been kidnapping them and taking them to a foreign country. Maybe Caroline had been so distraught by the recent revelations that she couldn't think of any other way to stop him.

She needed some help in this.

"There's someone I'd like you to meet," she said to Beth as they walked into the wide elevator. "He's . . . his name is Michael and he's a good friend . . ." She stopped for a moment as she pressed the button for the lobby. "He's more than a friend. He's the father of my baby," she corrected "And I hope you'll like him."

"Okay," Beth answered.

As they rode the elevator down to the hospital entrance, Claire wondered what had happened to her organized life she'd thought she could control. That seemed so long ago, almost like a dream. Now things were happening so fast she could barely keep up with it all.

Time, as she had known it, now took on a different meaning.

It appeared to be speeding up.

§

Everything in her wanted to hibernate with Beth, keep the outside world at a distance. There were too many intrusions, too many people who wanted to ask questions. Her phone started ringing the afternoon they'd come back from the hospital. Reporters. One actually told her he'd gotten her name from Alicia Williams. It seemed everyone wanted to know the details the police were not yet revealing, why David was quietly buried next to his father, without a funeral. Claire, disgusted with her mother, refused to answer anything and stopped picking up even her cell phone unless she recognized the number or thought the call was urgent. Like from Caroline's doctor, who said he was working with his patient and she was making progress, yet it might be another month before Caroline could consider leaving the hospital.

As an adult, Claire knew hibernation wasn't a real option.

Tina kept leaving messages about looking for her wedding gown. The last few had sounded desperate.

Shelly left a voice mail about the office gossip, the pool that was organized to bet on whether or not she returned to work.

Even Jim Doherty left a message, saying it was vitally important that she contact him as the partners were asking questions he couldn't answer.

She couldn't hide out forever. And, *and* Michael wasn't appearing, even when she wished he would. What if she'd been abandoned? What if she was now all alone in this pregnancy, which was proceeding at an alarming rate? None of her clothes fit and she'd actually gone shopping at night to buy shorts and cropped pants with elastic waistlines. Thank goodness hippie-style tunics were back in style. She'd always been more tailored, but even leaving her blouses out wasn't working anymore. She couldn't button the bottoms across a belly that kept expanding. She'd even had to buy old-school underwear to accommodate her increased waistline. And her breasts! Anyone who knew her would think she'd had implants!

No, she couldn't keep this a secret any longer. Plus, she needed some help.

It was definitely time to call an emergency meeting of the Yellow Brick Road Gang.

She called Cristine, told her she was babysitting a ten-year-old, not to ask any questions yet and could she just please arrange the meeting.

The next night she and Beth showed up at Cristine's house twenty minutes early. Cristine didn't hide her surprise when she opened the door. Introductions were made and Beth immediately fell in love with Angelique. After a few minutes the two of them disappeared upstairs into the baby's room and Claire told Cris to wait for an explanation. When they were finally alone, Claire flattened the tunic around her belly and said, "It's not natural, Cris. If I keep gaining weight like this, I'm going to be as big as a house! Already my boobs are flotation devices. They actually *float* when I'm in the pool! And I'm never going to have a waistline again, so I . . . Hey! It's not funny! Did I laugh at you?"

Cristine covered her mouth, but couldn't hide her laughter. "I'm sorry and, yes, you did. You said I was going to be so big they could use me in the Macy's Thanksgiving Day Parade."

"Well, it would take the whole West Side to hold the ropes on me. This is crazy. I swear I feel kicking. I keep telling myself that it's just digestion, since now I'm eating whole grains and broccoli and all this nutritious stuff that tastes like crap. I'm dying for a cheese steak and fries."

Cristine shook her head while grinning. "I told you, everything was going to be accelerated, Claire. It probably was kicking. You look like you're five months pregnant."

"Five months? *Five months*?" Her jaw dropped. "It hasn't even been one month! So . . . what? I'm going to have this baby *next month*?" she asked, noting the hysteria coming into her voice. "This *is* crazy!"

"No, it's not crazy, Claire. It's unusual."

"Gimme a break! This is beyond unusual. So *am* I gonna have this baby soon? There are no guidebooks on this stuff!"

"I don't know," Cristine answered with a giggle, pulling Claire into the kitchen. "Now sit down while I get the cake ready."

"Cake? Do I look like I should eat cake?"

"It's not for you," Cristine said, pulling out a white bakery box. "It's just a small cake to celebrate Tina's engagement. You beat me in calling a meeting, so I thought we'd combine things tonight."

"Cris . . . Cris . . . I'm about to tell them I'm pregnant Don't you think that just might be stealing Tina's thunder? Her news is happy news. Mine is . . ."

"Happy news," Cristine supplied. "You just have to get used to it. I'll admit Paula, Tina and Kelly are going to be . . . surprised, but—"

"Shocked," Claire interrupted, supplying the right term. "I don't know how to explain it. Do you think we should just tell them the truth, about . . . you know . . ."

Cristine turned away from the counter. "Would you have believed it, if it hadn't happened to you?"

Claire just stared at her friend. "Probably not," she muttered eventually. "I would have thought you and Isabel were delusional. Truthfully, I did think that about you in the beginning." She watched Cristine transfer the cake to a serving plate. "So what do I tell them?"

"Stick to the truth, as best as you can. That's what I did. You met someone special and now you're pregnant and you're keeping your baby."

"That sounds like a Madonna song, not the words of a semi-intelligent forty-three-year-old." She paused for a moment. "Who am I kidding? Semi-intelligent? What kind of intelligent woman gets pregnant by a being from another dimension? There's real intelligence."

"Hey! Me, and there's Isabel. And we're intelligent women." Cristine shrugged, licking icing off her finger. "I guess it doesn't matter how old you are in this situation. And speaking of situations, who's the little cutie upstairs with Angelique? I can't wait."

"I'll explain that later. Maybe I shouldn't say anything tonight and just let this be a night of congratulations for Tina's engagement."

Cristine grinned. "Honey, they're going to take one look at you and you're going have to explain yourself. You haven't seen anyone in what? Three weeks? The change is remarkable, Claire."

"Gee, thanks," she muttered, hanging her head. "I feel *real* good now."

"Claire, you're beautiful. You always were and you still are. You're positively radiant. *That's* what I'm talking about. You could explain away a weight gain, maybe not easily, but I mean it's in your eyes, your face. You're different. You glow."

"It's probably just the flop sweat that keeps popping out all over my body."

Laughing, Cristine came over and placed her arm around Claire's shoulders. "Don't worry so much. I'll support you."

"You haven't told anyone yet, have you?"

"I promised."

"Not even Issy?"

"Not even Issy, and I was dying to tell her. She's going to be so happy for you."

"She's not the one I'm worried about."

"Who is?"

Claire sighed. "Tina. I'm supposed to be her matron of honor, her little wedding lackey, and I've let her down miserably."

"Not so. Tina told me how you'd arranged things with Isabel to hold the wedding in Issy's backyard. She said you had lists and—"

"And I don't think I can keep doing it," Claire interrupted. "With Beth staying with me, and me expanding every minute like a big mound of rising bread dough, I just don't have the time to do it right."

"Then do it the best you can, Claire. Nobody expects perfection."

Claire raised her head. "Are you kidding me? What bride doesn't expect perfection? They have that new term *bridezillas* for a reason, Cris."

"Tina is not going to be a *bridezilla*," Cristine said with a laugh, just as the doorbell rang. "Especially when she finds out you're pregnant. Stop worrying so much, will you? This is the hardest part, trying to explain to people, then it gets so much easier." She gave Claire a quick kiss on the side of her head and hurried to her front door.

Claire heard them entering, the raised voices when they all got together, the laughter that came so easily. She looked down to her red high heels, designer heels, which looked particularly odd with white crop pants and a white tunic. She wished she really could click them together and be back in her own home along with Beth. Hibernating felt especially enticing now.

"Well, Miss Claire! It looks like you've come out of hiding finally. What's up with you?"

She grinned at Tina with a guilty expression. "I'm so sorry, Tina. I'll explain everything once the whole Gang gets here."

Tina leaned down and kissed Claire's cheek. "Well, whatever it is, it suits you. You look great."

Grateful that Tina wasn't angry with her, she murmured, "Thanks." Claire was still seated on the stool, leaning her elbows on the counter, and she wondered if they could have the meeting in Cristine's kitchen so she wouldn't have to get up and display the bottom half of her body. "So how's the wedding plans coming?" she asked to distract her friend, even though the question made her feel more guilty for not helping as she'd promised.

"Great. I got a florist and that caterer Issy recommended. They put me in touch with the rental company for the tent. Now it's just the music and the dress."

Claire sort of grimaced. "I know I promised, Tina, we'd find it weeks ago. I've just been so busy, kind of overwhelmed."

"What's this meeting about, Claire? Cristine said you called it and it was an emergency?"

Claire was saved from answering as Kelly and Paula came into the kitchen, followed by Isabel and Cristine.

The Gang's all here, she thought. For the first time, she dreaded it.

"We've got the liquid refreshments," Kelly said as she and Paula placed two wine bottles on the counter.

"What's the emergency?" Isabel asked, kissing Claire's cheek and adding, "You look . . . different."

"I was going to say the same thing," Paula remarked, staring at Claire.

Claire waved her hand. "First, we have some important business to take care of . . . Cristine?" She looked at her friend meaningfully. Probably pleadingly.

"Right . . . right," Cristine muttered, pushing past the

women to get back into her kitchen. She picked up the cake and placed it in front of Tina.

The white cake was decorated with real, tiny pink rose-buds and in the center were two gold wedding bands connected by an intricate sugar ribbon.

"Wait, wait," Kelly called out. "We need to open the bottles first!"

"Right," Paula added, going to Cristine's cupboard and bringing out wineglasses. She handed them to Cristine and Isabel who put them on the counter surrounding the cake.

"You guys shouldn't have done this," Tina protested, but Claire could see she was really happy.

Again Claire felt guilty, not doing her matron-of-honor duties. And it suddenly dawned on her that someone should be planning a wedding shower. Was that up to her too? God, she'd have to ask Cristine, because if it was, she was going to need even more help.

When Kelly had opened the first bottle, Paula poured what turned out to be champagne into the glasses.

Everyone held up her glass to Tina.

"To our sister, Tina, who so deserves the very best that life can bring her. And that turned out to be the good Dr. Ramsey," Kelly said with a laugh.

"Hear! Hear!" Cristine added. "To Tina."

"To Tina," everyone cheered.

Claire barely sipped the champagne. She probably wasn't supposed to have that, either. She really was going to have to buy a book or something. But what book could help explain *her* situation?

"Thanks, everybody. This is really sweet. And where did you get that cake, Cris? It's beautiful. I'm looking for a good baker."

"There's a new bakery that opened and I heard they were pretty good."

"Well let's try it out then," Tina said, picking up the cake server. She cut into it and everyone held her breath as Tina brought out a perfectly thin triangle that looked delicious.

"It's a pound cake with a Linzer torte filling," Cristine murmured, anxious for a reaction.

Tina served everyone and then picked up her fork. She closed her eyes, savoring the taste. All watched as she opened her eyes wide and grinned. "It's fabulous. Taste it!"

They did, and they agreed.

Tina was telling them about her plans, the caterer, the florist, the rental company. "I still have to get the music, the photographer and my gown, but I think I've made great progress so far."

Again, the guilt hit Claire.

"I promise as soon as I settle a few things, I'll be right there at your side and do whatever I can."

"That right," Paula said, looking at Claire. "What's the emergency?"

"Hold that thought," Cristine called out. "I'm going to take some cake upstairs and look in on the kids."

"Kids?" Isabel asked with a grin, as though Cristine had made a mistake.

Cristine shot Claire a look and then cut two small pieces of cake.

"I'll explain when Cris gets back," Claire said, digging into her cake and realizing she was probably blowing all her good intentions with nutrition on this one piece of cake. Filling her mouth, she figured it was a small price to pay for a diversion and putting off the dreaded discussion. Maybe she really was a coward at heart, because as she watched Cristine hurry out of the kitchen and listened to Kelly questioning Tina about live music or a DJ, she felt a sense of reprieve.

These were her friends, her soul family as Tina had labeled them. They weren't going to attack her, she reasoned, and then felt Isabel staring at her with a quizzical expression. She simply smiled in answer to the unasked question. Even Issy was going to be shocked at first. But she knew she could count on her later. Isabel would help ground her, even if she had to hypnotize her to get her to accept the unexplainable.

And that was just it. For three of her best friends—Tina, Kelly and Paula—there simply wasn't any way to explain it. The truth was beyond reason.

Stick to the truth as much as possible, Cristine had said. It wasn't just the pregnancy. She had to explain Beth. That meant the whole ugliness of the past.

Unconsciously, she sighed deeply and wished it was over, everything out in the open.

"Are you okay, Claire?" Kelly asked.

"You seem . . . I don't know . . . impatient," Paula suggested gently.

Realizing everyone had heard her sigh, Claire nodded. "I'm okay. I'm sorry. I just have—"

"All right, I'm back," Cristine announced, cutting off Claire's words. She looked at Claire. "Everything is fine," she said, glancing up at the ceiling, indicating Beth and Angelique.

"Will *someone* tell us what's going on?" Paula asked.

"Right," Tina agreed. "This is getting too mysterious. What's the emergency?"

Everyone, including Cristine, looked at her. Claire felt like she was on the witness stand. Silence pervaded the room as they waited for her to speak.

Taking a deep breath, Claire said, "Okay, you might want to sit down for this."

"Oh geez . . ." Paula muttered, "I don't know if I like the sound of this."

"Where? The dining room or the living room?"

"How about the dining room?" Claire answered. "Bring your cake and the champagne. You're definitely going to want a drink."

Kelly said, "Not a good start."

Walking into the dining room with her plate and wine-glass, Isabel answered, "Let's just hear what she has to say."

Claire waited until everyone was seated and then stood in front of an empty chair on the side of the table, across from Isabel. "I have a lot to say, so please don't interrupt me un-til I get it all out. And, yes, I can see how you're looking at me since I've stood up. I've gained some weight and—"

"But so quickly? I just saw you a few weeks ago and—"

"No interrupting," Cristine interrupted.

Tina clamped her lips shut.

Claire held onto the back of the chair and breathed deeply. "This is hard for me," she murmured. "I don't now where to start, so I guess I'll begin at the beginning. You know I don't talk about my family. Some of you may not know that I even have one, considering, to me, they didn't exist anymore. I hadn't seen or talked to anyone in almost twenty years. Well, last month I was visited by a lawyer who told me my stepfather had died and I was mentioned in the will. I fought within myself about even going to the reading, knowing I'd have to see members of my family that . . . that I held no good will toward. I was . . ." She stopped and swallowed, thinking if Beth could forgive and go on, she had to. "I was raped repeatedly as a child by my stepbrother and my mother didn't believe me."

"Oh, God, Claire!" Cristine whispered in shock and sym-pathy.

Claire held up her hand and tried to smile. "No interrup-tions, remember?"

She could see the stunned faces of her friends and swal-lowed the bitterness in her throat. "I'm sorry to dump all this on you guys, but there's a reason." She paused to regain her composure. "There was a great deal of ugliness that fol-lowed my telling, so I didn't see anyone after I left that house for college. I built a life for myself without them in it and I was happy. Well, as happy as I could be. I had a pretty good life, a great job, terrific friends, a nice house, good investments. And then my stepfather dies and it's all back in my face. To make a very long story short, Eric, my stepfather, left a written note. In it he mentions his granddaughter, Beth, my stepbrother's daughter, and asks that I get to know her and thinks I will bond with this child. It was all very cryptic to me until I looked down the conference table at this little girl and, somehow, I knew."

Again, she swallowed the tightness in her throat and refused to let tears overwhelm her. "It was like a lightning bolt," she said, seeing Isabel hold her stomach and Tina's hand come up to cover her mouth. "I knew my stepbrother was abusing his daughter and Eric somehow must have known and wanted me to connect the dots. I . . . I asked that Beth leave the room and I told everyone what I suspected. I sort of backed the lawyer into a corner and said as an officer of the court he had an obligation to report it to the authorities. So—"

"Good for you!" Kelly said.

"Shh!" Paula admonished. "Go on, Claire."

Again the silence seemed almost palatable as they waited for her to continue.

"So . . . I was right, unfortunately. The authorities found things in my stepbrother's house and he was supposed to turn himself in with his lawyer, but he decided to kidnap his wife and daughter and was trying to get to JFK when . . . there was an accident." No one needed to know Caroline's part in it.

"I think I read about this," Tina whispered and was shushed.

"He died of complications in surgery," Claire continued. "His wife was injured, but really is suffering from shock and guilt that she didn't know what was happening in her home, and I . . . I got a phone call at work from my mother.

We don't get along at all. Like I said we hadn't communicated in twenty years, and I've come to accept we never will. She said she couldn't take care of Beth and told me I had to pick her up and tell her about her father's death."

"Oh, my God . . ." Isabel murmured, shaking her head.

"So that's what I did. I now have a ten-year-old living with me while her mother recovers. She's the sweetest girl with a heart of gold and she's teaching me so much about forgiveness. It's, quite frankly, amazing and more than a bit overwhelming."

Still holding onto the back of the chair for support, Claire hung her head as tears filled her eyes and slid down her cheeks.

"Good heavens, Claire. I . . . I'm stunned. I don't know what to say. No wonder you haven't been picking up your messages."

It was Tina's voice and before she completely broke down in front of them, Claire lifted her head and said, "Oh, yeah . . . and I met someone and I'm pregnant and I've quit my job. There. That just about says it all."

She pulled out the chair and plopped down into it, leaning her elbows on the table and covering her face.

Everyone started speaking at once.

"Pregnant! By whom?"

"What can we do?"

"Who's the father? Where did you meet him?"

"Don't worry, you're not alone in this."

"You poor thing. How can we help!"

"*Who* is the father?"

Cristine said this was the hardest part and it would get easier afterward.

Right now it felt like the seat of her chair was burning hot and her friends had turned into benign inquisitors.

She slowly raised her head and wiped her eyes on the

sleeve of her white tunic sleeve. It didn't matter that black mascara stained the material. "All right," she said, taking a deep breath. "First, the father's name is Michael and I met him in a video store. He doesn't . . . live around here. Just visits."

She saw Isabel look pointedly at Cristine.

"Well it must have been quite a visit," Paula murmured in astonishment.

"It was, Paula," she answered as calmly as possible. "I can't tell you everything about him because I don't know everything about him."

"Does he know you're pregnant?"

"Yes, Tina, but the last time we talked he only knew how unhappy I was about it and he didn't know if I was going to continue the pregnancy."

"You have to contact him," Kelly pronounced. "Obviously, you're what? Four months?"

"I don't know," she answered in a tiny voice. "And I don't want anyone lecturing me on that. I had . . . a lot happening in my life, so give me a break."

"But you have to see a doctor," Paula said. "You need . . . I don't know, vitamins and . . . and an ultrasound at this point and, well, just reassurance everything is okay."

"I will take care of myself, Paula. I promise." She gulped in air, as though she'd been deprived during the telling of her story. "I called you all together because I'm going to need your help. Paula, Kelly, do you think you could help out Tina with her wedding plans?"

"Sure."

"Absolutely," Paula answered. "I'd love it."

Claire looked at Tina. "I promise you and I will find that dress, but we're going to need their help with the rest. Please don't be upset with me."

Tina, who looked close to tears, stood up and reached

across the table to touch Claire's hand. "I wish you would have told me. I wouldn't have been pestering you with phone calls and—"

Claire squeezed Tina's hand in return. "You weren't pestering me. How could you know my whole life was turned upside down?"

"Wow . . ." Kelly said. "It really has been, hasn't it? You lost your job?"

"She quit her job," Cristine corrected. "And I can see why now. Good God, Claire. I wish you would have confided in one of us."

Claire wrinkled her nose and shook her head. "How could I? It was this terrible little secret I'd kept from everyone. I would have had to explain and . . . and it was too painful to even remember. I thought I was done with the past, had buried it solidly six feet under, but I guess the past wasn't done with me. In some ways, and I can't believe I'm going to say this, but in some ways all this has been healing. Beth, that remarkable little girl upstairs, has shown me it's possible." She sniffled, thinking about the child. "Hey, she even calls me Aunt Claire. Can you imagine? Me, an aunt?"

"I can imagine," Isabel said softly with a knowing smile. "You're a wonderful woman, Claire, beyond your tough exterior. We've all known it for years. I'm glad you're going to be getting a chance to see it for yourself now. You'll be a terrific mother."

Claire couldn't hold it back anymore and the tears flowed. "You think?"

"Yes!"

"Of course!"

"You can do this!"

"That's right, you *can* do this, and we'll all be there to help."

"You're going to be fine, Claire. Stop worrying."

She sniffled and smiled. "Thanks, guys. I knew I could count on you."

Paula leaned in closer to the table and whispered, "Can we meet her?" She looked up at the ceiling.

"Yeah, Claire. I'd love to meet her."

She looked at Cristine. "I'll go up and get her and I'll bring Angelique with me."

She pushed back her chair and left the dining room.

She wasn't five feet away before she heard them beginning to whisper.

Grinning, Claire wasn't upset. She would have done the same thing to any one of them who had just dropped that news. She almost laughed. Let Cristine field the questions for a few minutes.

According to her, the worst was over.

Chapter
16

IT'S FUNNY SOMETIMES THE WAY THINGS WORK OUT. Beth was so reluctant to leave Angelique that Cristine invited her to spend the night. Cristine said they would improvise a nightgown and Claire could pick up Beth in the afternoon. A part of her didn't want to let Beth out of her sight, but she saw the pleading look in the child's expression and caved. Besides, it might be nice to spend the night alone and maybe, just maybe, Michael might show up.

She'd taken a shower and slipped into an old nightshirt, one big enough to accommodate her belly. Looking at herself in the mirror, she sighed in surrender. Whatever was happening to her body seemed out of her control now. It was as if the baby was taking over, growing and thriving.

Thriving?

Hmm . . . so maybe everything really was okay?

She pictured Cristine and Isabel pregnant. As bizarre as their pregnancies had been, they'd survived. More than survived. Both of them were happy.

Thinking of her friends, Claire decided the emergency meeting had gone well, better than she'd imagined. No one really pushed her for more information after she'd introduced Beth to the Gang, and she thought maybe Cristine and probably Isabel had something to do with that. She was just grateful. No more explaining in person.

She'd call Jim Doherty tomorrow and have him arrange a conference call with the partners. If they didn't want her working part time and fired her, so be it. She'd have to get health insurance on her own, or maybe she'd pick up on the foundation's insurance policy Cristine used. Whatever, she wasn't going to worry about it now. As soon as she crossed off the work issue, she'd be free to finally start preparing for the arrival of her daughter.

Even thinking about it brought a rush of awe.

Soon—she hoped not too soon—she was going to have a baby.

She ran her hands over her expanding bump. "Hey you in there . . ." she whispered. "Have a little patience, okay? I have to prepare a place for you and I need to fix things with your father."

"There's nothing to fix, Claire."

She spun around from the mirror and inhaled with appreciation. There he stood, looking wonderful and . . . if she wasn't mistaken, wearing a new designer outfit.

"You . . . you look great," she murmured, smiling at him. "What's the label say?" she asked stupidly, trying to postpone a deeper discussion.

As if not expecting that question, Michael seemed startled for a moment. "I believe it says Hugo Boss."

"Great choice," she said, impressed and taking in his casually tailored appearance. Why was it that a well-dressed man was such a turn-on for her? "You really do look great," she repeated.

"So do you," he answered, stepping closer. He stood about twelve inches from her and looked into her eyes with a tender expression. "I am in awe of you, Claire, and what you have done."

Unprepared for compliments when she thought she was going to have to eat crow and apologize, Claire could feel herself actually blushing. Blushing! *Her!*

"I . . . I didn't do anything for you to be in awe of," she answered haltingly, embarrassed with his praise.

"No? You didn't step in and take care of a child who was terrified by what was happening to herself and her family? You didn't help her to see that her father was unbalanced and therefore not thinking sanely? You didn't illuminate a way for her to forgive the transgressions against her, saving her from years of torment? You didn't open yourself to her, and tear down that protective barrier you had erected when you were as young as her?" He reached out and cupped her face in the palm of his hand. "Claire . . . you are able to love, really love, again. And, to me, that inspires awe."

She reached up and held her hand over his. "I'm sorry, Michael. I . . . I was so scared about what was happening to me, getting pregnant, and I took it out on you. And I shouldn't have, but—"

"There is no need of an apology," he interrupted, pulling her closer until he wrapped her in his arms. "I simply chose not to engage in conflict and empower it. Do you think I wouldn't have been able to comprehend your fear? To feel it overpower you? I know what has happened to you and what has happened in your life has been overwhelming, and you needed time to integrate it. I stayed away to allow you to process what you were experiencing with Beth and within yourself."

She clutched his shirt. "But, look at me! I'm huge! All this is happening too quickly. It takes nine months for a baby to be born normally. Cristine says I look five months pregnant and . . . well, that can't be! Can it?"

"I don't control this, Claire. The child is developing at her own pace, not yours and not mine, so your pregnancy will not be what is considered as normal because our daughter will not be what you term normal. She will be extraordinary and will never forget her true identity."

She raised her head and looked up at him. "You said *our* daughter."

He smiled down at her. "And is she not our daughter, conceived in an act of exquisite union?"

Claire nodded her agreement and swallowed deeply. She had to ask what was burning inside her head. "But, Michael, will you be here for her? For us? Or, will I be raising her alone?"

"We are linked now, Claire, into eternity. I will always be connected to you, and to our child."

She still didn't get the answer she wanted. Sighing, she said, "Look, I am prepared to raise this child alone. I just want to know if you're going to be a part of our lives, like now, in a physical way."

"A physical way?"

"Yes," she answered, putting her hands on his shoulders and shaking him. "Like you are now. So your daughter will know you."

"She already knows me and the physical manifestation is—"

"I *want* the physical manifestation, Michael," she interrupted, pulling out of his arms and trying not to feel hurt again. "I want my child's father to be *in* her life physically."

He appeared puzzled. "Claire, I cannot become physical. I can maintain it for a short while, but to stay in this physical body permanently is impossible. I belong in a different dimension and, as in all of creation, I am striving to evolve to a higher one."

"So, you're going to . . . abandon us? Just evolve right on out of our lives?"

He took a step toward her, but she held her hand up like a crossing guard and stopped him.

"I would never abandon you, Claire. Can't you understand

that once we achieved unity you became a part of me, my energy, the very force that makes me who and what I am. You are imprinted upon my soul."

She sucked in her bottom lip. "Then I don't understand," she said. "Are you or are you not going to be here for me? You can't impregnate me with this extraordinary baby and then confuse me like this. I need to know. I can do it alone if I have to, Michael. I just don't want to have to."

He ignored her defenses and came up to her. Pulling her back into his arms, he kissed the top of her head and whispered, "I love you, Claire. I know you need reassurances right now and the best I can say is that I intend to be here for you, but it won't always be in the physical. I can't maintain this form as you would wish."

"Daniel and Joshua do. Cristine says Daniel is getting better and better, staying longer and longer."

"I am not Daniel, or Joshua."

She knew she was beginning to sound like a clinging pregnant woman, but couldn't seem to stop herself. "Will you at least *try*? This is an awful lot to drop on a woman, any woman. I need help, Michael."

"I will always help you," he murmured, still cradling her in his arms.

"Then can you at least tell me if the baby is okay? I thought I felt a kick, but it's impossible so soon. I just need to know before I see a doctor. I should be taking vitamins and getting ultrasounds and—" Her words were cut off by the sudden tightness in her throat. Those damn tears sprang to her eyes and her nose burned as she tried to stop it. She sniffled again for the hundredth time or more since he'd come into her life and muttered, "I'm so damn emotional now. I can't seem to control anything anymore."

"It's all right, my love," Michael answered, leaning back from her and wiping away her tears with a smile of compassion. "Stop trying to control and just allow it to *be*. You haven't come to this dimension to control anything, but to create everything, from the infinite sea of possibilities that surrounds you in each moment. Haven't you seen how what you might perceive as challenging can turn out to be exactly the opportunity for expansion that was needed? Now let me check."

He turned her shoulders until her back was against him. Slowly his hands came around what was left of her waist until his fingers were spread out over her belly.

Claire closed her eyes with the sudden feeling of pleasure mixed with peace, as though this place in his arms, this moment, was what she was born to experience. It made her feel connected to another so completely that her mind was filled with joy. She tilted her head back to rest on Michaels chest and felt him exhale when he said, "Ahh . . . yes. You can rest assured, Claire. Our daughter is progressing well."

"She is?"

"Have faith."

Faith? How long since she'd had faith in anyone or anything? She'd rejected so much in her life that she had instinctively felt was another's system of belief, whether it was the way her mother lived to impress others or the rules of a religion that didn't seem to have a place for a female who had her own mind. Could she have faith in Michael, in her daughter? Was she ready for that, believing in something she couldn't prove? How does one verify love?

Michael turned her around. "May I tell you something?"

She looked up at him and smiled, forgetting that moments ago she had been so worried. "Sure."

"I have missed you greatly, Claire. I am pleased to find you alone this evening."

"You are?"

He nodded, his smile becoming sexier as his dimples appeared.

Or maybe that was just hopeful thinking on her part.

"And why is that?" she asked in a teasing voice, wishing she wasn't wearing her old ratty nightshirt.

"Because I have come to crave the way your body responds to my touch, the look in your eyes, the expression on your face. When I become physical like this, it is difficult now for me not to pick you up and place you on your bed."

Thank God she'd at least taken a shower!

"Who's stopping you?"

He grinned so broadly that she barely had time to register it when he scooped her up in his arms and she yelped in surprise as he carried her to the bed.

Laying her down gently, he murmured, "I never expected this, Claire."

"Expected what?" she asked in anticipation.

"This great attachment, this yearning for you, the feel of you, the marvelous way this body reacts to yours." He reached for the hem of her nightshirt and began pulling it up.

Suddenly, Claire's hand came down and clasped his to stop him from proceeding. "Wait!"

"Wait?" he asked, confused.

"I . . . I'm not the same, Michael. I've gained so much weight and . . . and you might not find me as attractive."

"Not find you attractive?" he asked in a shocked voice. "Claire, you're beautiful. You are carrying our child," he said, lifting her shirt even though she hadn't let go of his hand. He lowered his head and kissed her belly, right above her pubic bone.

Claire moaned, her hand falling away as the pleasure raced instantly to her brain.

"I intend to kiss all of you," he whispered against her. "I have done research."

"Re . . . research?" she mumbled, as his kisses trailed over her.

"Uh-huh," he answered and the timber of his voice against her sent bolts of shivers throughout her body.

Just don't let him stop, she prayed, thanking the source or the force or whatever created him to be intelligent enough to *do* the research.

No matter what happened between them, she had this night, this unbelievable connection. Someone might actually cherish her.

And suddenly she had faith.

Somehow, in some strange and bizarre way, everything was going to be okay.

No matter how it all fell out.

Chapter

17

IT WAS THE LATEST STOP ON THE BRIDAL HUNT where two well-seasoned shoppers were able to enter a store, easily size up potential targets, dispose of them quickly and move on to the next destination. It was, in fact, the fifth store they had entered that day and one of the shoppers/ hunters felt as if her time had come to be put on an iceberg and floated out to sea. She was too far out of condition and holding her own was becoming a challenge.

Claire sat in a chair and waited for Tina to exit the dressing room. They were in Bala Cynwood, the last shop, their last hope for finding a wedding gown on the Main Line before expanding their search to Philadelphia. Resting her hands on her belly, a now convenient ball that was beginning to cover her upper thighs, Claire prayed they wouldn't have to go into Philly. Carrying this extra weight in summer was bad enough going from car to store, but in Philly it would be walking in the streets, trying to flag a cab and then more walking. The heat and humidity would surely do her in.

Please, please, let this be it, she prayed to the wedding gods, who surely would take pity on a woman in her position. She didn't even want to think about what she would be wearing as matron of honor. She'd tried to back out of it, telling Tina she would be too big to be waddling down an aisle in a month, but Tina stood firm, saying they would find her a dress or even have it made.

Have it made? Hmm . . .

Claire thought of the jar of prenatal vitamins that had appeared on her night table after Michael had come back into her life. He'd simply said he'd *accessed* what she had meant and manifested them for her since she had been worried over not taking them. Claire remembered being impressed and flattered that he wanted to show her his support. But if he could conjure up vitamins . . . what about a dress if she showed him what she wanted?

Would a dimension traveler become her personal dressmaker?

He manifested clothes for himself to wear, why not her?

Excited by the idea of not having to schlep all over two counties trying to find a gown that would accommodate her ever burgeoning bump, Claire picked up a bridal magazine from the stack on the table next to her. She began thumbing through them, looking at designs. Something off the shoulders, drawing attention away from her middle. She almost laughed at the thought. Nothing was going to accomplish that. Her middle was the most prominent part of her now.

She saw one gown with a halter neckline with soft folds of silk falling gracefully from under the breasts. *Something like that,* she thought. In pale, pale green, one of Tina's accent colors. Claire looked around the upscale store and began to slowly, quietly, tear the page from the magazine. She needed it to show Michael and was almost finished with her theft when the large louvered door to Tina's dressing room opened.

"Tina!" she breathed, forgetting about her own dress as her jaw dropped in admiration. "You look . . . fabulous!"

Tina, dressed in a cream two-piece gown with a strapless bodice that accented her breasts and came to her hips in a point, beamed as her hand fluttered around the long A-line skirt with soft graceful folds of creamy silk. "I think I love it," she whispered, looking for Claire's agreement.

"You ought to love it," Claire said, unable to stop grinning. "That top is gorgeous. I love the way it's dotted with tiny seed pearls. Nothing outrageous, just tasteful and . . . God, it looks wonderful against your skin too. You're beautiful, Tina," she added, feeling her throat beginning to close with emotion.

Tina came to stand in front of the big three-way mirrors. She twirled around slowly and Claire could see the happiness in her friend's expression.

Tina looked at Claire. "You think?" she asked hopefully.

Claire tore the page of the magazine completely and stuffed it into her purse. She hauled herself upright and came to stand next to Tina. Looking at her in the mirror, Claire wrapped her arm around Tina's waist. "Oh, yeah . . . I definitely think it's the one. It accents your great bustline and minimizes everything else. No one will even be looking at anything else. And the back pleat takes care of that trunk you were so worried about. Oh, I love it, Tina!"

Tina started to giggle like a much younger female. "I can't believe I finally found it!"

"It's perfect," Claire declared, still looking in the mirror at Tina and touching the skirt part of the gown. "What's the material?"

The salesperson who was standing to the side said, "Silk faille. And the bodice has hand-sewn genuine seed pearls. It's from our premier collection."

Claire picked up the little sales tag that was attached to the bottom of the bodice like a little formal calling card. She gulped when she saw the price.

"I don't care," Tina murmured, still falling in love with her reflection.

"It's worth it," Claire answered. "Now, are you doing a veil or not?"

Tina shook her head. "I think I'm little past the virginal veil."

"No tiaras!" Claire pronounced with a laugh.

Tina joined her amusement. "No tiaras. This is about as close to a princess as I'm going to get. What do you think about doing my hair up and having tiny pearls put into it to match the bodice?"

"I think it would be beautiful," Claire said.

"Shall we look at shoes?" the saleswoman asked.

Tina held up her finger to postpone answering the woman. She looked at Claire and said, "Do you think it would be totally crazy if we all wore our Yellow Brick Road heels?"

Claire laughed. "Yes!"

"Really?" Tina looked disappointed. "I just thought we do it for meetings but also for special occasions. My wedding's a special occasion."

"Honey, we'll all do whatever you want. If you want wacky red high heels, then that's what you're going to get. At least no one will see yours until the reception."

"Now what about you? Honestly, Claire, it's a good thing we didn't pick out a gown for you before now."

Claire ran her hands over her bump, which technically should now be termed a mound, as she'd definitely left the bump stage weeks ago. "I think I'm going to have it made. What do you think about pale subdued green. I can't do pink now, Tina. I'd look like a big party balloon."

Tina clicked her tongue. "You would not, but I like the idea of pale green. Maybe we could have our flowers wrapped in pale pink ribbon."

"Great!" Claire said, thankful not to have to wear anything pink. The color was just too cutesy for a big pregnant woman. "I still say you should think about having someone else be your matron of honor, Tina. These wedding pictures are going to be around for a long time and I'll be hogging all the space in the camera's viewfinder."

"Oh, shut up," Tina said, twirling around one last time. "I can't believe it doesn't even need alterations. It's like it was made for me."

Claire grinned. "It was. Now let's think about underwear."

Tina cupped her breasts. "They don't have a strapless bra in my size here, so we're going to have to look elsewhere. Oh, and a long slip. Where are we going to find *that* in my size?"

"Saks is right up on City Line Avenue. We'll go there next."

"You really are sweet about this, Claire. I know you must be tired."

"Go take off that perfectly gorgeous gown and we'll take care of the rest. We'll both feel good knowing it's done and then you can concentrate on all the details for the reception."

"Did I tell you I'm having trouble getting the air conditioners?"

Claire sighed. "We need air conditioners, Tina."

"I know, I know. It was one of the first things my future mother-in-law asked when we told them it was going to be an outside wedding."

"How did that dinner go? Meeting the new family?"

Tina's expression changed. "I'll tell you on the way to Saks. Let's just say I have a sneaking suspicion the first Mrs. Ramsey, his mother, had someone different in mind for her doctor son."

Claire opened her mouth to protest and then shut it. "Tell me in the car. And I know you hate to take it off, but it's time to get undressed," she added, pointing to the dressing room. "We need to drive to Saks and then get back on the turnpike before rush hour starts out of the city."

"Yes, ma'am," Tina answered, walking to the dressing room. Right before she entered, she turned around to Claire and said, "It really is perfect, isn't it?"

Claire chuckled. "Yes. You look like a fairy princess,

without the tiara and wand. Take the thing off. You can try it on every day for the next three weeks and admire your beautiful self."

Laughing, Tina went into the dressing room and Claire closed her eyes as she paid homage to the wedding gods for helping Tina find her perfect bridal gown. It really was a mini miracle. What other bride got away with no alterations?

With Tina's treasure safely secured in the trunk of her car, they drove to Saks, their last stop on this bridal hunting trip.

"So, what did Louis's mother say?"

"It wasn't so much what she said, and she had a lot to say—questioning me on my family, my schooling and why I would waste a master's on real estate—it was more how she acted. As though Louis was the golden fleece and I was stealing it away from her. Honestly, Claire, you should have seen her hanging onto him."

"Maybe that's the way all mothers feel about their sons," Claire answered, trying not to dislike someone she had never met. But anyone, mother-in-law included, that disrespected her friend who had already achieved so much in her life was skating on thin ice in her mind. "Once you're married she'll come around."

"I don't know," Tina answered in a worried voice as she pulled into the parking lot of Saks. "She actually had the nerve to ask if there was a reason we were getting married so quickly."

"You should have told her you were expecting triplets and you wanted to make sure she was still young enough to babysit them for you."

Tina chuckled. "I wish I'd have the courage to say something like that. The woman scares me."

"What does Louis say about this?" Claire asked, pointing to an empty parking space in the next aisle.

"He says she's always been overprotective because he's the youngest in the family. His brothers' wives seemed nice, but it was as though no one wanted to go up against the mother and tell her she was inappropriate or out of place."

"So she scares everyone, and she probably knows it and uses it to get her way."

"I don't know, but my dad is so great, welcoming Louis into the family so easily, that I'm . . . I don't know, almost jealous that everything is so easy for him. I'm doing all the wedding planning, running around for everything, and the one place I could use something easy is with his family. She says she doesn't understand why I wouldn't have a church wedding. I tried to explain that a minister will be there and that Isabel's garden makes a beautiful church, but she's got that disapproving attitude that makes me feel like I'm not good enough for her son."

Just as Tina was about to turn off the ignition, Claire grabbed her wrist on the steering wheel. "Hey! Stop it! Do not allow anyone, including Louis's mother, make you feel insecure about yourself. *Do not allow it.* You're a grown woman, Tina, an accomplished woman." She removed her hand and unbuckled her seat belt. "The only way you feel like that is if you allow it. Don't let her win in whatever mind game she's playing. You're marrying her son. Period. Maybe if she'd had more time to get to know you, she'd be different, but you two are grown-ups now and making your own decisions without her input. She'll have to get used to it, or she'll lose her son. Her big fear will come to pass. Wait and see how she is after the wedding. I bet she comes around."

They got out of the car and walked toward the store's entrance.

"I just wished she liked me."

"You know what? You can't make her like you the way you want. That's her choice," she said, opening the door to the store for Tina and walking in behind her. "It's your choice to—"

"*Claire?*"

Frozen by the voice, she felt like she was in a nightmare. Here she'd been talking about not making someone like you and coming out of Saks with her nurse pushing her was her mother! It was too incredible. What were the chances?

Unfortunately, since they were on the Main Line, pretty good.

Claire simply stared at the two of them. The nurse, obeying Alicia's upright hand, blinked in confusion as she looked at Claire's belly. Her expression was no match for Alicia's.

"I see you're up and about shopping," Claire remarked, thinking someone had to say something.

"What's happened to you?" Alicia demanded, waving her hand at Claire's mound.

Claire instinctively put her hand over her belly as if to protect it from the evil witch in the fairy tales. "What happened to me is I'm pregnant."

Tina stood at her side, expecting to be introduced. Claire knew she should make the introduction, but didn't.

"I can see that," her mother stated, screwing up her mouth as though someone had forced something distasteful on her. "We should take this outside," she added, looking over her shoulder. "Get the car while I speak with my daughter."

Tina gasped at the revelation and then smiled weakly.

Claire turned to her friend as the nurse pushed Alicia out of the building. "Why don't you get started? I'll find you in a minute."

"Sure," Tina said, confused and seeing how upset Claire was. She walked into the cosmetics department and left the Claire to follow her mother back outside.

Alicia was alone and Claire saw the nurse walking to the parking lot.

"There's nothing to take outside," Claire stated. "This has nothing to do with you."

"Are you saying I'm about to be a grandmother and it has nothing to do with me?" Alicia, wearing very expensive teal slacks and a silk print blouse, was carrying a Saks package on her lap that she clutched between her bony fingers.

"You already have a granddaughter, one you shoved out of your house at a critical time in her life. Do you even care how Beth is?"

Alicia brushed aside the question. "But you didn't even look pregnant at the reading of the will. How did you get so . . . *big* in such a short time? It's astounding. Are you having twins?"

No, Mother, I'm having a litter. She wanted to say it, but didn't.

When Claire didn't answer her, Alicia said, "Well tell me you are at least married."

"I'm not." That should do her in. "And I have no intention of getting married."

Alicia shook her head with an expression of disgust. "You always did everything the hard way. Is this too to get back at me?"

"Get back at you? Not everything is about *you*! I'm thrilled with this pregnancy."

"And Beth sees this . . . this shameful behavior? You're certainly not a good influence on the child." Alicia sighed, looking for her car. "You've always been a bitter disappointment, Claire, and an embarrassment. I refuse to endure any more."

She wanted to be civil. She really did, but hearing her mother's ugly accusations, especially about Beth, did in her good intentions.

Claire leaned down to the wheelchair so her face was mere inches away from her mother's. "Now you listen to me, don't you dare ever, *ever*, criticize me again. I am a grown woman, no thanks to you. You made your choices a long time ago and didn't give a shit who you hurt in the process. I'm grateful to you for giving me life, but that's where it ends now. I don't know why it makes you feel better to judge others so harshly. Maybe so you never have to look at yourself with any degree of honesty. So keep paying your nurse, because that's the only way anyone can stand being around you. You've become a miserable old woman, and I couldn't give a flying fuck what you think of me or my life. Your opinion holds no value, because you have to earn respect. And I respect myself too much to participate in your insanity for one minute longer." Breathing heavily, she stood upright and added, "And I'm really sorry you never learned how to love anyone except yourself. You've missed out on so much."

She then turned and walked into the store, her heart pounding and the baby kicking.

I'm sorry, I'm sorry, she mentally apologized, running her hand over her belly. It had to be done. It was the final break. She simply would not allow that woman to manipulate her ever again into feeling guilty or not good enough. Michael was right. Her mother would never love her the way she had foolishly hoped so long ago. Too many years and too much pain had passed between them. It was strange to think they shared the same DNA. Her family now consisted of people not related by blood, people who knew her, accepted her and loved her. And they supported her in whatever decisions she made.

Some things couldn't be fixed.

In a flash she realized the only way to fix it was for her to capitulate to her mother's judgments and bitterness. She would have to become someone else, someone who wouldn't stand up for herself and allow her mother the power to make her life a living hell. And while she would be doing that, pretending everything was okay out of misplaced loyalty or respect, who was being Claire? Nobody. She would simply disappear to play the false role her mother demanded.

It was over. Finally. Some relationships, even mother and daughter, will always be like fire and ice. And if she was the fire, she wasn't about to allow her mother's cold ice to freeze any more of her soul.

The woman had done enough damage. Now that she was going to be a mother herself, she was going to protect herself and her child. No matter what anyone thought.

She found Tina in the lingerie department.

"I am so sorry about that."

Tina spun around. "Are you okay, Claire?" She touched Claire's arm. "*That* was your mother?"

Shaking her head in exasperation, Claire said, "That was Alicia Williams. My mother disappeared a long time ago when my father died. The woman I had it out with just now doesn't know the first thing about being a mother."

Tina grimaced in sympathy. "You fought?"

"She criticized and judged. I told her I couldn't give a flying fuck what she thought of me or my life. If it was a fight, it was the final showdown."

"I'm sorry. I can't imagine . . ."

"She actually said I was a bad influence on Beth because I'm pregnant and unmarried. This, coming from a woman that threw the child out of her house because she didn't want to be bothered taking care of her."

Tina sighed. "Claire, you just told me about not allowing anyone to manipulate me with their disapproval."

"I know. Is that not ironic? Maybe I meant it for myself. They say you try to teach what you most need to learn." She paused for a moment and then chuckled. "Of course being pregnant and spewing words like *flying fuck* didn't improve my image, but I couldn't help it. I mean, I don't see this woman in twenty years and she thinks she has any right to judge me?"

Tina wrapped her arm around Claire's shoulders. "Don't get any more upset. Think of the baby."

"I know you're right. It was the Beth thing that really got to me. All she's ever cared about was security and keeping up appearances for her wealthy friends." She caressed her belly. "I was just told I am now an embarrassment."

Shaking her head, Tina said, "Okay, look, I found the slip. It's up at the register. And here's the bra. I have to try it on, 'cause this is too far to come back if it doesn't fit. Hold on for a few minutes and then we're out of here."

Nodding, Claire said, "I could use a drink."

"You're not serious."

"Of course I'm not serious. But I could use one. Go try on your bra. I can't wait to get back on the turnpike."

"Right," Tina said, hurrying toward the dressing room.

Claire looked around the department, hardly noticing the lovely lingerie offered for sale. She thought about Beth, over at Cristine's again, so she and Tina could go on their intensive bridal-wear hunt. She wanted to get Beth and hold her close against her body for protection. Soon she was going to leave, as Caroline was now in a rehabilitation center and improving under the guidance of counselors.

It was going to be hard to let Beth go home to her mother, Claire admitted. She'd become so attached to the child and would miss her greatly. She knew she wanted to stay in Beth's life and hoped Caroline would allow it. On their last visit at the center Caroline had been much more friendly and involved in the conversation. She never mentioned the accident and neither did Claire. Caroline talked about moving into a new house and, when Beth had asked if they could have a pool, Caroline had said it was a great idea.

Beth . . . dear, sweet, courageous Beth had shown her so much.

And thinking about that, Claire knew now she forgave her mother for what she'd done to her all those years ago, or what she hadn't done to protect her child. She knew the fear behind her mother's choices back then. She simply wouldn't allow her mother to continuing hurting her now as an adult. It had been time for a reality check. For both of them.

You could forgive someone and not have anything to do with her.

Forgiveness didn't mean you had to make nice, or enter into someone's insanity.

Forgiveness meant you no longer carried the weight of another's transgression. She was free. Finally, thankfully, she was free.

So it wasn't going to be a tidy little happy ending between them where they wrapped each other in their arms and cried. This was real, not some movie on Lifetime where everything is tied up nicely in the end. In reality, she accepted what is, simply is, but it didn't have to influence the rest of her life.

"It fits."

She spun around and saw Tina clutching the beige-colored strapless bra.

Smiling, Claire said, "Then let's pay for it and get outta this place."

It was time to go home to her sanctuary where, if she was lucky, Michael would be waiting for her.

She actually felt better, lighter, as she followed Tina to the register, as though a huge weight had been lifted from her shoulders. Maybe everything did happen for a reason . . . even the tough, unexpected challenges.

Chapter

18

BETH FELL IN LOVE WITH MICHAEL AND EVERY TIME he was around, the girl seemed to want to follow him or sit by his side. Claire couldn't blame her, but she was glad Beth was out at the pool, for she had a few things she needed to discuss with him in private.

"And I want this . . . and this . . . and maybe this to change diapers." She looked up at him. "You are going to learn how to change diapers, aren't you?"

Michael blinked a few times. "Diapers?"

Claire nodded. "A baby wear diapers, Michael, for at least a year I think." She looked down at the magazine in her lap, or what was left of her lap. "Maybe longer. I'll have to ask Cristine. I don't know when you start toilet training."

"If you show me, I will learn," he answered. "I am finding there are many things a being needs when she enters this dimension as a human."

"See?" Claire nodded. "It's not so easy, is it?"

His arm was around her shoulder as they sat together on the sofa, picking out baby furniture. "I never thought it was going to be easy, Claire. Especially for you." He squeezed her shoulder. "I will help as much as I can. Are you sure you want to purchase these items? I can easily manifest them and—"

"No," she interrupted. "I want to go into a baby store and pick out everything. I've waited a long time for this and finally it's my turn."

"All right. We shall do whatever you desire."

Perfect opening, she thought. "There's two things I desire," she said casually.

"And they are?"

"First, I think you should check in on the baby again. Since I haven't gone to a doctor or even had an ultrasound, I'm depending on you. Cristine and Isabel said they did the same thing, so I don't feel like a bad mother, but I want to be sure everything is proceeding right."

"It is my pleasure," he said, standing up and holding out his hand to her.

She pushed herself to the edge of the sofa and let him haul her upright. "Talk about being as big as a house," she muttered, pulling down the gauze tunic top that had ridden up her mound.

He took her hand and led her in front of the fireplace where there was more room. "So now you are a *brick house*?" he asked innocently.

She burst into laughter as she turned around in front of him and took his hands to place on her belly. "I don't think I'm what the Commodores had in mind, Michael. Though I am definitely *lettin' it all hang out,*" she added.

"But you insinuated that it was a compliment being a *brick house*. I'm afraid I don't understand."

"First of all, you don't have to keep saying it like you're on stage and singing the words. Just say brick house. It's fine that way. And in the song, it is supposed to be a compliment. But not about pregnancy. I'm sure you've observed there actually are women whose bodies are round and full, women who are not pregnant, but curvaceous. I hope I get to keep these though," she said, looking down at her breasts, then seriously thought about it. "Maybe not, or I'd have to buy a whole new wardrobe."

"Claire, you are confusing me. Is it a compliment or not?"

She chuckled. "It is, and thank you, Michael. Now check in with our daughter."

She closed her eyes and let her head fall back to his chest, reveling in the feel of his hands upon her, the sudden infusion of joy that swept through her body. "I love this," she murmured, realizing that she insisted Michael check in at least once a day. She was probably driving him to distraction with her requests, but she didn't care. Since she was the one carrying this extraordinary child, she felt she had some right to indulgences, especially this one. It was better than any ultrasound.

"She is progressing well, Claire. All organs and electrical systems functioning soundly. She is thriving and in good health."

Claire exhaled deeply in relief. It didn't matter how many times she heard it, she still worried something bizarre was going to happen. Maybe all expectant mothers did. As much as she hated to leave his embrace, she said, "The second thing I desire may be a little more challenging."

He kissed her temple. "And what is that, my love?" he breathed against her skin.

"I need you to make me a dress. A gown, actually."

He seemed to freeze. "A gown?"

She slowly turned around and looked up at him. "I've been putting off asking because I don't want to make this like Cinderella and you're my fairy godmother, but I'm desperate, Michael. Look at me! How am I supposed to find a gown to fit when I'm this big? You *have* to help me."

"I will help you," he said, putting his hands into the pockets of his trousers. "I just don't know what you mean."

She held her hand up. "Wait! I have an example." Hurrying

to the foyer—well, hurrying for a woman her size—Claire picked up her purse and took out the folded page she'd been keeping. "The bridal shower is this week at Cristine's, and I'm running out of time. I just know you can do this, Michael."

He came to meet her on the other side of the sofa. Taking the page from her hand, he studied it. "And you want this . . . gown for the bridal shower?"

"No, I want it for the wedding. I told you I have to stand up with Tina and Louis and Louis's brother to be a witness. Do you think you could do it? Like you've done for yourself with the clothes I showed you in that catalogue? It should be simple, right?"

Michael studied the picture for a few seconds. "All right."

And before Claire had any time to give him more instructions, the blue halter gown was on her, over her clothes, while an electrical energy frizzled throughout her body. Stunned, Claire looked down at the bodice pushing her breasts tightly together and the seams of the skirt looking ready to split open at any moment.

"Wait . . ." she commanded, wondering how the hell she was ever going to get out of it when it seemed as if it was molded to her body. "Not the *exact* dress. The dress in that picture is for someone who isn't over thirty pounds over-weight and a pregnant brick house!"

"It does appear uncomfortable and—"

"And *tight*?" she supplied. "Get it off me!"

In a fraction of a second the dress disappeared and Claire felt like someone had released her from one of those cans of biscuit dough. As her body expanded, Claire took a deep breath. "There's some alterations I'd like to discuss."

"But it *was* the gown you showed me."

"I understand, Michael. But this time you need to make it bigger, big enough for me, and if it's possible I'd like it to be green, a really, really soft green color. Okay?"

"Bigger?"

She nodded.

"Soft green?"

Another nod.

She prepared herself for his magic and then held up her hand. "Same material. Silk."

"Silk," he repeated, now nodding his head.

"Maybe I should take off this top, so you can fit it right."

"All right," he answered, looking very serious, as though he was trying to fit her requests into the equation.

She started to pull up the tunic, but the gauzey material got stuck on her protruding belly like it was Velcro. With her hands, arms and face covered, she called out, "Help!"

He pulled the shirt completely off her and smiled. "Shall we try this again?"

Taking the tunic from his hands, she threw it over the back the of sofa and nodded. Wearing her bra and maternity shorts, Claire knew she made quite a strange picture, but pride had to be thrown out the window for necessity. There was no other way she was going to find a gown she liked.

She held her arms out and closed her eyes. "Go for it."

She felt that electricity passing through her again and the silk, lovely soft silk, seemed to fold around her. Opening her eyes, Claire gasped.

It was beautiful!

And it fit!

At least it felt like it fit, she thought, picking up the hem and walking over to the mirror in the foyer.

She blinked at her reflection.

She looked . . . almost beautiful, even with her hair sticking out all over the place from pulling off the tunic. Her breasts were encased in soft tiny pleats of silk that crisscrossed into the halter around her neck. The empire skirt fell gracefully to the floor. It was simple, yet tasteful and flattering. She turned sideways and, yes, she did look pregnant and overweight, but she also looked pretty. The soft pastel green was perfect against her skin.

Spinning around she grinned at Michael and hurried back to him.

"It's perfect!" she exclaimed. "I should let you make all my clothes!"

"You look lovely, Claire," he answered, obviously pleased with his effort.

"Thank you, thank you, thank you," she kept saying, standing on her tiptoes and kissing his face. "I was so worried and you've made everything just right!" She giggled with happiness. "You've turned into a great fairy godmother."

"Godmother? I don't understand."

She waved her hand. "Doesn't matter, just a silly reference to a childhood fairy tale. I'm trying to say thank you, Michael. I love it!"

He kissed the tip of her nose. "I keep telling you to have a little faith, Claire."

"I know. I know." She suddenly felt the baby kick hard, as though to get her attention. Rubbing a foot or a knee or an elbow that seemed right under the surface of her skin, Claire said, "I think I have it."

Michael grinned. "And that is?"

"Faith," she answered. "What do you think about Faith for our daughter's name?"

He reached out and pulled her into his arms.

"I do think you've got it, Claire."

She grinned back up at him. "That doesn't mean your assignment here is completed. You *are* hanging around, right?"

"I've told you, Claire, I am not leaving you."

Sighing, she rested her head on his chest and felt very feminine.

She had her man. Well, almost a man. And she had her baby.

Faith.

She'd let the future take care of itself.

Oh, and she had the perfect gown for the wedding!

§

Cristine's backyard looked lovely at night, her beautiful garden leading to her new pool. Everything was professionally backlit and it was breathtaking. The women attending the bridal shower were seated at round tables with tablecloths woven to look like a Monet watercolor. At the center were small copper lanterns surrounded by pink and white freesias with greenery and baby's breath. The small white candles inside the lanterns were lit and cast soft flickering shadows on the tables.

Claire thought Cristine had outdone herself and she looked down the garden to the pool area. The men stood around drinking and talking. A part of her worried that Michael might say something strange to Louis's relatives and friends, but she saw Joshua and Daniel standing with him and thought they would help out any sticky conversation.

She tried to hide her pleasure as she remembered introducing him to everyone, the way the Gang's eyes widened with approval, the way Michael had seemed like the perfect mate as he held Claire's hand and made a personal comment to each of her friends, repeating things Claire had told him so long ago, like what a good mother Paula was and inquiring about her thesis.

Everyone loved him.

Even Tina's future in-laws seemed to fall under his charming spell.

The food was eaten. The gifts were opened. And now everyone was seated and talking about the wedding.

"Do you think I can come to the wedding?" Beth asked,

seated next to her. "Maybe I won't be here if my mom comes home."

Claire put her arm around Beth's shoulders. "We'll ask your mom and if she says yes then you can stay with me for the wedding."

"Can I go and get Angelique? Cristine said I could watch her when we're done eating."

Grinning, Claire released the child. "Go. Have fun."

She watched Beth get up and walk over to Cristine, who was holding Angelique on her lap. She saw Cristine smile and nod and watched as Angelique held Beth's hand as they walked off into the garden to catch fireflies.

Everything seemed perfect, Claire thought with satisfaction. Even the bugs and mosquitoes were absent, though she would bet Daniel had something to do with that.

"And you're the matron of honor, I hear," an older woman, one of Louis's aunts, stated with a friendly smile.

Claire smiled back at the woman across from her. "Yes, I am." Claire wished she could remember her name. Once, not so long ago, she had been very good with names. Her business demanded it. Business . . . now the foundation was her only client. Somehow, all of it was okay. She was enjoying the extra time with Beth and Michael and preparing for her child.

"Have you known Tina long?" the woman asked, interrupting her thoughts. "Did you go to school together?"

Claire kept smiling, knowing she was being grilled. "No, Tina and I met through Cristine years ago. This is Cristine's home. It's so wonderful all of you could come tonight."

"Well, this is a big deal . . . our Louis finally getting married."

"And he couldn't have met a more wonderful woman," Claire answered. "Tina is intelligent, warm, witty and has a heart of gold. She's waited a long time until the right man came along."

"I don't understand people waiting so long to get married. In my day we found our man and had our babies while we were young."

Claire couldn't detect any criticism of her, so she just smiled and said, "I know for myself I wanted to be sure."

"Sure? Do you really think you can ever be sure? I think you just have to take the plunge and hope you're both good swimmers."

"That's a good way to put it," Claire answered with a grin as she looked at Tina chatting with one of her future sister-in-laws. "I think Tina and Louis are good swimmers. I know Tina and she's missed her mother all these years. I'm glad she'll be marrying into a family of strong women."

"That she will," the older woman said, picking up her glass of punch. "Tell her from Aunt Leslie she's got my support."

"Thanks," Claire said. "I will tell her. I know she's anxious to make a good impression on Louis's family."

Leslie leaned in to the table and Claire stretched her neck to hear whatever the older woman was about to impart. "And tell her to not worry about my sister. Sarah takes such great pride in her youngest. I don't think she'd be happy if he was marrying Cleopatra herself. Just tell Tina to bide her time and hold her ground. Sarah will come around."

"She is worried that Mrs. Ramsey might not like her, so she'll appreciate your words." Claire didn't think she was gossiping. At least she hoped not. She just wanted someone in Louis's family to know how hard Tina was trying to fit in.

"So you think you're going to make it to the wedding?" Leslie asked, grinning and looking pointedly at Claire's belly. "Looks to me like you're ready to pop any minute now."

Claire leaned back and held her hand over herself. "Oh, don't say that! I *have* to make it past next week."

"Well, you hold on, honey, and tell that baby to stay put.

Keep your feet up and don't allow anybody to drive you over any bumpy roads. Let somebody pamper you until after this wedding. Rest up. Lord only knows, when the baby comes that's when the hard word begins. Are you going to breast-feed?"

Claire blinked. She should have thought about that. "I guess so."

Leslie chuckled. "Then be prepared. It'll be a good day if you can take a shower and shave your legs. They're always hungry."

Maybe she wouldn't breast-feed.

Leslie nodded. "It's best for them, I know, and I was glad I did it back in the day. Gives them extra immunities too. But it sure felt like all I did all day long was feed a baby."

Immunities. Okay, maybe she would. And Michael would help her. But he couldn't breast-feed. "I should buy some bottles, I guess. Just in case."

"No, no, you should breast-feed. Unless you intend to pump your breasts."

Ouch. Just the thought of that made her muscles contract. "I . . . really don't know."

"You'll know," Leslie said confidently. "When you see your child, look in its face, believe me, you'll know."

Claire could only nod.

"There's no reason for you to look scared," Leslie said with a smile. "It's the most natural thing in the world."

"What are you two chatting about?" Cristine said, taking Beth's empty seat.

"Breast-feeding," Claire said with dread.

Cristine laughed. "Glad that's behind me."

"Gee, thanks, Cris."

Cristine put her arm over Claire's shoulders. "Now you know everything is going to be fine, Claire. Stop worrying." She looked at Leslie. "It's her first."

"I figured that."

Claire glanced over at Cristine. "You've only got one."

Cristine looked like the cat that swallowed the canary. "Right now I do."

Claire's jaw dropped. "Do you mean . . . ?"

Cristine's eyes sparkled as she nodded.

"I . . . I don't know what to say!" Claire exclaimed.

"How about congratulations?"

Claire wrapped her arm around Cris's waist and kissed her cheek. "Congratulations! Wow! Another baby!"

Leslie pushed her chair back. "This must be the fertility table and I'm too old for that. Congratulations, Cristine. I'm going to get to know my future niece a little better and then I'm sending her over to you two. Sarah would be thrilled with another grandbaby."

"Thank you, Leslie," Claire said as the woman rose. "It was nice speaking with you."

"Please don't say anything yet . . . about me," Cristine asked. "This is Tina's night."

Smiling with approval, Leslie nodded and walked away.

Claire turned to Cristine. "So when did you find out?"

"Last week. I think we can keep this under wraps until after the wedding. I don't want anything to take away from Tina's day."

"Are you kidding? She'll be thrilled for you. Who else knows?"

"Just Isabel. I had to tell someone and she's sworn to secrecy."

"Just me and Issy?"

"Just the two of you. Besides, you two are the only ones who would understand . . ." Cristine took Claire's hand and placed it on her lower abdomen.

Claire felt the bump. "Already?"

Cristine giggled. "Daniel said since time is speeding up

all over the planet, so will the pregnancies. Look at you. You're hardly three months in real time."

"Oh, God . . . real time," Claire repeated. "It's hard to remember that. What have we gotten ourselves into?"

Cristine turned her head to the pool. "Look at them, Claire. Is your heart not bursting with love?"

Claire looked down the yard to the men at the pool, all in conversation. Sighing, she said, "You're right . . . as corny as it sounds, I'm bursting with love."

"I think," Cristine whispered, "what we've gotten into is the best time of our lives and I intend to ride it to the fullest. I never knew I could love like this."

"Me, either," Claire whispered back.

Cristine turned around to Claire again. "I know you're scared about what's ahead of you. I was the same way. You don't know if Michael is going to be there for you, whether you'll wind up raising your daughter alone. You can drive yourself crazy, Claire, with the 'what ifs,' or you can just trust in the love you and Michael share and know everything is going to work out for you, maybe better than you could ever have imagined."

"I hope you're right," Claire answered. "Because this is a whole different way of living. It's always been so hard for me to trust in the unknown. I always thought if I had a plan, if I could play the future like a chess game and think out all the possible moves, I could focus and make what I want happen. Now, I don't know . . . it seems I'm just trying to deal with whatever shows up."

"I know. You're talking to the queen of plans, and I've abdicated. I had to throw that out the window, right along with logic. Here's what Daniel told me. Think of whatever comes your way as energy you can choose to dance with, and then dance as gracefully as you know how at any given moment."

Claire almost snorted with laughter. "I'm not exactly in any shape to be dancing."

"You know what I mean. Deal with whatever comes your way with grace."

"Grace was never my strong suit, even before I became pregnant."

"But you're learning. I've watched you, especially with Beth. You're a natural, Claire. Don't doubt yourself."

Isabel came up and stood behind Cristine. "I say we go over there and break up that manly conclave." She tilted her head toward the pool.

Cristine pushed back her chair and stood up. "I agree. Let's get Tina and the rest of the Gang. It's time to mingle. Are you coming, Claire?"

"Sure, if you get a crane to hoist me up."

Issy laughed. "You're not as big as I was," she said, putting her arm under Claire's and pulling.

When she was standing, Claire said to Isabel, "Cristine's told me her secret."

"Isn't it great?"

Nodding, Claire looked down to the men. "Who would ever think it, Issy? The three of us in love with . . ."

"Angels?" Cristine supplied when Claire hesitated "Angels?"

Cristine and Isabel, with big grins on their faces, nodded. Claire's jaw dropped.

Angels?

"It's just a label," Isabel whispered, leaning closer to Claire's face. "But I have to admit, as goofy as it might sound, Joshua is simply divine."

Cristine laughed and said, "Okay, enough gushing. I'm going to get the others."

Claire stared after Cristine. "Are you guys kidding? Making a joke?"

"What do you think, Claire?"

She blinked, staring at Isabel to find any trace of facetiousness in her expression. She then looked at the men.

"It's just a word," Isabel murmured and squeezed her arm. "If it makes you feel any better none of them claim to be angels."

"Then why did you say that?"

"Because they are enlightened beings from another dimension," Isabel said in a low voice, leading her down to the garden. "In the past, some attributed the word *angels* to those like them. What do you care about what label they are, Claire. One of them loves you unconditionally, and you're carrying his child."

She felt the baby kick and jumped in surprise at the strength of it.

"I think your daughter agrees with me," Isabel said, touching Claire's belly.

"I'm coming to think she hears everything and makes herself known." Claire tried caressing the tight knot in her side to ease up.

"Of course she does. Like mother, like daughter."

"Oh, don't put that on her. I was hoping she'd be more like Michael, at least in her temperament." Claire reached for a firefly, but it eluded her as her attention was captured by Beth leading Angelique to her father. "Of course," she murmured. "Angelique. It makes sense now."

"Stop putting so much importance on names."

She watched Daniel scoop his daughter into his arms and the men surrounding him grinned. She saw Michael hold out his hand to Beth and watched as she casually allowed him to bring her closer to him.

Her eyes filled with tears of gratitude.

"I don't care what he is," she murmured. "I've never loved like this before."

"There you go," Isabel answered as they came to the pool. "Just go with the love, Claire. You can't go wrong with that."

She walked up to Michael and Beth and smiled.

Michael wrapped his arm around her shoulders and

brought her into the manly circle as Joshua reached for Isabel.

"We were just speaking about you," Michael said with affection.

"I'm afraid to ask," she answered, snuggling under his arm and grinning at Beth.

"Michael was saying you have become even more beautiful with your pregnancy," Daniel related. "We all agreed."

Even Louis's relatives and Paula's Hank nodded their heads or held up their drinks.

Embarrassed, Claire answered, "Well considering the state of the Phillies' slump, I guess you men had nothing better to talk about."

"We've already discussed the sorry state of the Phillies," Hank said. "We really were talking about our wives and how they just seemed to radiate during pregnancy."

"You're radiating," Isabel said with a laugh. "Just say thank you for the compliment, Claire."

"Thank you for the compliment," she repeated obediently, then couldn't resist adding, "You'd be radiating too if you were carrying around all this weight in August. It's called sweat, fellas."

She was so much more comfortable with laughter than with praise.

Still, it felt wonderful to know Michael still thought she was beautiful.

Yes, whoever he was, whatever he was, she was blessed.

Or crazy.

Maybe crazy in love.

Chapter

19

CLAIRE FOUND BETH SITTING ON HER BED WITH THE large duffel bag and a small shopping bag at her feet containing all her things. She looked so miserable, staring down at the wooden floor, that Claire felt her throat tighten with emotion.

"It's okay, honey," Claire said, coming into the room and sitting on the edge of the mattress next to the child. "You can come back any time."

Beth just nodded.

"Your mom is coming home, isn't that exciting?"

"She's not coming home. We have to stay with grandmom and granddad."

"That's because the doctor thinks it's better for her to be with her parents for a little while. And her arm isn't completely healed. Everyone thought this was the best plan for now."

"I want to go home or stay here."

Claire put her arm around Beth. "I know this is hard. Everyone's making decisions about you, but you know how much your mom loves you and she misses you. It's been almost two months now. Besides, the two of you can now go look for a new house with a pool. That'll be fun, right?"

Beth only nodded again.

Wishing she could makes this easier on the girl, Claire looked around the second bedroom. "Hey, this will always be your bedroom, okay? It's always going to be here for you. We're buds now, right? You can call me anytime."

"I won't be here when Faith is born," Beth murmured.

Claire bit her bottom lip. "No, you won't. But I'll call you right away and you can see her anytime you want." She squeezed Beth's shoulder. "I'm gonna need a good babysitter, you know, and Cristine thinks you're a great one."

Beth seemed to perk up a little. "Maybe we could look for a house around here and then I really could babysit."

"That's a great idea. Talk to your mom about it. And if she says she's willing to look at houses in Haverton or close by, Tina and Cristine would be the persons to call. They sell houses. But wait until after Tina's wedding, okay?"

"She said I can't go to it."

Claire sighed. "I know. I think your mom misses you so much that she wants to make up for the time she lost while she was getting better. Don't be upset with her, Beth. She's trying to make a whole new life with you and I think it's a little scary for her right now."

"But I wanted to go. I'll miss everything."

"No, you won't. Tina is hiring a photographer and a video cameraman. You can see everything. I promise. Next time you come over, we'll have a little after-the-wedding party. We can get dressed up and I'll get some of the wedding cake and freeze it, and we'll have a great time."

Beth started sniffling and wiped her nose on her wrist. "It won't be the same."

"No, but it will be the best compromise I can do, Beth." She paused, searching for something to make her feel better. "You know, I'm going to miss you too. I love you, kiddo."

Beth rested her head on Claire's chest. "I love you too, Aunt Claire."

Nodding, Claire tried to keep her composure. "And Faith is going to want to see her cousin, so we'll definitely get together as much as we can, but now we have to think about your mother, Beth. Imagine how she feels, being away from you."

Claire couldn't add that she wanted to keep Beth with her and not let her go. She'd become so attached that she was actually fighting being possessive of another woman's child. Clearing her throat, she stood up. "C'mon, honey. You carry one bag and I'll carry the other. The sooner you see your mom, the sooner the two of you can start making plans."

She picked up the duffel bag filled with clothes and watched Beth pick up the other.

"You know, sometimes what we think isn't what we want turns out to be just the right thing in the end. You have to have faith, Beth, that this is the right thing to do."

Beth reached out and kissed Claire's huge belly. "Bye, Faith. I love you too."

And just then Beth started giggling when she felt a hard kick against her cheek.

In the end it would all work out, Claire thought.

It had to.

§

Tina's wedding day turned out to be bright and sunny in the mideighties with low humidity, for which Claire was extremely grateful. Isabel's backyard looked magnificent. The gazebo was in full pink clematis bloom and the inside was decorated with pale green and white fabric with tall, full bouquets of white calla lilies on pedestals flanking the entrance.

Right outside the gazebo was the huge white tent that peaked like a castle in a storybook. Inside the tent were ten large round tables on either side of a wooden dance floor. Tina got her wish and on each table was a tall arrangement of white and pink wisteria mixed with freesia. It really did resemble a graceful floral umbrella, high enough so guests could see each other.

Claire turned away from the upstairs window as the waiters offered glasses of chilled wine while guests held their place cards with table numbers and mingled.

"Everything looks fabulous, Tina," she said, coming back into Isabel's bedroom, which they were using to get dressed.

Tina, with her hair up and wearing her bra and long slip, sat in front of Isabel's dressing table and looked at Claire in the mirror. "I'm not worried anymore about out there."

"And you shouldn't be worried about anything in here, either. Your hair looks great. Your makeup is flawless. You're just waiting for everyone to arrive and then you're going to put on that perfect dress and marry the man of your dreams. What is there to worry about?"

"I don't know . . . if I'm ready for this."

Claire blinked, seeing the fear in her friend's eyes. "It's just wedding jitters. Every bride feels them." Please, please, let it be nerves.

"What do I really know about him, Claire? What if there's this dark side to him that's moody or, even worse, he wants someone to take care of him like his mother?"

Claire stood behind Tina and answered her while looking in the mirror. "He is going to be moody sometimes. And so are you. And he will want someone to take care of him once in a while, just like you want to depend on him. He doesn't want a mother, Tina. He's got one. He wants *you*." She patted Tina's bare shoulder. "This is nothing but wedding nerves. Do you want a glass of wine?"

Shaking her head, Tina said, "He had his bachelor party last night with his brothers and his friends from the hospital. I called at three in the morning and then four, and there wasn't any answer. This morning I reached him and he was hungover and asked me not to nag. *Nag! Me?* Like I don't have a right to know what my husband is up to the night before he gets married!"

Claire swallowed, then shook her head slowly. "Guys . . . It's their tradition to blow off a little steam at these things. So what? It's over and he's here, downstairs, ready to make a commitment to you in front of God and everybody he knows."

"But do I want to be committed to someone who the night before he marries me does God knows what with God knows whom? And I don't care if it's tradition or not, I'm scared to death now of the honeymoon and whatever nasty thing he might have caught."

"Tina? I think you're blowing this all out of proportion," Claire said as calmly as she could manage, because Tina looked pretty serious and was getting worked up. "Did he say he did anything . . . nasty?"

Tina looked at her in the mirror and raised one perfectly arched eyebrow. "Like he would."

Just then they heard through the closed window the trio of violinists begin to play. The classical music should have soothed her nerves, but Claire felt flop sweat begin to pop out of her pores even though the house was air-conditioned. "Okay, I'm going to go downstairs and get you a glass of wine. We'll settle this, I promise."

Thankful she was already dressed, Claire opened the door and headed for the stairs. By the time she reached the bottom she felt a tug at her lower back and blew it off as she smiled at everyone in the groom's wedding party and made her way into the kitchen. She found the catering staff busily working arranging trays and touched the sleeve of one pretty young woman dressed in black slacks, a white shirt and a black bow tie.

"Excuse me, do you think I might get a glass of wine for

the bride?" She grinned feebly, knowing she was asking a favor in the midst of organized chaos. "Wedding jitters."

The woman nodded and smiled back. "Sure. Give me a minute."

Claire pointed to the front of the house. "I'll be right out there."

She left the kitchen and walked through the dining room that was filled with china and glasses and all sorts of catering stuff. The three-tiered wedding cake was on its own table out of the way and was beautiful, she thought as she entered the large living room. Walking up to Louis, who was in conversation with his groomsmen, she tugged on the sleeve of his tuxedo jacket. "Louis?"

He turned and grinned. "You look wonderful, Claire."

"Thanks, but can I speak with you in private for a minute?"

"Sure." He left the group of men and followed her into Isabel's office. "What's up? Tina's not having second thoughts, right?" he asked with a laugh.

She stared at him.

"You're kidding!" he demanded in disbelief.

"Listen, Louis, she's really upset about last night."

"But I didn't do anything!"

"I'm just the messenger. Don't shoot me. She said she tried calling you at three in the morning and then four, and when she finally reached you this morning you asked her not to nag you." Claire screwed up her nose. "Not a great answer, Louis."

"I did? I don't remember. I had such a headache, all I could think about was a shower and coffee." Louis now looked as worried as Tina had.

"Okay, her imagination is on overdrive right now and she's worried you might have picked up something from . . . I don't know . . . a stripper or something, and—"

"*Nothing* happened, Claire. I swear it!"

"I'm not the one who needs to hear that. So give me a few

minutes and then get your sorry behind up there to her and explain yourself. No bride can walk down the aisle with these concerns."

Louis ran his hand nervously over his forehead. "I should have called when I got in, but it was so late I didn't want to wake her."

Suddenly a light flashed and they both were startled.

They looked at the doorway and the wedding photographer grinned. "Thanks, Tina said she wants candid shots." He walked back to the other guests gathered in the living room.

"Well there's a picture I'd pay to hear you explain to the grandkids," Claire mumbled.

"I should have called her!" Louis repeated, oblivious to what had just happened.

"Obviously she's had less sleep than you, so let's factor that in too. I'm getting her a glass of wine and then you come up and knock on Isabel's bedroom door. It's in the back of the house, the only door upstairs that's closed."

"Right. Thanks, Claire."

She looked him straight in the eye. "Hey, we're all trusting you with one of the finest women we've ever known. You treat her like the queen she is, and you'll be one happy man the rest of your life. She deserves nothing less."

"I know, I know," Louis repeated, looking toward the door as the woman from the catering staff held a silver tray with Tina's glass of wine.

"And there's my cue," Claire said, thanking the woman and picking up the glass. She looked back at Louis and raised her thumb. "You can do it."

Nodding, Louis raised his thumb in return. But he still looked worried.

Claire headed back to the stairs. Looking up, she sighed. Now to haul her own sorry behind up this flight of stairs, while holding a crystal glass of wine. She could do it. She had to do it. She took the steps slowly, dragging her weight up each one. The heaviness in her back increased and she was thankful her home was one floor. She wondered where Michael was right now. He and Daniel were assigned to the valet parking, making sure each guest had his or her ticket as the parking staff drove away the cars to a nearby school parking lot. They then were to direct the guests to the backyard. Was that done? Were all the guests here?

Tina had thought of everything, except Louis staying out all night.

Suddenly, lost in her thinking, Claire stepped on the hem of her long gown and felt her body falling forward as she tripped up the stairs. It happened in a split second and all she could think about was saving the glass of wine for Tina. She landed three steps from the top, her left elbow breaking her fall, while her right hand held the glass of wine above her head. More embarrassed than hurt, Claire put the wineglass on the next step and hurried to right herself before anyone noticed.

No one did, thank heavens.

She pulled the hem of the gown over her left arm and picked up the wineglass, then used her right arm to hold onto the banister and drag herself up the remaining stairs. She tried not to concentrate on the pain in her arm, shooting up to her shoulder, or the tightness in her back that now increased on her left side.

"Sorry, baby," she murmured, thinking she should have kicked off her heels before attempting this. "I'll watch my step from here on out."

She knocked on Isabel's door and opened it. "Here's your wine," she announced, as if it were the Holy Grail she'd saved from destruction.

"Thanks," Tina said, turning her attention away from the window. "Everything does look fabulous, doesn't it?"

"Every single detail is perfection, Tina," Claire answered,

handing over the wine and sitting on the edge of the bed. Only one more trip down those stairs, she vowed, and it had better be for the wedding ceremony.

"You should see Paula and Kelly and Isabel, acting as hostesses, showing people where their tables are. Everyone's been so wonderful . . . Oh, Claire! Look!" Sighing with disappointment, she said, "It's gone now."

"What?"

"A hummingbird. My mom loved hummingbirds." She blinked a few times. "Remember Isabel said I'd get a message from my mom? Do you think?"

Claire grinned. "It wouldn't surprise me. Everything today is just as you'd wished."

Tina sipped her wine. "Except for the man I'm supposed to be marrying."

"I really think you're blowing everything out of proportion and—"

A knock on the door interrupted Claire.

She and Tina stared at each other as they heard, "Tina, baby? It's me. Can I talk to you?"

"He can't see me!" Tina whispered in alarm. "It's bad luck!"

Claire, wishing she could take Tina's wine and finish it off in one gulp, called out, "You can't see her, Louis. It's bad luck."

"Will she listen to me?"

Claire raised her eyebrows to Tina.

Tina shrugged.

"She'll listen, Louis. Make it good."

There was a pause. Tina put her wine on a night table and began walking over to the door, her hands twisting in nervousness.

"Hon, I'm so sorry about last night. And this morning. I . . . I didn't want you to walk down the aisle thinking I disregarded your feelings."

Tina's head turned back to Claire. "You talked to him, didn't you!"

It really wasn't a question, so Claire dragged herself up and walked to the window, waving off Tina's accusation. "This is your business. Settle it. Do you want me to leave?"

"No!" Tina answered in a whisper, then turned back to the door. "What about last night, Louis? I know when a man doesn't want to talk about what he did the night before, he's got something to hide."

"I didn't do anything, Tina. I promise. You can ask anyone there. All we did was drink a little and—"

"A little?" Tina interrupted.

There was a moment of silence.

"Okay, more than I should have. But nothing else happened. I would never disrespect you like that, Tina. You've got to know that. I love you. I've waited all this time to find you and all I want to do is marry you and make our lives together the best they can be. Please . . . will you forgive me for being a total jerk last night and this morning?"

Claire looked over her shoulder and saw Tina touching the door. "You said I was a nag."

"I asked you not to nag me and you can stuff the cake all over my big mouth for that stupid remark. I'd just woke up. Baby, you never nag and I promise never to say that to you again for the next fifty years. Please, Tina. Forgive me."

Tina grinned and looked at Claire. "Ain't he sweet?" she whispered.

Claire stifled a groan. "Yeah. Real sweet. Now put the man out of his misery and get dressed. They're almost ready out there."

"Louis, I forgive you for being a total jerk and you are going to pay for that when we get to St. Lucia. I'll have the whole plane ride to think of something completely wicked."

"I can't wait," Louis answered in a sexy voice.

"Now go outside and get ready. I'm about to become your wife."

"Thank God," he said in a relieved voice. "I love you, Tina."

"I love you too."

Claire walked over to the bed and picked up the skirt of Tina's bridal gown. "*Now* will you please get your ass into this thing?"

Tina clucked her tongue. "You shouldn't talk to a bride like that right before she's about to walk down the aisle. And you, with child."

Claire rolled her eyes. "You're right. Wedding slave apologizes to the bride. Just get dressed, all right? Everyone's waiting."

Tina's eyes sparkled with happiness. "I'm gonna miss having you for a slave," she said with a laugh. "Think you can take all the presents over to my place while we're in St. Lucia?" She turned around and stepped into the silk skirt, pulling it up to her waist.

Claire zipped it quickly. "Think you can think sanely for five seconds? Do I look like a pack mule? My emancipation begins when you say *I do*."

Tina laughed and reached for the gorgeous bodice. "I was kidding. Louis's brothers are going to do it. Here," she added, holding the bodice together at her waist. "Button it up."

"Yes, ma'am." Claire began buttoning the tiny pearls that ran from under Tina's shoulder blades to the top of her behind. It fit like a handmade glove and Claire's fingers were aching by the time it was completely fastened. "There," she pronounced, shaking her hands to bring the blood back into them. "Go look at your gorgeous self."

Tina walked over to the mirror and stared.

"It's not complete without these," Claire murmured, handing her the bridal bouquet of long graceful calla lilies held together with a soft pink satin ribbon twirled around the stems.

"Gosh . . ." Tina whispered, looking at her reflection.

Claire giggled. "Gosh?"

"I mean . . . look at me."

"I am. You're an exquisite bride, Tina."

Tears came into Tina's eyes. "It's all come together, hasn't it? Just like I'd imagined."

"Maybe better," Claire whispered back, picking up her single calla lily and grabbing a tissue from the box on the dresser. "Blot your eyes, girl, before you ruin that makeup. You know the photographer is waiting at the bottom of the stairs to take your picture."

Tina gulped and dabbed under her eyes with the tissue. "You go down first and make sure Louis is outside." She turned her head and stared at Claire with a shocked expression. "I'm going to do this."

"Yes, Tina, you *are* going to do this," Claire answered, taking the tissue out of her hand and throwing it on the table. "We are going outside and you are going to become Mrs. Louis Ramsey, doctor's wife." She kissed Tina's cheek. "Just don't get all snooty on me or I'll have to tell Louis about the time we were coming home from New Hope and we couldn't find an open bathroom and you pulled the car into a corn field and—"

"Stop!" Tina commanded with a laugh and then sobered quickly. As Tina looked at Claire, her bottom lip trembled. "I love you like a sister, Claire. Thank you for everything. Today wouldn't be possible without you."

Claire bit her lip, trying to control her own emotions. "Well, sistah, let's get this show on the road."

Tina sniffled, nodded and smiled. "Give me two minutes and I'll follow you."

"Have a happy life, Tina," Claire whispered, feeling the

bridge of her nose begin to burn as she lightly kissed Tina's cheek. "You, above everyone, deserve it."

She left Tina in Isabel's bedroom and headed for the stairs. This time she took off the red high heels and held them as she slowly descended. She didn't even care that the photographer caught her in her bare feet. Looking at Louis she called out, "We're ready. She'll meet you in the gazebo."

Louis and his older brother hurried to the back of the house, and Claire saw Mr. Andrews, Tina's handsome father, waiting expectantly. "She'll be right down," she said, as he offered his arm while she put on her shoes.

"You look lovely, Claire," he said with a smile.

"Thank you, Mr. Andrews. But wait till you see your daughter. She's—"

"Magnificent," he supplied, now looking up the stairs.

Claire turned around and watched Tina descend amid the photographer's series of flashes. Mr. Andrews left her side and held his hand out to his daughter.

When Tina came to the last few steps she reached for her father's hand as he said, "You're absolutely beautiful, baby girl."

Claire's eyes welled up with tears. Wow . . . to be thirty-eight years old and still be your father's baby girl. That's being cherished. There really were good men of integrity and decency and sure enough of themselves to love their daughters unconditionally. And, in the moment, she missed her own father, regretting he would never see her in love, never see her have children.

She vowed her daughter would grow up to be a woman and still know she was loved as much as when she was a precious baby girl.

"Are you ready, Claire? Shall we lead the way?"

She blinked away her tears and threaded her arm through Tina's brother's. "Let's go, Jake. Somebody's got to get this thing started."

She and Jake walked outside to the violins playing Delibes's "Flower Duet." As they entered the backyard, smiling faces became a blur until she focused on Michael, beaming at her with such love that she almost stumbled. Jake kept her steady as they walked up to the gazebo, joining Louis and his older brother, in perfect timing for the music to end.

All waited until the musicians began playing the traditional bridal march and everyone watched as Tina and her father entered the tent from behind and walked down the center of the wooden floor. Guests stood at their tables and smiled in appreciation. Tina was radiant, smiling at everyone, and Claire noticed that even Louis's mother looked happy.

It was all turning out exactly as Tina wanted, and Claire looked for the Gang. They were each seated with their partners at different tables, having been instructed by Tina to keep the flow of conversation going, or maybe Tina just wanted them separated like naughty children who would giggle and disrupt everything.

Tina focused on her future husband as they neared the gazebo. It was hard not to cry with happiness as Claire saw Tina's love reflected in her expression. *It was almost holy,* Claire thought, clutching her lily. That total trust in committing your life and love to another.

"Who gives this woman in marriage?" the minister asked as the violins faded away.

"I proudly do," Tina's father announced in a firm, yet emotional voice. He then placed Tina's hand on Louis's. Kissing Tina's cheek, he nodded once and then backed away.

Everyone turned their attention to the minister, who repeated several verses from Scripture about love and marriage. Claire noticed from the corner of her eye, one of Louis's friends place a decorated broom at the bottom of the gazebo steps.

The vows were traditional, with the love, honor and cherish part, and Claire watched the couple exchange wedding bands.

The minister then declared them husband and wife and they kissed amid cheers and applause from the guests while the violinists loudly played the triumphant exit march. Laughing, Tina and Louis held hands as they walked down the two steps and then paused.

It was really something to behold.

The roar of a hundred people filled the air as together, united, they jumped the broom into married life.

Chapter

20

IT WAS THE BEST WEDDING.

It wasn't just Claire's opinion. Everyone said so. The sit-down dinner menu gave guests a choice of citrus-dusted filet of red snapper or pan-roasted mignon of steak cullotte. The champagne flowed freely while the violinists continued to play during the food service. Then the toasts, sentimental and hilarious, came from family and friends. The cake was wheeled out and Tina did smash a piece into Louis's face, only to immediately get a napkin and wipe him off. A DJ took over and dance music ranged from old-school Motown to present-day hip-hop. Everyone was laughing, reminiscing or just plain old gossiping at different tables while the younger crowd took over the dance floor and showed off their skills.

Claire smiled at everyone, mingled like a good matron of honor, but couldn't wait to sit down at her table again. Her back really was bothering her and she thought she should have Michael check her, just to make sure. That fall on the stairs didn't help.

She saw Michael standing with two of Louis's brothers, Vernon and Jake, talking by the dance floor. Determined to make her way to him, she walked around a couple of teenagers who were gyrating in perfect time to the grinding hip-hop beat. She had to admire them and wondered if she'd ever get her figure back and be able to strut her stuff on a dance floor again.

Just then the music segued and Claire felt her wrist caught.

"C'mon, Matron of Honor . . . you can't have a wedding without the Electric Slide. Especially this wedding. Will you look at the grande dames getting up to dance, even my mother-in-law!"

"I . . . I can't," Claire protested as Tina dragged her to the dance floor. People were lining up in rows, mostly women, and Tina was waving at the Gang to join them. "Honestly, Tina. I'm too tired. I can't do this."

"Of course you can," Tina insisted, only half listening as Paula and Kelly and Isabel and Cristine lined up next to her. "Let's show 'em how it's done!" she pronounced in a voice that said this was her party and she was going to have a blast with all her friends.

"C'mon, Claire," Kelly said, moving in step to the side.

To do anything else would have made a scene, as everyone was looking at the dance floor. Claire, as sedately as possible, began to dance, keeping up with the turns, the dipping, the sliding. Her lower back was protesting the exercise and she wished she was on the end of a row and could just slip away between the tables. Instead, she kept up with the rest of them. She saw the Gang laughing at each other, the happiness of her friends, and didn't have the heart to complain. It would be over soon and then she and Michael were going to go somewhere private in the garden and take a breather from all the festivities.

Her feet were killing her with the extra weight she was carrying and she wished she'd kicked off her heels before being hijacked into dancing. Still, she put up with the pain and concentrated on keeping a smile on her face as the photographer and video camera were capturing the dance for posterity.

Let it end, she prayed. *Please!*

Within less than a minute her prayers were answered.

Despite the air-conditioning blasting in the tent, flop was breaking out all over her and Claire waved her hand in front of her face as everyone on the dance floor started to disperse.

"Wait, *wait*," Tina called out to the Gang, grabbing Isabel's arm. "I want a picture of the Gang together."

Claire's shoulders drooped in surrender. A few more minutes and she could make her escape. Tina got the photographer's attention and then gathered her friends.

They stood in a group, smiling, as the camera took their picture.

"Now all of us should do a kick, showing our Yellow Brick Road heels," Tina pronounced.

Claire, standing next to Isabel, said, "Unless you're prepared to hold up my leg, Tina, I'm not in any shape to kick."

Tina got the message. "Okay, how about this? We all stand together in a tight circle and put one foot out." She turned to the photographer. "Would give me your camera and I can take the shot looking down at the circle of red high heels?"

The man made an adjustment on his camera and handed it over.

The Gang stood with their arms around each other's waists in a tight circle. Each one put her right foot out so the toes of their high heels were almost touching.

"That's it," Tina exclaimed and shot the picture.

"Oh, I love it!" Paula said. "Can I get a copy?"

"Me too," Isabel agreed. "I want to blow it up and frame it for my office wall."

The DJ played a slow song and Claire moved out of her circle of friends. She looked for Michael and caught his eye. He must have read her fatigue, for she saw him excuse himself and quickly make his way to her.

"Are you all right?" he asked, concern showing in his expression.

He looked so handsome in his Armani suit. The man was acquiring real taste in clothes on his own.

She met him on the edge of the dance floor between two tables. "I'm just really tired," she answered, holding onto his forearm as she slipped out of her heels. She bent down to pick them up, heard Michael saying he would do it, but before she could answer, Claire felt a rush of liquid come out of her.

Bent over, she froze in fear.

"Oh, my God . . ."

"Claire? *Claire? What's wrong?*"

She tried to straighten out, but she felt like the small of her back was locked into a spasm of pain that was slowly wrapping around her belly.

"Don't be embarrassed," Michal whispered, bending down to her. "I'll get you out of here."

"I didn't go to the bathroom! My water broke . . . I . . . I can't leave *this* on the floor," she gasped, reaching onto one of the tables and grabbing a napkin.

"What's wrong?"

She heard Kelly's voice behind her and, reaching back, she grabbed Kelly's arm to bring her down to her level. "My water just broke."

"Good God!" Kelly muttered, grabbing every napkin off the table and throwing them onto the floor. "Cristine! Isabel! Paula!"

"Don't call attention to it!" Claire managed to get out as the spasm lessened. She straightened out as best as she could and leaned her hands on the back of a chair.

"What's going on?"

"What's . . ."

"Oh, sweet Jesus, here we go again!" Paula exclaimed. "Tina!"

Claire closed her eyes in humiliation as Tina came over with several other guests.

"Her water just broke!" Kelly said.

"Well somebody do something!" Tina pronounced.

"I *am doing something!*" Kelly shot back. She looked at the other deserted tables. "Everybody grab napkins! Hurry!"

"I'll get Louis," Tina said, turning around.

"No, don't get him. It's his wedding," Claire whined as tears came into her eyes.

Tina ignored her as Cristine lifted Claire's gown and a flurry of napkins landed around her wet feet.

"Claire, let me carry you out of here," Michael said, caressing her back in small circles.

"Carry me *where?*" Claire demanded. "Is anyone going to call 911? I would really like to have this baby in a clean hospital."

"Hank!" Paula called out in a loud voice. "Call 911!"

From the corner of her eye, Claire saw the entire wedding reception grind to a screeching halt and she groaned in mortification.

Tina's new aunt Leslie stood on the other side of the table and clucked her tongue. "You should have kept your feet up, child."

"I tried," Claire mumbled, unable to stop the tears from falling down her cheeks.

"Never you mind. This is the best of luck, a baby coming into this world at a wedding. Best present you could have given your friend. Now the marriage is truly blessed."

"Amen!" another older woman pronounced, holding up her hand.

Claire tried to nod, but her embarrassment was overwhelming. She turned her head slightly. "Michael, please get me out of here."

"Absolutely," he said, and scooped her up into his arms as though she weighed nothing.

"Umm-umm-umm, will you look at the strength of that fine man," another woman declared

"Good gene pool," someone else added.

"Take her into the house," Isabel directed. "She can wait there for the ambulance."

She buried her face in Michael's neck. "Tell them to go back to partying," she murmured. "I can't bear that I've ruined Tina's wedding."

Turning around, Michael said in a loud voice, "Claire and I would be honored if our child came into this world while you continue to enjoy yourselves. Please, let her hear the sounds of celebration."

No one moved for a few seconds, then Aunt Leslie called out, "You heard the man. Let's get back and party, folks! A baby's coming!"

The DJ spun a new song and before they left the tent, Claire and Michael heard people singing *celebrate good times, c'mon . . .*

"Michael," Claire whispered, her head still cradled into his neck, "I'm scared."

"Don't be frightened, my love. I'm with you and everything is going to be fine."

She started crying. "How can you say that? I haven't even seen a real doctor and . . . and . . . Oh, God, oh, God . . . put me down!"

"Down?" he asked in confusion.

"Yes!" she demanded, almost pulling herself out of his arms.

Michael waited until her feet touched the grass before releasing her legs. She grabbed hold of his arm and bent over, gasping.

"What wrong?" he asked in a barely controlled voice.

"What's happening?" Isabel called out from the kitchen door she was holding open.

Michael looked at Cristine, who was holding Claire's red high heels.

"She's having a contraction, I think," she called back. "Are you having a contraction, Claire?" she asked, bending down so her face was close to Claire's.

Claire couldn't speak, but she grabbed Cristine's shoulder and dug her fingers as hard as she could into it, as though it would lessen the pain to hold onto something else.

Cristine seemed to shrink as she tried to withstand Claire's grip. Seeing Claire's grimace of pain was all Cristine needed. "It's a contraction, all right," she yelled to the others. "Anybody time it since the one at the table?"

"It can't be more than a couple of minutes," Kelly said in a worried voice. "What if the ambulance doesn't get here?"

"*Don't . . . say . . . that,*" Claire gritted out between clenched teeth.

"At least Louis is here," Cristine added.

Claire felt the contraction ease and slowly tried to straighten out. She had a death grip on Michael's hand and let up the pressure on him and Cristine. "I'm gonna need drugs," she panted. "I can't do this . . . I never knew . . ."

"You'll do it," Paula said reassuringly. "We all get through it somehow. Just think what's on the other side of it."

"We've got less than three minutes to get her into the house," Cristine said. "Michael, get her up and get her in the house."

Michael immediately obeyed, scooping up Claire again, even though she moaned in pain and panic. Quickly he walked up to the kitchen door.

"How's she doing?" Isabel asked, just as Tina and Louis arrived at the same time.

"We think the contractions are three minutes apart, maybe less," Cristine said as Michael took her through the door and past the stunned catering staff that was cleaning up.

"We weren't timing them," Kelly added.

"Somebody get my bag," Louis called out. "It's in the trunk of my car."

"I'll get Hank . . . wait! All the cars are at the school parking lot, except for the limo."

"Put her down," Louis ordered when they were in the dining room.

Michael did as he was told and gently eased Claire into a standing position.

She held onto the edge of the table as Louis took off his tuxedo jacket and began rolling up the sleeves of his dress shirt.

"I'm sorry, Claire. I know this is going to be embarrassing, but I have to see if we have enough time to wait for the EMTs. I'll be as quick as I can." He turned to Cristine. "Get her underwear off."

"Right," Cristine said, already rolling up the skirt of Claire's damp gown.

"And, Isabel, do you have rubber gloves? Clean, unused ones?"

"I have a whole pack. The thin kind that you throw away. I use them for gardening."

"Bring them."

"Oh, God," Claire murmured, now totally humiliated. She grabbed Michael and buried her head at his side. She felt Cristine grab the edges of her panties and pull them down.

"Step out of them, Claire."

She tried doing as she was asked, but that pain came back with a vengeance, like steel claws wrapping around her middle. She gasped, pulling on Michael's jacket as he tried to support her.

"She's having another contraction," Kelly needlessly announced.

"Try breathing, Claire," Cristine said. "Like this . . ."

She couldn't pay attention to any of them. She was in the throes of such pain that she thought surely death must be easier. At least there's an end to that! She wanted to scream, yell at them all that this was unfair. No one should have to go through this hell on earth. At least she should be in a hospital with *drugs,* lots and lots of drugs, and then thankfully, mercifully, it began to ease and her moaning became whimpers.

"Claire?"

It was Louis's voice. She turned her head.

He was kneeling in front of her. What . . . ?

He looked concerned. "I'm going to examine you now, okay?" He showed her his gloved hands.

"But . . . how . . . ?"

He lifted her skirt and put his hand underneath the silk. "Spread your legs, if you can."

She looked at Tina and began crying. "I'm so sorry!" she blubbered, figuring this was the absolute worst thing that could happen to Tina . . . having her brand-new husband stick his hand into her friend's vagina. What could be worse?

She shouldn't have even thought it.

Tina waved away her apology, waiting for her new husband's words.

Louis took his other hand and pressed on Claire's abdomen. He looked up at her. "The baby has already crowned. We can't wait."

"What do you mean you can't wait?" Claire demanded in a near hysterical voice. "The ambulance. It's coming, right?"

Isabel was ordering the catering staff to remove everything from the dining room table. "I'll get towels and somebody boil water, or *something!*"

"I'm not having my baby on your table!" Claire pronounced, though no one was paying attention to her as chaos descended and all she saw was a blur of hands grabbing serving dishes and big plastic boxes with glasses rattling. "This is crazy," she nearly yelled.

"Calm down, my love," Michael whispered, rubbing her back again.

"Don't tell me to calm down! They're . . . they're saying I'm going to have the baby *now, here*!" She held onto his jacket and looked up at him. "Do something! Tell them I can't have my baby in front of everyone, in a *dining room*!"

He bent down and said, "Claire, I can't control this. Our daughter is coming now. We are fortunate Louis is here and can assist you."

She knew everything he was saying was true, but *still*! Before she could protest again, the pain came back, sharper, more intense, and she couldn't help crying out in pain.

"Hurry, hurry," Tina commanded, waving her hands at the catering staff.

"We have long rolls of plastic wrap," one of the women said. "It's three feet wide. Maybe we could protect the table."

"Great idea," Tina answered. "Let's get it."

Within minutes, Claire was hoisted up onto the edge of the dining room table. Louis was covered in a tablecloth tied around his neck. A big bucket was at his feet. Michael was supporting her back, while Cristine and Kelly were holding back Claire's legs as Tina stood behind her husband, wringing her hands. Paula and Isabel stood on either side of her, their arms wrapped around her waist.

Louis pulled back the skirt of Claire's gown to put a towel on her belly when he stopped and said, "What is this?"

Everyone leaned in closer for a look.

Claire lowered her head and saw several bruises. "I fell going up the stairs before the wedding." She felt guilty as they all stared at her.

"No wonder you went into labor, Claire," Cristine said, still holding back her leg.

"Why didn't you tell me?" Michael asked softly.

"I don't know . . . I didn't think it would . . . oh, *noooooooooooooo*!"

The next contraction came and Claire thought she was going to faint from the horrible burning pain. She moaned and groaned and wished for oblivion to knock her out, for she felt like something had taken over her body, something alien and torturous.

"Claire, I want you to take a really deep breath on the next contraction," Louis said.

"Pay attention," Paula called out. "This is all normal."

Claire glared at her. She didn't care how many kids Paula had popped out of her! Nothing about what was happening resembled anything close to normal!

When the contraction eased, she started crying profusely. "I can't do this!" she moaned, shaking her head from side to side. "I can't . . . Michael, can't you do something? You and Daniel, Joshua, *something*?"

"Our daughter is in control now," Michael answered, wiping the sweat off her forehead with a small towel. "Soon, my love, soon . . ."

"Doesn't *anybody* have any drugs, painkillers, cocaine, morphine, *crack*?"

Kelly laughed nervously. "It's too late for that, Claire. You're ready to give birth."

"I am?" she asked hopefully, her mouth so dry she would kill for some spit.

"When the next contraction comes, I want you to push, Claire."

"Really?" The burning sensation was so intense and it didn't ease up this time.

Louis nodded. "Really. The baby's head has completely crowned. We're going to see if we can get her head out."

"Her head," she repeated, looking up at Michael's right next to her own.

"Soon," he murmured, kissing her temple. "You're doing so well. I'm so proud of you."

"Really?"

"Really," he answered, nervously kissing her sweaty cheek.

Claire turned back and looked at Tina, Kelly and Isabel behind Louis. "You . . . you guys look sick," she muttered and heard sirens in the distance.

"The ambulance. Thank God," Cristine said.

"Oh, God, here comes another," she moaned, not even caring that the ambulance must be carrying drugs and sterile equipment of some kind. Nothing mattered but the pain consuming her body.

"Deep breath!" Louis commanded and it seemed everyone in the room inhaled along with her. "Now push while I count to ten. One . . . two . . ."

Claire felt like she was trying to push a watermelon out of her as she grabbed her knees and Cristine and Kelly held her shins back. Why was Louis counting so slow?

"Five . . . six . . ."

She would never make it to ten! Her cheeks felt like they were going to explode! Hurry! Hurry!

"Eight . . . nine . . . ten."

Claire let her breath go, cried out with pain and collapsed against Michael's chest, almost missing Tina pronounce, "The head is out!"

She looked around at her friends; all of them were crying along with her. She wished she could take their hands and feel their strength.

"Okay, Claire, one more push for the shoulder," Louis called out. "Big, big breath, the worst is over."

Claire inhaled as much air as her lungs would allow.

"Now, push! One . . . two . . ."

"Push, Claire."

"You can do it!"

"C'mon, Claire!"

"Almost there!

"Five . . . six . . ."

"A shoulder!"

Her eyes were clamped shut and she was in such intense concentration that she was only vaguely aware that the sirens had stopped and there were other voices in the room. Male voices.

And suddenly, mercifully, she felt a whoosh coming out of her and it seemed that everyone inhaled as one in awe.

"Our daughter, Claire," Michael whispered as Claire opened her eyes. "Thank you, thank you . . ." he murmured against her temple.

Claire could only blink as everyone bent over Louis's hands.

There, squirming and shiny wet, was this tiny little being.

"Is . . . is she all right?" Claire barely whispered. "Why isn't she crying?"

"She appears perfect to me, and full term," Louis proclaimed with a big grin. He looked at the EMTs who stood at his side. "Glad you showed up. Just in time. I need to clamp the umbilical. You want to take over?"

Claire couldn't care that a strange man was now working between her legs. All she could see was her daughter in Louis's hands. She didn't feel anything as the baby was separated from her.

Isabel held out a white towel and Louis placed the baby inside it.

"She's beautiful."

"So sweet."

"And good. Not even a cry."

"A happy baby."

"A blessed baby girl," Isabel whispered, handing Claire her child.

Claire looked down into the towel in awe. She was speechless.

"Isn't she beautiful?" Kelly asked with a sniffle.

Claire could only nod as she was cleaned up and covered in a paper blanket, while the other EMT wrapped a blood pressure cuff around her upper arm.

"She looks just like her mother," Michael said, pulling back the towel from the baby's face. "Beautiful."

"See?" Christine asked all teary eyed. "Everything turned out better than you could have imagined."

Claire couldn't stop the tears of joy as she looked up from her daughter. "Thank you so much, Louis. I'm sorry this happened and took you away from your wedding."

Louis pulled the plastic gloves from his hands and removed the tablecloth from his neck. "I wouldn't have been anywhere else. And neither would my wife," he added, pulling Tina into his arms and kissing her cheek.

"I would have been so upset if you went into labor while I was on my honeymoon. I would have had to race home, so you saved me the trip," Tina said, beaming with happiness. "And you blessed our wedding, Claire, so I'll be grateful to you for the rest of my life. There isn't a soul out there who will ever forget this."

Claire shrugged helplessly. "Well, it wasn't planned."

"Best-laid plans always seem to go astray anyway," Kelly murmured, peeking over Claire to get a better look at the baby. "This was much more exciting than rushing to a hospital."

"I know," Paula said. "First time for a home delivery."

"Let's make it the last," Cristine declared.

Claire smiled at Tina. "I'm so glad you're not upset by this. I don't think anyone would argue that you and Louis are going to be the godparents."

"Yeah, we'll give her that," Paula said. "Her wedding and everything."

"But this is the baby's real family, all of us here," Claire murmured. "The Yellow Brick Road Gang."

"Right. And this calls for a big celebration," Tina proclaimed and walked to the kitchen door. Out came Hank and Joshua and Daniel. "Now we're all here."

Surrounded by love, Claire kissed Michael's cheek then looked down at their daughter, their beautiful, precious, extraordinary gift.

"So what's her name?" Hank asked.

Looking back up at her family, Claire smiled broadly and said, "Faith."

It was Isabel who said, "Let's all welcome Faith into the world."

As one, even the EMTs, all called out, "Welcome, Faith!"

And, as if on cue, the catering staff brought in silver trays of champagne.

"To Faith," Louis proclaimed, holding up his glass.

"To Faith," everyone resounded.

In the midst of such a touching moment, Claire suddenly remembered her promise. "Somebody get me a phone," she ordered. "I have to call Beth." She looked down at Faith and said, "And get the photographer and I need someone to save two pieces of cake and . . ."

"Well it was nice while it lasted," Cristine interrupted, handing Hank's cell phone over. "She's transformed back into the bossy woman we all know and love."

"Hey, I'm keeping a promise!" Claire said in her defense, while dialing the number she had memorized.

"That's what we love about you, Claire," Isabel said. "You're nothing if not faithful."

Claire blinked, then looked down at the miracle in her arm. "I *am* faithful, aren't I?"

Michael whispered in her ear, "She's the best parts of you."

Tears sprang into her eyes again while the phone rang. "I love you," she muttered, meaning it for Michael, Faith, the Yellow Brick Road Gang, the catering staff, every single person in the dining room.

And then she saw her child gazing up at her and a strange recognition washed over her body.

It was her, Claire, looking back at herself, and yet so much more . . . a precious unique human being who would never forget that she was cherished.

Hearing a child's voice brought her back to the present.

"Hey, Beth," she said, trying to hold back a giggle. "Guess who I'm looking at?"

Twenty minutes later she was being wheeled into the ambulance when Michael said, "Listen, Claire . . ."

The EMTs stopped and all of them heard a hundred people in the tent singing "Happy Birthday" to their child.

It wasn't the way she would have planned it, certainly not disrupting her best friend's wedding and delivering her baby on an antique dining room table, but it had turned out better than she could have imagined.

All she had to do was let go of everything, all her perceptions about the way things are supposed to be . . . and have a little faith.

She lowered her head and kissed her daughter's.

"Happy birthday, baby girl."

Acknowledgments

Christine Laidlaw, my sister, for lightening the load. See you in South Africa.

Victoria O'Day, my sister-in-law, for her editorial input and her daily encouragement.

Kristen and Ryan Flannery, my children, for always believing in me.

Michael R. Wolf, dear friend, for bringing out the laughter, no matter what.

Richard Curtis, my agent, for his enthusiasm, for always seeing the bright side.

Anna Genoese, my editor, who had to put up with my family emergencies, pneumonia and a hard drive crashing. Thank you, Anna, for your extreme patience and your skill in editing this trilogy.

And I would like to acknowledge you, the reader. You are the reason I sit down every day in front of my computer. Many of your e-mails have brought tears to my eyes, and I am forever grateful you continue to allow me to rent space inside your head for a short while. I never take that for granted.

Love is magic